D0876657

Re:ZeRo
-Starting Life in Another World-

When Crusch hurriedly looked, the land dragon Subaru and Rem were both riding was galloping, cutting across the vanguard.

"All hands, follow that pair of fools!!"

Then, with a roar, it chased after Subaru and Rem.

"Whoaaaaa—?!"

There was an overwhelming amount of pressure as it chased them from the rear.

"Were you laughing at me?"

"......"

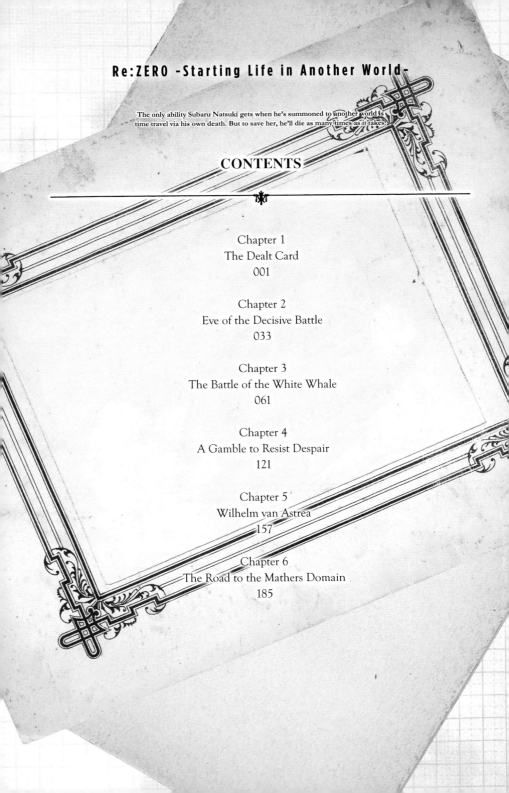

Re:ZERO -Starting Life in Another World-

The only ability Subaru Natsuki gets when he's summoned to another world is time travel via his own death. But to save her, he'll die as many times as it takes.

CONTENTS

Re:ZeRo

-Starting Life in Another World-

VOLUME 7

TAPPEI NAGATSUKI
ILLUSTRATION: SHINICHIROU OTSUKA

YEN ON

NEW YORK

Re:ZERO Vol. 7

TAPPEI NAGATSUKI

Translation by Jeremiah Bourque
Cover art by Shinichirou Otsuka

This book is a work of fiction. Names, characters, places, and incidents are the product of the author's imagination or are used fictitiously. Any resemblance to actual events, locales, or persons, living or dead, is coincidental.

Re:ZERO KARA HAJIMERU ISEKAI SEIKATSU Vol. 7
© Tappei Nagatsuki 2015
First published in Japan in 2015 by KADOKAWA CORPORATION, Tokyo.
English translation rights reserved by YEN PRESS, LLC under the license from
KADOKAWA CORPORATION, Tokyo, through Tuttle-Mori Agency, Inc., Tokyo.

English translation © 2018 by Yen Press, LLC

Yen Press, LLC supports the right to free expression and the value of copyright. The purpose of copyright is to encourage writers and artists to produce the creative works that enrich our culture.

The scanning, uploading, and distribution of this book without permission is a theft of the author's intellectual property. If you would like permission to use material from the book (other than for review purposes), please contact the publisher. Thank you for your support of the author's rights.

Yen On
1290 Avenue of the Americas
New York, NY 10104

Visit us at yenpress.com
facebook.com/yenpress
twitter.com/yenpress
yenpress.tumblr.com
instagram.com/yenpress

First Yen On Edition: June 2018

Yen On is an imprint of Yen Press, LLC.
The Yen On name and logo are trademarks of Yen Press, LLC.

The publisher is not responsible for websites (or their content) that are not owned by the publisher.

Library of Congress Cataloging-in-Publication Data
Names: Nagatsuki, Tappei, 1987– author. | Otsuka, Shinichirou, illustrator. |
ZephyrRz, translator. | Bourque, Jeremiah, translator.
Title: Re:ZERO starting life in another world / Tappei Nagatsuki ; illustration by
Shinichirou Otsuka ; translation by ZephyrRz ; translation by Bourque, Jeremiah
Other titles: Re:ZERO kara hajimeru isekai seikatsu. English
Description: First Yen On edition. | New York, NY : Yen On, 2016– |
Audience: Ages 13 & up.
Identifiers: LCCN 2016031562 | ISBN 9780316315302 (v. 1 : pbk.) |
ISBN 9780316398374 (v. 2 : pbk.) | ISBN 9780316398404 (v. 3 : pbk.) |
ISBN 9780316398428 (v. 4 : pbk.) | ISBN 9780316398459 (v. 5 : pbk.) |
ISBN 9780316398473 (v. 6 : pbk.) | ISBN 9780316398497 (v. 7 : pbk.)
Subjects: | CYAC: Science fiction. | Time travel—Fiction.
Classification: LCC PZ7.1.N34 Re 2016 | DDC [Fic]—dc23
LC record available at https://lccn.loc.gov/2016031562

ISBNs: 978-0-316-39849-7 (paperback)
978-0-316-39850-3 (ebook)

1 3 5 7 9 10 8 6 4 2

LSC-C

Printed in the United States of America

R0452784361

CHAPTER 1
THE DEALT CARD

1

In life, you can only play the game with the cards you've been dealt.

This held true no matter the circumstances of a person's birth, appearance, talent, reputation, or the skills they cultivated.

Subaru Natsuki was keenly aware that he was lacking in every single one of those categories.

Through some kind of mistake, Rem had completely accepted Subaru, but he knew all too well that the Subaru Natsuki she saw was an ideal far removed from the real thing. Compared with the man she envisioned in her mind, the cards that the real Subaru held were few in number, and poor in quality—

But he learned, now that he stood at the playing table, no one cared about his personal problems.

All anyone in his position could do was try to win with the cards he was dealt.

The rest came down to simply how well each person played, their timing, and if they used any bluffs.

"—The White Whale."

Of all the cards in Subaru's hand, he chose the one that resulted in the greatest effect on the others.

His declaration changed the faces of those around him in different ways.

They were currently in the reception room of the Duchess of Karsten's villa in the royal capital's Nobles' District.

Not counting Subaru, five were participating in the discussion—first, Crusch Karsten, lady of the manor, accompanied by her two retainers, Ferris and Wilhelm. Also in attendance was Russel Fellow, one of a tiny handful of influential movers in the royal capital, acting as an adviser for Subaru.

And...

"..."

...the fifth was Rem, who was touching Subaru's sleeve, providing limitless strength by inspiring the courage within him.

The conversation between those six in the capital quickly began hurtling toward an intense climax.

In short, the objective of the discussion was to form an alliance between the Emilia camp and the Crusch camp. The Crusch camp was taking a cautious wait-and-see stance toward the Emilia camp's request of cooperation to resist the universal menace of the Witch Cult. Subaru's invoking of the White Whale's name was his trump card for breaking that stalemate.

Crusch's eyes narrowed in profound interest; Ferris looked at his master with gloom-filled eyes. The deeply mercantile Russel knotted his brows, whereas Wilhelm—

"—?!"

After an instant, Subaru involuntarily held his breath when a thick, dark hostility permeated the room's interior.

Feeling sick to his stomach, as if his intestines were about to be rearranged by the tip of a sword, Subaru lifted his face to see the source—and saw the white-maned, old man exhaling deeply and lightly shaking his head.

"...Forgive my...gross indiscretion. It would seem that I, too, still have room for improvement."

Wilhelm closed one eye and apologized without any change in expression.

The aged swordsman pushed the malice away, leaving no traces remaining even in the farthest corners of the room, then touched the sword on his lap as if ashamed.

"I have no excuse for interrupting. Say the word and I shall remove myself."

"No, stay. I wish to hear your opinion."

Crusch personally stopped Wilhelm from excusing himself. "You do not mind?" he said, shifting his eyes to Subaru, who answered as well with a nod of agreement.

"Now then, the term *White Whale* has been thrown out rather suddenly. May I take it that the White Whale of which you speak is the Demon Beast of Mist, one of the three great demon beasts?"

"Yeah. A monster that spews out mist and swims around in the sky—that White Whale. I know when and where it'll show up next. I want to offer that information as part of the deal for an alliance."

Is she gonna bite? wondered Subaru, his nerves on edge as he waited for Crusch's reaction.

The lady of the house put a hand to her chin in contemplation. Before she rendered judgment, someone cut in.

"Apologies. May I ask you some minor things?" Russel raised his hand and sought permission for questions.

"Sure thing, ask anything you like."

"First, there is a matter I must verify… Mr. Natsuki, do you have an accurate assessment of what value to place on your knowledge of where the White Whale shall next appear?"

"…It could reduce the number of people caught up in the White Whale's damage. Merchants and land dragon cargo runners can revise their routes, and it would improve the condition of a lot of victims, I think?"

"Yes, precisely. However, that only earns you a score of fifty."

Russel's assessment of Subaru's mostly timid reply was rather harsh.

"Are you aware of just how much blood has flowed due to the Demon Beast of Mist to date?" he continued. "The unlucky caravans, which the White Whale's mist swallowed up, vanished without a trace! The royal knights assembled to dispatch the White Whale failed, routed by the beast! Until a few decades ago, it appeared near villages and cities, swallowing them and their entire populations whole. It was not uncommon for cases where it was impossible to ascertain the truth of what had happened. The White Whale is more than a very large demon beast."

Russel's words, explaining the menace of the White Whale, were hot—almost excessive. Subaru, prone to hiding his negative emotions behind a facade of denial, understood the desire to have others understand such feelings.

Faced with an enemy too vast to fathom, people tried to extoll the vastness of its existence to protect their fragile spirits.

"With such a demon beast, the most crucial measure is never to encounter it. Many merchants and travelers fear nothing greater than mist covering their path. The White Whale is a symbol of calamity, and any mist itself is a veritable evil omen. If one could see ahead to know where it would appear, it would be worth an immense fortune! However…"

Having clenched his fists and spoken with such zeal to that point, Russel suddenly looked down at Subaru with cold eyes.

"Information is assigned value from its trustworthiness. Mr. Natsuki, how can you prove such a thing? Without proof, it cannot be seen as anything but fiction."

"Most of which I wished to express would only repeat Russel Fellow's words. I was about to ask if you could prove your claim."

With thin smiles, Russel and Crusch both questioned the basis of Subaru's tip.

Is the information true or false? Posed this question, Subaru felt a cold sweat against his back. But he could not reveal his anxiety. Returning a bold smile their way, he managed to keep himself from letting weak thoughts trickle out as he put his next card on the negotiating table—just like he'd elaborately simulated many times over in his preparations beforehand.

"The reason I can know where the White Whale will come out beforehand…is this!"

Suddenly, he took something out of his side pocket and slapped it on the table.

Subaru displayed his evidence on the table. He felt the expressions of everyone staring at it tighten briefly, but the next moment, bewilderment came over them.

"Subaru Natsuki."

"Yeah."

When Crusch quietly invoked Subaru's name, he puffed his chest out without a hint of fear. Without commenting on Subaru's impudent demeanor, she pointed at the proof Subaru had placed at the center of the table.

"What…is this?"

It was a gleaming piece of cutting-edge future technology encased within a white, metallic body.

—She did not take her eyes off the cell phone for a single instant as she quizzically tilted her head toward Subaru.

2

Subaru's knowledge of precisely when and where the White Whale would appear was truly the fruit of repeated coincidence and the mischief of fate.

The decisive instant came on that misty night during the third loop—when he encountered the White Whale face-to-face.

While sitting in the driver's seat of a dragon carriage, he had retrieved the cell phone from his hand baggage and activated it to use it as a light source.

"It was then, right before that."

The first time Subaru set eyes on the White Whale, he'd been trying to check on the dragon carriage running beside them, had vanished. His eyes struggled to pierce the darkness at the time, so he thought to use the light of his cell phone.

Even in the present, he found it hard to forget meeting the thing in the dark, eyeball to enormous eyeball.

Right after that moment, the demon beast roared. Then, its first attack blew Subaru and Rem's dragon carriage away, turning it into wood chips. As Rem grasped him by the collar and they sailed into the air, the scene seared itself into Subaru's eyes as everything moved in slow motion.

And with the world crawling forward one frame at a time, Subaru saw it crystal clear: his cell phone, knocked out of his hand in the initial blast, twirling through the air—and displayed on its backlit screen, 3:30 PM.

After arriving in a new world, the clock function of his cell phone had lost all meaning. But if he used it as an indicator of a determined future event, it was more accurate than anything else available there.

More importantly, the cell phone played the role of an irreplaceable device.

"It's no fault of yours for not knowing what this is. This is one of those metia thingies, unearthed in my homeland. This is the proof for what I'm saying."

It was the very fact that the cell phone was from an unknown land that turned it into a valuable weapon for negotiations.

"...May I touch it?"

Russel was the first to swallow his saliva and reach out toward the cell phone. Subaru gave permission with a nod. The man timidly took the cell phone in his hand, checking the feel for himself.

"Oddly, it is quite comfortable to the touch. It seems to be metal, and yet it seems warm... The surface is glossy yet also soft... This spot...opens up?"

Russel unfastened the flip-up phone and marveled at the light flowing from the screen.

Before the conversation started, Subaru had changed the display on the screen to that of a more orthodox clock. Even with skilled operation, there was little else to extract from it save for a few phone numbers.

"There is a glow, and the picture is changing... Ah, but I cannot determine the contents. Are these characters I have never seen? Or wait… *Is* this a picture?"

Bit by bit, the screen showed the second hand of the clock moving. But the human beings of that world used very different devices to tell time, so Russel could not understand the display. The same went for the numbers indicating the time. His best guess about the Arabic numerals was probably that they resembled a child's scribbles.

Subaru knew how he felt. After all, he'd gone through the same thing day after day.

"They're special characters, so I don't think anyone here can read them."

"However, you can use it properly… Is that it?"

"I actually can't fully use *all* its functions."

When Crusch posed the question, Subaru employed caution, carefully choosing his words.

There were a number of conditions for successfully completing these negotiations, but one reigned supreme. He could not let Crusch, who possessed absolute confidence in her keen eyes, detect any falsehood within him.

Subaru needed to do everything in his power to avoid stepping on any land mines.

"In other words, you are saying the following: This metia acts like a warning crystal that indicates the approach of the White Whale."

"I don't recall ever hearing about these warning crystals, but I think so."

Judging from the name, they were probably some sort of alarm crafted from magic crystals.

"A metia that signals the approach of the White Whale, eh? What does the expert think?"

"In truth, I must admit I am at a loss. Individual metia differ greatly, and it is rare for any two to work precisely the same. The manufacturing of conversation mirrors is an exception because a method to reproduce them has been discovered, but the costs involved make mass production simply unfeasible even for those. At the very least, this is the first I have heard of this variety of metia."

Russel avoided making any careless statements about an object he knew nothing of. For the moment, he played the role of a benevolent third party, intervening in neither Subaru's favor nor Crusch's.

Naturally, Russel's eyes were exceptionally critical when it came to discerning whether siding with Subaru or Crusch would accrue him the most profit.

"Therefore, I cannot see any method of determining the veracity of the information. Which means your assertion becomes difficult to swallow at face value. Now then, what shall you do?"

"Yeah, that is a tough situation. It'd be great if I at least had a way of proving it, but..."

In response to Crusch, Subaru raised both hands, his gesture indicating that there was no hope for that.

"Hmm. Perhaps try to see if it rings at the approach of an actual demon beast? Or maybe you have another way of proving that this metia is indeed a device that reacts to demon beasts?"

"I'm gonna correct you about one thing."

Subaru raised a finger and swayed it left and right, as if enjoying a chance to get back at Crusch.

"This metia doesn't react to demon beasts themselves. If it did that, any demon beasts hanging around would make it ring all the damn time. It turns on for only the important ones."

"—Surely you are not saying it reacts when a demon beast is threatening the user?"

Crusch reacted to Subaru's assertion, adding a laugh, as if such a function was too good to be true. But there was yet another reaction that followed Crusch's.

"—Ah."

Standing at Subaru's side, Rem let out a tiny voice of comprehension. Then, immediately after, she lowered her face, apparently ashamed at having disturbed the negotiations.

"That reaction makes me wonder, Rem. Did that remind you of something?"

When Crusch pressed for an answer, Rem's eyes ran over the side of Subaru's face for only an instant. Hints of worry and gratitude filled her gaze, so Subaru smiled to give her visible reassurance.

"It's all right. If you have something to say, go right ahead, 'kay?"

"—Yes. If you say so, Subaru."

Rem lifted her head, turned toward Crusch, then indicated the cell phone on the table.

"I shall omit the fine details, but recently, there was an incident within the Mathers domain caused by demon beasts. When it occurred, Subaru was the one who acted the swiftest to bring the situation to an end. He had not been with us very long, so I thought it strange he grasped the circumstances before the landlord himself, Master Roswaal, but..."

"With this metia, he noticed the incident beforehand?"

"It was an open question, as it was a little too convenient for him to notice without any tangible basis."

Meekly, Rem tilted her head very slightly, glancing Subaru's way. She clearly harbored doubts over how Subaru had sniffed out the Urugarum incident in a very Rem-like way. The learning of the metia's existence had just erased those doubts.

"..."

On the other hand, that reply drew Crusch's piercing gaze right to Rem. Her eyes gave off a sharp, penetrating stare that seemed to slip inside people's innards, as if she could see their very soul.

In terms of actual time, only a few seconds passed. And yet, Subaru felt like each took a heavy toll on his endurance when finally—

"—You have not...spoken falsely."

Crusch displayed a certain level of trust and comprehension toward Rem's statement.

Hearing her assessment, Subaru struggled with all his might not to show the relief he felt on his face. On the inside, he could not stop clenching his hands and pumping his fists.

In other words, it had all been a bluff.

If that fact came out, negotiations would immediately be cut off, and it would not have been odd for him to be sliced into thousands upon thousands of bits for his insolence. However, Subaru had glossed over it all by using his words to direct everyone toward a different topic.

Subaru had not spoken a single falsehood in response to Crusch's questions. After all, the cell phone really wasn't a device that rang in response to demon beasts in its proximity. Moreover, Subaru, someone who had barely even used his cell phone to send messages, certainly could not use its full potential.

Rem had unwittingly allowed herself to be exploited for the greatest hurdle Subaru needed, which was confirmation from a third party. Even if the contents of what she said differed from the truth, she had no intent to deceive, so it was not a lie per se.

"You've gotta admit, though, you said that like you can tell if a person's lying or not."

"At the risk of boasting, that is correct. One might call it having perceptive eyes, but in actuality, I have been graced with the blessing of wind reading."

"…What did you say?"

The completely serious reply Subaru received was not at all what he'd expected, recalling how in the past she had chewed him up and spit out the leftovers. During the previous loop, Subaru had chalked up Crusch's self-described "ability to discern falsehoods" to her perceptive eyes, but…

"Reading the wind allows me to judge that which cannot be seen by the eye. By nature, I am able to discern the wind that envelops the other party. Those who speak lies have a telltale wind that blows from them—there is none of this around Rem."

"R-really, is that so? I didn't know that. Had no idea."

"An unsettling wind does blow from you, Subaru Natsuki. That said, standing at the negotiation table while unaware of my wind reading was simply too unfair toward you."

Subaru's smile twitched at how rotten Crusch's personality was for her to reveal that ability at the height of negotiations. A blessing that provided a way to determine whether the other party's words were true or false was practically cheating. It also explained the sharpness of the barbed words that had cut Subaru so deeply the last time around.

"Rem's words contain no hint of deception. At the very least, this certainly proves that you possess the means to detect a demon beast menace in advance."

But in this one instance, her confidence in that blessing was a double-edged sword.

Subaru was balancing atop a tightrope, embodying the very idea of letting his opponent get their cuts in as long as it meant he could hit back even harder.

"So can I take it that you believe in this metia now?"

"That would be speaking too soon. Even knowing there is no collusion, it does not change that I must protect all my vassals. This is a decision that might determine the outcome of the royal selection, or even the fate of the kingdom itself. I shall not proceed lightly."

Unsurprisingly, she fended off Subaru's attempt to quickly close the deal.

He'd achieved a bare minimum of trust that his proclaimed metia could provide information about where the White Whale could appear, but that only meant they would consider the proposal seriously rather than laugh it off.

What would build on that level of trust and bring the negotiations to a successful ending was—

"—Sooo, how about letting me in on this metia talk, too?"

The reception room was seized by surprise when a voice suddenly interrupted.

When the speaker stepped into the room, she elegantly smiled in response to their startled gazes.

"Aren't you a funny one, Subaru, looking the most shocked when you're the one who invited me?"

Addressing the wide-eyed Subaru, the charmingly smiling girl ran her fingers through her wavy mane.

Her light-purple hair seemed as soft as down, reaching all the way down to her hips. With such a gentle face, she could easily put others at ease. However, the girl's eyes meticulously surveyed everything—a clear sign that she was not to be underestimated.

"—Anastasia Hoshin."

Knowing who she was, Crusch shut one eye and addressed her by name. Anastasia responded to the greeting with an easy "thanks."

"It's unfair that while I was busy hurrying over after getting word, you just went and started talking without me. With such an interesting, profitable conversation going on...you'll let me join, won't you?"

Phrasing her request in a pleading way, Anastasia's words and subtext contained genuine delight. After considering her presence, Subaru subconsciously glanced behind her.

"If you are wondering about Julius, you can rest easy."

"—!"

As he did so, the mischievously grinning Anastasia seemed to read his mind.

"Currently, Julius is under house arrest by order of the captain of the royal guards. He's currently undergoing punishment for smacking around someone else's boy without my say-so. That knight of mine is quite a handful."

"House arrest..."

Now that she mentioned it, Subaru recalled the night when Reinhard had told him the same thing. As a result of his private duel with Subaru, Julius was being disciplined with house arrest. Apparently, that was why he hadn't accompanied Anastasia to the current meeting.

"I see. That's...very...unfortunate."

Subaru was too pathetic to keep the look of relief off his face. But even then, he was unable to summon any words he might have for the next time they met.

"You said you were invited here. By Subaru Natsuki, I take it?"

Crusch addressed Anastasia, ignoring Subaru's wounded feelings. Anastasia sat in a chair offered to her as she stroked the fox-fur scarf hanging around her neck.

"More precisely, it was the girl with him. Normally, I'd have just sent her away…but I couldn't wave her off after she said there was super-important stuff concerning the White Whale."

When Anastasia finished chatting with a smile, Crusch turned to Subaru.

After bringing two royal selection candidates to the same table, Subaru gripped his fist at the drastically altered situation.

This is it. Everything starts from here.

All the necessary parties were in the same room together. Subaru could finally begin the true negotiations.

However—

"Pardon me, Mr. Natsuki, but there is one thing I would like to ask you."

Naturally, Russel did not find the invitation of a rival merchant to the meeting very amusing.

"Go ahead, Mr. Russel."

"Mr. Natsuki, I would like to hear your true motive for calling Lady Anastasia to this place. As she is both a candidate in the royal selection and president of the Hoshin Company, possessing great influence with the merchants in the royal capital, my position here has become highly…indistinct. Surely it could not be…"

"You're wondering if I'm weighing other options?"

The instant Subaru responded to Russel's doubts, the atmosphere in the reception room grew taut.

Of course, Russel felt slighted, but his grave expression spread to Crusch as well.

"In other words, you are saying this: You shall select your alliance partner based on who bids higher for the information on the White Whale, my house or Anastasia Hoshin?"

"_____"

"If so, that is an exceedingly imprudent choice, Subaru Natsuki."

With Subaru silent, Crusch slammed him with the force of her will, rising to her feet and gazing down sharply at Anastasia.

Amused, Anastasia tilted her head slightly as she spoke. "Oh my, Crusch. If you look at me like that, I'm going to get excited… That's a face that people in the lead get when they're worried about their competition catching up soon."

"You have questionable hobbies. Perhaps it is the correct decision for someone like you—openly motivated by personal greed—but my principles shall not be swayed."

After fending off Anastasia's taunt, Crusch turned back toward Subaru with a serious expression.

"It is as I said, Subaru Natsuki. If you expected a bidding war between my house and the Hoshin Company for your information, let me say that you will be disappointed. I have no intention of cooperating with your sch—"

"Wait, wait, you're jumping to conclusions! Both of you calm down, okay?"

Subaru scrambled to stop Crusch from breaking off negotiations and wrecking all his efforts so far.

"Jumping to conclusions...? Mr. Subaru, so it was not your intent to draw two candidates to compete against each other?"

"Of course not. I'm not so overconfident to think that I can make people dance in the palm of my hands. I ain't Buddha. Really, with what I have..."

Subaru gave a little wave before making a show of holding Rem's hand as she stood beside him. The touch conveyed a body heat that sent courage flowing into him, calming the faint trembling of his fingers.

"All I can manage with hands my size is holding on to another person, like this."

"Ahh, yes, yes, very touching. So where do you plan to take the conversation from here?"

"Er, I guess that was a pretty lame line..."

When he tried loosening his grip, Rem fiercely resisted letting go, so Subaru left it at that while using his free hand to slap the table before continuing.

"I've played the White Whale card, and I've invited two people who represent the merchants in the capital. That makes the situation a big deal already...but I want to propose one more thing."

Subaru tapped his fingers on the table while sending a fierce smile Crusch's way, blatantly hiding all the frail, weak-kneed parts of him behind a bold, confident front.

"Willing to listen?"

"I am the one who rushed to conclusions and interrupted you. I have an obligation to listen. Say what you will."

The sense of an oppressive wind blowing from Crusch intensified. On top of that, even Anastasia showered Subaru with similar pressure. It seemed like he would buckle at any moment.

He had no doubt that if he was alone, he would've laughed, made light of it all, then promptly run for the hills.

"_____"

He felt a squeeze from the warm touch of the hand clasped around his.

She could not call his name, nor could she offer any words. All she could do was convey her feelings. That made him happy.

As long as he had that, Subaru could probably take on even the Witch.

"_____"

He closed his eyes, held his breath, and keenly felt thoughts and oxygen coursing through his brain.

I'm pretty sure she'll bite.

After thinking about it over and over, incessantly recalling what happened on the first, second, and third loops, he pieced together his accumulated knowledge, then drew out what he expected to happen onto a blank, white canvas.

He wasn't…absolutely sure. It wasn't like anyone had told him that's what would happen, either. But combined with the pieces found scattered throughout the ongoing negotiations, the vague image pointed to only one possibility.

It was either a convenient delusion or a miracle he had obtained after suffering death three times.

It comes down to this.

"Crusch, I think…"

"_____"

"...I think my information will be extremely useful for your plan to hunt down the White Whale."

Subaru's future information and the objective Crusch harbored—these formed the basis of his decision. Subaru would become a suitable ally for Crusch Karsten, as a comrade in arms against their mutual foe: the White Whale.

3

In the instant after Subaru spoke, the room fell into silence as each person in attendance sank into thought: Crusch, Anastasia, Ferris, Wilhelm, Russel. Each closed their eyes, as if digesting the words Subaru had just given voice to.

The moments that passed amounted to several seconds, but the incredible pressure of that quiet tied Subaru into knots.

This is it. This'll decide everything.

Unlike the events so far, simulations in his mind wouldn't cut it. Unable to determine the other parties' probable reactions, he was left with no choice but to react instantly to what they did then and there.

"I shall ask you about one thing, Subaru Natsuki."

As he'd expected, it was Crusch who broke the silence.

Crusch unfolded her arms and raised a single finger, turning it toward Subaru.

"From where did this extraordinary idea come? Why do you believe that my house has crafted such a plan? It is not a statement you can simply walk away from."

Her uninflected voice betrayed no alarm or bewilderment, nor any emotions. Awed by her statesmanship, Subaru's gaze wandered as he breathed in and called out a name.

"Rem."

"Yes."

"Give my back a good, hard smack, would you?"

"Yes."

The moment he finished talking, Subaru thought to himself, *Uh, a good, hard smack might be overdoing it*, but it was too late. With an

incredible jolt and a dry, explosive sound, the force shooting through his back made him wonder if his guts were about to spill from his belly.

He felt something hot press against the center of his back in the shape of a small hand. Using the pain and heat to gather his wits, Subaru bowed his head to all the confused people watching.

"Sorry you had to watch that. I was losing my mind a little there."

"Everyone can remember one time or another when they needed to rally themselves after faltering before a great challenge. I was taught long ago to write 'enemy' on my palm, then to swallow the word to steel myself…"

"Lady Crusch, Lady Crusch. That's the charm Ferri taught you a long time ago. You still remembered that?"

"What…? Was it…a lie?"

"It wasn't based on anything concrete, but if the charm helped dispel any doubt in your heart, then it was no lie, Lady Crusch. Ferri's really happy to have been a help to mew."

"I see. So you were thinking of me. In that case, I forgive you."

Seeing how easy it was to cajole Crusch made the earlier discussion about her blessing rather suspicious. Though after many years together, Ferris probably knew exactly how to exploit the loopholes in her lie-detecting ability.

"Gotta say, though, this kind of talk is in a different dimension compared with the negotiations earlier…"

"It's not that strange. I do the same thing before I begin working on any important business deal. Jingling a sack of gold coins by my ear brings out my courage… What's with the face?"

"I was just thinking that if we cut off the conversation here, no one would guess that you guys are competing for control of a kingdom right now."

Subaru pretended not to notice how trivial their chat was compared with the important matters they should have been focusing on. Anastasia pouted at Subaru's reaction, then sighed deeply before continuing.

"All right then. Now that we've had a nice change of pace, let's leave it at that and let you pick up where you left off."

"Yeah...thanks for being so considerate."

Crusch and Ferris were simply talking as they usually did as master and servant, but Anastasia's benevolent humoring of the off-topic conversation had bought Subaru precious time to organize his thoughts into something coherent.

"There were a bunch of things nagging me while staying at this mansion for the past several days. First is the number of people passing through. The volume of visitors and goods going in and out has been more than just a little high."

"That's only to be expected once news that I am a royal candidate was made public. Surely you understand this?"

"That explains the guests during the day. But what about the ones who came in the dead of night? After you've changed into your evening clothes, the only thing left for you is heading off to bed... Can you really claim that guests arriving at that hour are there just to talk?"

One night, during the first time around, Crusch had invited Subaru to a drink in the evening. Having changed into a nightgown before sleep, Crusch was incredibly feminine, and Subaru recalled finding it awkward not knowing where to look, along with the conversation they had, of course. But that wasn't the only thing he remembered.

He distinctly recalled being together with Crusch, a wineglass in her hand, while noticing the presence of people coming and going in the yard below.

"Given your personality, you'd never even think of drinking alcohol if you were receiving guests. So how do you explain all the people moving around the mansion after you'd gotten tipsy? They were there for something besides seeking an audience."

"_____"

This time, Crusch did not have a response for Subaru's deductions. Having tentatively seized the right to guide the conversation, Subaru tapped the table with his hand.

"Another thing that bugged me was the market for metalwork here in the capital. According to a merchant I know, the price of various metal goods has been spiking. In other words, that means weapons and armor."

Subaru had drawn this conclusion from disparate fragments of information he'd gleaned from his first, second, and third times around.

"So I'd bet that you've been gathering up a big amount of dirt-cheap combat gear. I heard that from that shop I know, and from traveling merchants coming here to visit you, Crusch."

Maybe she's preparing for a war, said some traveling merchant or other he'd journeyed with, laughing it off.

"It's significant enough to affect the entire market, so it seems like you're buying up quite a lot. If you're going as far as to buy weapons from outside your own lands, common sense says that something's up, right?"

"Mentioning my house in the same breath as the White Whale is far too great a leap from only that much circumstantial evidence. You've barely compiled enough to even speak the first letter in its name. It is a fact that my house has been acquiring weapons, but that is not proof that I plan to hunt down the White Whale. Perhaps I am amassing military power so that I may ignore the results of the royal selection altogether and seize the throne by force of arms."

"You don't have any reason to plan something so violent, and even I can tell you're not that kind of person."

Crusch, who was the living incarnation of words like *sincere* or *noble*, was one of the last people willing to violate the trust of others like that.

"Though I must say, I am somewhat surprised."

Crusch, who shouldn't have known what Subaru was thinking, sighed in admiration. She crossed her arms, tilted her head quizzically, and looked Subaru over from head to toe before speaking again.

"I had firmly believed that you went into the capital during the day purely as a diversion...but it was most definitely my own eyes that did not see clearly."

"Nn! Yeah, that's right. It's not like I spend all my time playing around."

Crusch's open praise struck Subaru with heavy pangs of guilt. In truth, Crusch's initial assessment was exceedingly correct. She judged that he was gullible and spoiled. All he could do at the moment was to respond, turning a blind eye toward the truth.

"Anyway, when I first realized you were gathering weapons, I thought you were preparing for war. The real question was who you were planning to fight...but a slippery merchant let something fall from his lips."

"A slippery...merchant."

"Just to be sure, to avoid any misunderstandings, allow me to affirm that it was *not* I."

When Crusch glanced at him, Russel directly denied the misgivings that were undoubtedly on the tip of her tongue. Apparently, Crusch sensed no hint of deception in his words, because she grudgingly showed that she believed him.

As expected, Crusch's intuition was very sharp—but her suspicions were actually both correct and incorrect.

The merchant who'd let it slip from his lips was indeed Russel, just as Crusch had suspected. However, it was not the Russel currently standing before them but the Russel Subaru had met during a previous loop.

"*Should Lady Crusch succeed in her current endeavors, we would feel nothing but delight.*"

Russel had spoken those words on the way out after his negotiations with Crusch had broken down. Subaru had pondered the meaning behind those words for a long time.

If Crusch had stated she expected to succeed the royal throne, it was difficult to imagine that would cause negotiations to break down. But if Crusch's and Russel's mutual goals were aligned, then—

"If you go by popular rumor, a lot seem to think you're practically running alone in the race, Crusch. But it looks like the merchants don't seem as eager to call it as regular folks do."

"I do not deny it. It is only sensible that the wealthy are the most reluctant. I acknowledge that the tax rate on commerce is high within my lands. Naturally, I use those funds to defend the peace and order…but I am well aware of the difficulty in conveying this benefit to other parties."

"So unlike the people benefiting from your rule in the Karsten domain, people who aren't swayed by fame can only judge what kind of person you are by how you appear to be, huh?"

It was entirely true that Crusch was a capable ruler who managed her territory well. But beyond those who could confirm her true skill for themselves, people had to rate Crusch based solely on second-hand bits and pieces of information.

Much like Emilia, often judged based on the mere fact that she was a half-elf, Crusch alienated those who were able to see only the negative side of her austere way of life.

"So I figured it's like this. I don't think you care much for people who judge based only on what's visible on the surface, but in a royal selection, you need to persuade even those people to come down on your side. So what should a girl do to convince people like that to see you in a better light…?"

"Well hey, if people judge only from appearances…then all you need to do is slap on a fresh coat of paint, right?"

Anastasia picked up where Subaru left off, bringing his point to its logical conclusion.

"Well, that's pretty easy to say, but it's not so simple to actually do it. In the first place, chances are good this is all a miscalculation. After all, you're wording things to be pretty convenient for yourself there, Subaru."

"I…can't argue with you there. There's no mistaking that Crusch is gathering weapons together for some big plan to somehow court the merchants to support her. But maybe tying that together with the White Whale is just a lot of wishful thinking on my part. I could have just convinced myself it's related to my knowledge about when and where the White Whale's gonna show up…"

Then, Subaru trailed off with a final "But..." while staring directly at Crusch.

Crusch kept her emotions off her face, and he couldn't get a glimpse of what lay in her mind. However, she hadn't refuted anything he had said yet.

That made the gamble worth it.

"I'll say it again. In return for an alliance between Emilia and Crusch, the Emilia camp offers the magic crystal mining rights in the Great Elior Forest in addition to information on the time and place the White Whale will appear—in other words, the honor of hunting down the demon beast that has threatened this world for far too long!"

"_____"

"If any part of what I'm saying is off the mark, then just go ahead and throw it right out. If I'm wrong, then you can go ahead and simply consider the info I have on the White Whale as a plain bargaining chip for us to haggle over."

Perhaps the two merchants present could simply take that information alone and turn a fine profit; Crusch herself could surely use that information to improve her reputation with merchants as a whole. It had at least that much value.

"But if what you're after is in line with what I'm hoping for, then—"

Subaru raised his right hand and offered it, inviting Crusch to take his hand—to tear down the wall between them, and to prove the future Subaru had seen was worth something.

"We should take out the White Whale—let's go on a hunt."

Subaru was proposing to Crusch that they hunt a creature of legend, a symbol of calamity to traveling merchants. That enormous, nightmarish Demon Beast of Mist that Subaru hated for its link to one of his abominable memories.

"Allow me to...ask you one thing."

Crusch examined Subaru's presented hand and raised her finger, pointing it toward him.

Subaru instinctively understood that the question Crusch would pose him was the final gate barring his path.

"You claim...to know when and where the White Whale shall appear. Is this absolutely certain?"

"—Yeah, it's true."

Subaru released the breath he had been holding as he gave his answer.

The final question was no accident—Subaru could not lie.

"I guarantee I know when and where the White Whale will show. You can bet your...life on it."

In fact, it really was information he had literally paid lives for—whether his own or those of others, over and over. There was no doubt about how reliable it was, nor could Subaru show weakness now that he had come so far.

"...Though there are still some points about which I have doubts, you have done well to see through my plans."

With a small sigh, Crusch closed her eyes as she replied, seemingly giving in.

At first, Subaru was unable to grasp exactly what she meant. But as the words slowly permeated his mind, their meaning gradually took shape and became clearer.

"Then that means..."

"I have misgivings. I have doubts. There are many elements I cannot comprehend, which makes accepting immediately difficult. However—"

Crusch lowered the hand with which she had used to point at him and positioned it against Subaru's. Now, Crusch's slender, pale fingers were firmly grasping the hand he had offered earlier.

"—I shall trust in your eyes and the spirit that leads us to the current state of affairs."

The negotiations had succeeded.

Seeing both of them shake hands, it was actually Russel's shoulders that visibly relaxed first. With an exaggerated breath, he was beside himself as he shook his head before he started speaking.

"There were a number of rather close calls, but it seems you have come to terms. Mr. Natsuki, can I assume that the promise you made prior to this meeting is still firm?"

"Yeah. Sorry it's not much of a deal. You were a big help, Russel. Just like I promised, I'll give you my cell phone after we're done hunting the White Whale."

Subaru responded to the devious smirk that came over Russel with one of his own. Noticing the exchange, Crusch had an exasperated expression on her face as she sighed.

"So you really were working together."

"Hey, I'm the one who invited him. I just asked him to give me a tiny helping hand."

"Please do not think poorly of me. In point of fact, I did my utmost to avoid any unnatural interference during the negotiations. At worst, I merely looked ahead to after you established an alliance."

Crusch shrugged her shoulders at Subaru's and Russel's nonchalant replies.

Subaru had gotten in contact with Russel immediately after exchanging information with Rem. Once he got a hold of Russel, whose negotiations with Crusch had similarly failed during Subaru's third time through the loop, they agreed to help each other during the meeting. That cooperation rested on the condition that Subaru would eventually hand over his cell phone.

Properly speaking, Russel also had a false understanding of the cell phone's capabilities, but Subaru came to peace with it by seeing it as a chance for Russel to get his hands on an electronic device made with future technology.

"Now then, it is your duty to clear up these remaining areas of doubt."

Crusch shifted her eyes from the link between Subaru and Russel, turning them toward Anastasia. Anastasia noticed that doubting gaze and tilted her head in an open question.

"Mm? You look like there's something you don't understand. But about what, I wonder?"

"I understand that Subaru Natsuki and Russel Fellow have goals that align. This makes your position suspicious. What, pray tell, were you invited here for?"

"Well, guess I see your point."

Anastasia embraced her scarf, pouting with an adorable *mmm* before continuing.

"There are two royal selection candidates and one of the capital's leading merchants assembled. If you have alliance negotiations with this many heavy hitters…it's not like nothing you say goes outside of that place, huh. But just having me here gave Natsuki's words weight, didn't it?"

"W-well, I did have a little bit of that in mind…"

Giving an evasive answer, Subaru hoped to muddy the waters even as he broke out into a cold sweat once she pointed out exactly what he had been thinking.

In actuality, he had another reason for calling Anastasia over, albeit closely related to the one she had just mentioned.

It was not to keep Crusch from saying anything carelessly. Subaru wanted to make sure Crusch didn't assume that anything he said was thoughtless and unfounded. By assembling so many important figures in one place, he felt it would lend greater credence to his words.

Though given Crusch's and Anastasia's particularly sharp intuition, he was afraid to ask just how much it had actually worked.

"Then there was another reason as well. And that was?"

"That's super-simple—it's because I'm a merchant."

Putting a hand over her lips, Anastasia smiled as she practically hopped forward. Then, she put both of her hands over Subaru's and Crusch's hands, still clasped together.

"I have big expectations for this hunt for the White Whale. For merchants like me, the White Whale is a matter of life-and-death, so if you're gonna take it out, I'll lend you two a big helping hand. Incidentally, you might want to consider the various products the Hoshin Company has on hand and ready to go?"

"Please wait. Surely the Merchant's Guild of the royal capital has precedence in this deal. Lady Anastasia, I would kindly ask that you refrain from interfering in this matter."

Russel rebuffed Anastasia's blatantly mercantile probing. As sparks flew between the competing merchants, Crusch looked at

Subaru, seemingly having deduced something from the mutual exchange.

"Wait. Listening to your words, it would seem that we are rather short on time."

"Well, I never heard a thing about that, either. I just thought it felt that way from how the conversation was going. But you're actually pretty hard-pressed, aren't you?"

With both Crusch and Anastasia staring at him, Subaru licked his dry lips.

Now that they'd formed an alliance, there was no point hiding the information anymore.

"—Yeah, that's right. According to the metia, the White Whale will appear about thirty hours from now. The location is...the area around the Great Flugel Tree."

"Thirty hours...!"

"The Great Flugel Tree—"

Crusch ground her teeth at the incredibly tight schedule. Anastasia tried to wrap her head around the name of the location.

Yes, the rest was a race against time.

"Within thirty hours, we need to deploy our forces to the Liphas plains, and strike at the White Whale with a coordinated attack just as it appears. For that..."

Crusch, quickly adapting to the situation, turned her head only to see Wilhelm nodding. The aged swordsman broke his previous silence and spoke.

"With regards to the attack force's organization, it has already been on standby in the royal capital for several days. In the first place, it had assembled in the royal capital to coincide with the timetable of the White Whale's expected appearance. Lady Crusch, I believe you are blessed that this should coincide with the beginning of the royal selection, but..."

"That was fast! But what? Is there a pattern to when the White Whale shows up?"

Though Wilhelm's news was a lifesaver, what Subaru heard also surprised him. As far as he knew, the time and place of the White

Whale's appearances were completely random. Its tendency to pop up anywhere, anytime was a part of the Demon Beast of Mist's greatest menace, but…

It was Ferris, advancing to Wilhelm's side, who answered Subaru's question.

"Figuring out the times and places the White Whale comes out is all Old Man Wil's hard work, *meow*. He's spent the last fourteen years living with only the thought of giving it a good pounding, *meow*."

Ferris's cat ears twitched. Then, he peered into the face of the broad-shouldered old man and spoke again.

"Thanks to Old Man Wil, I'm not worried about the morale or training of the troops, but I can't say the same for our logistics network. I mean, if people figured there was an army under Lady Crusch's command here in the capital, there'd be a huge fuss over it, so we've had to sneak stuff in bit by bit."

When Ferris pointed that out, Wilhelm's sharp eyes shifted Subaru's way.

"Certainly, I cannot say that our weapons and equipment preparations are completely in order… Sir Subaru, did you bring Mr. Russel and Lady Anastasia to the same table to address this?"

"Well, sometimes these things just happen… I wanted to say that at least once in my life, okay?"

Subaru scratched his head and returned Wilhelm's gaze with the answer he had prepared.

Russel, preeminent merchant that he was, accepted Subaru's reply and motioned to outside the window.

"I have already sent the guild notice to be ready to move. Preparations are happening as we speak. Allow us until tomorrow afternoon, and we shall gather everything that is necessary from the merchants here in the royal capital."

"Hey, the same goes for the Hoshin Company. Let's give merchants not part of the guild a chance to fill the gaps. You can expect various other things from us as well."

Anastasia followed Russel's words up with a strikingly powerful reply. Then, as Crusch folded her arms in relief, Anastasia smiled at her.

"I came here because it's an iron rule of commerce never to pass up a business opportunity. Selling things is nice, but, but, but, doing favors are number one! Intangible, no depreciation, no overhead—and more than anything, you can slap a price on it after the fact!"

"Hey, I'm glad she's on our side here, but hearing that makes me think 'Wow, this businesswoman's a real piece of work!' all over again."

Anastasia was a cute girl with an adorable blush to her cheeks, but she was a miser to the core and thus, very, very scary. Subaru couldn't even fathom the price she attached to her favors.

With Anastasia in a very good mood, Crusch glanced at her and nodded with an accepting look.

"So you prepared the path before negotiations took place. I see. So in this instance, it was I who lacked foresight and resolve. You have done well, Subaru Natsuki."

"I just crammed super-hard before the test. Me, I'm relieved to the bottom of my heart."

He'd schemed and prepared endlessly beforehand, but even then, successfully brokering the deal was still like tightrope walking across a knife's edge. Even with wild cards on his side, he still had an awful lot to learn. Even so...

"Guess I managed to save face for staying behind in the capital, Rem."

"Yes. You are incredible, Subaru, as I knew you would be."

He lifted up their still-clasped hands as he and Rem, the unsung hero of the negotiations, shared in each other's joy at their success.

There probably wasn't anyone happier at the result of the negotiations than Rem.

Originally, these negotiations had been Rem's appointed duty. He could easily imagine how being unable to divulge her task to Subaru and having to speak with Crusch day after day had whittled away at her spirit.

Subaru had continually rotted by himself while the future of the Emilia camp had been entrusted to her—she must have suffered under that burden.

He hoped that in some small way, this victory repaid the girl whose feelings had supported him for so long; if so, then for the moment, that was enough for Subaru to be happy.

"—Sir Subaru."

As Rem and Subaru celebrated together, a voice suddenly called out to him.

When he looked over, he saw Wilhelm, standing with his back straight as he watched Subaru with a serious demeanor. When the aged swordsman's eyes met Subaru's, emotions flooded onto Wilhelm's wrinkled, fearless face.

"Thank you."

With that brief statement, he went down on one knee on the spot.

The suddenness of it jolted Subaru. However, he was not alone in his surprise. Not only Crusch and Ferris, who knew Wilhelm, but even the others like Rem and Anastasia were startled.

"I offer thanks to you as deep as that I offer my lord, Duchess Crusch Karsten. I thank you for giving this elderly man an opportunity for vengeance."

"Uhh, that's...?"

"As wise a man you are, Sir Subaru, you have likely already deduced this, but allow me to reintroduce myself—"

Wilhelm paid no heed to Subaru's confusion, drawing his sword from its sheath. He lowered the blade onto the floor, then placed his hand upon it. It was the greatest possible gesture for paying the utmost respect.

Then, he spoke his name.

"Previously, I was known by Trias, my old surname. My true family name is Astrea. I took the previous Sword Saint, Theresia van Astrea, as my wife, sullying the family line of the Sword Saints—that is I, Wilhelm van Astrea."

After a breath, Wilhelm's eyes were filled with a glimmer of hope as he carried on.

"My warmest thanks, for granting this withered body a chance to slay the damned demon beast that robbed me of my wife."

Wilhelm deeply bowed his head, the emotions of his powerful, heartfelt plea slamming into Subaru all at once.

Everyone listening to the exchange was waiting in anticipation of Subaru's reply. To meet their expectations, Subaru drew a deep breath and answered.

"R-right…o-of course I knew. Naturally, that's how I was sure Crusch would agree to wiping out the White Whale!"

"Subaru Natsuki."

Crusch calmly interrupted Subaru's oddly flailing reply. Her amber eyes peered into Subaru's floundering expression when she sighed softly.

"A deceitful wind is blowing from you."

The power of the wind reading underscored how plain Subaru's paper-thin lie was.

CHAPTER 2
EVE OF THE DECISIVE BATTLE

1

—Slaying the White Whale.

With negotiations concluded, everyone involved acted quickly to make the word *hunt* a reality.

Just as the two merchants Anastasia and Russel had proclaimed, weapons and equipment were scrounged up from all over the royal capital, with Crusch mustering the punitive force she'd prepared beforehand. The rest, arranging dragon carriages to transport the additional people and supplies, was taken care of in short order.

"With so many dragon carriages being hired for this, no wonder I had so much trouble finding one to get back to Roswaal Manor."

As Subaru watched people and goods rapidly flow in and out of the mansion, he realized how much had been happening behind the scenes during the loop, completely without his personal involvement. During his previous trips through, Crusch and Wilhelm had already been preparing to fight the White Whale, even while Subaru was off in his own little world. Subaru had a rude awakening when he finally realized it after all that time.

He'd caused them trouble on three different occasions. He wondered if there was anything he could do to help.

"Hey, if there's anything I can…"

"Ehh, Subawu, there's nothing at all you *can* do, is there, *meow?*"

"Hey, I said if!"

Subaru, swept up by the busy atmosphere, was on the verge of offering some kind of help, but Ferris, concealing a yawn with a hand over his face, foiled Subaru's half-hearted attempt.

"Don't assume other people share your laid-back attitude. Even I must have something I can…"

"Preparing supplies and organizing troops are both outside your areas of expertise, aren't they, Subawu? And we can't have outsiders running all around, so sit and behave, okay?"

"Well, I can't do that. It's just that I'm the one who said 'let's do this' and everyone else is working into the dead of night while I'm…"

"That's where you're dead wrong!"

With Subaru all worked up, Ferris thrust a finger into the tip of his nose, interrupting with some terse words. Forced into silence, Subaru yelped as Ferris flicked his nose as he spoke.

"Ferri *really* doesn't like that it's-my-fault way of thinking. Or rather, I hate it."

"…I really am the reason why they're pulling an all-nighter, though."

It seemed strange for him to blithely sit around and quietly wait for the results.

"—Nowadays everything's all about the royal selection, but way back when, Crusch was just a normal, adorable princess without any thoughts of participating in kingdom politics."

"Huh?"

"Ah, did the princess part throw you off? She's always looked lovely, but Lady Crusch has become so strong and gallant since then that even men can't keep up…"

Subaru, bewildered by the topic's sudden onset, felt left behind as Ferris's cheeks flushed. Ferris let out a flustered sigh, swooning at the image of the young Crusch in the back of his mind as he continued.

"Lady Crusch is kind, wonderful, and invincible, earnest and valiant and more forthright than anyone...but the reason Lady Crusch turned into *this* Lady Crusch, strong enough to aim for the throne, is because she was at a certain someone's side."

"What are you talkin' about? And what do you mean, a certain someone...?"

"—His Highness Fourier Lugunica. This nation's late fourth prince."

Subaru, completely lost in this conversation, drew in his breath just a bit at Ferris's words. But he had more reasons for being at a loss for words than surprise at the name of a dead person he never knew.

"_____"

The fleeting, sad look on Ferris's face when he spoke the name had grabbed his attention.

His smile included a feeling of nostalgia and loneliness but, somehow, also a faint measure of pride. Even keeping his gender in mind, it was a beautiful sight that left Subaru short of breath.

"Watching you, Subawu, makes me remember Prince Fourier just a tiny little bit."

"...Was he someone with a mean-looking face?"

"Nah, he was handsome. You're not even in his league, Subawu. But the willful personality, the simplicity, the pure, blatant conceit... Well, I won't say any more, since it might insult him."

"I think that's already pretty insulting—and also a backhanded slap at me, too?!"

Apparently, it was their shared character flaws rather than similar faces that had gotten Ferris all sentimental. Sadly, Subaru couldn't deny any of them, but Ferris shook his head at Subaru's words.

"Prince Fourier was a confounding man to deal with, but he tried his very best. He always worried about how to act properly as a royal, and his inspirations caused all kinds of trouble for those around him. The prince wasn't talented, but he was full of drive, and he'd always listen to anything you wanted to ask him, *meow*."

"...Sounds like a pretty difficult guy to handle."

"That's right! He'd say, 'When everyone is working so hard, I simply cannot bear to be the only óne standing still!' Exactly like you are now, Subawu. But His Highness would never, ever say anything like, ''Tis my fault.' He wasn't someone to consider it, or even to think it at all."

The strained smile Ferris wore as his reminiscing words trailed off showed how much he cared for the prince. *Was that really such an important person?* Subaru wondered, before it finally dawned upon him.

The fourth prince of the Kingdom of Lugunica meant this Fourier person they were speaking about had died in the plague that became the impetus for the royal selection.

And if he was the reason why Crusch was aiming for the throne, that would mean—

"So this Prince Fourier and Crusch were…close?"

"They were similar in age, and Prince Fourier visited Lady Crusch's mansion a great deal. He'd drop in here and there, making an excuse every time, but he was bad at hiding things, so his real goal was obvious."

Ferris made a little smile as he cast his thoughts back in time, clueing Subaru in to how Fourier felt.

Ferris and Crusch's relationship went beyond that of mere lord and servant or man and woman. But for that Fourier person to be included in that relationship was no doubt very important to Ferris.

The relationship between the three was probably very special, and very precious.

"Ninety-five percent of the Ferri you see now is all because of Lady Crusch. But the most important part of that remaining five percent is thanks to Prince Fourier… That, I'm sure of."

The way Ferris gently lowered his eyes and put a hand to his chest as he spoke gave Subaru an odd feeling deep inside. Until then, he'd been firmly convinced that Ferris had never opened his heart to anyone besides Crusch. He thought it might be the healer's experience related to life and death that let Ferris dole out looks cruel enough to give people chills.

But when Ferris spoke of how he remembered Fourier, there was not even the tiniest trace of that.

"But what, you feel friendliness from me that's the same as what you felt from this Fourier person?"

"Hah? Why does that make Subawu and Fourier the same? I'll kill you."

"That's so mean it's scary!"

The sharp, impaling voice and dangerous look in his eyes made Subaru retreat a step, unnerved. Seeing this, Ferris cleared his throat.

"That's not how I meant it... I'm not going out of my way to talk to you about this right now because of that, Subawu... Aw, sheesh! Why don't you understand already, idiot!"

"Hey, that's not even the tiniest bit reasonable! The conversation jumped everywhere, so I didn't get it! What do you want from me, anyway?!"

Ferris stomped his foot on the floor in annoyance, with Subaru still cringing as a loud voice responded:

"Subaru, Master Felix, you are both speaking rather loudly, is something wrong?"

Rem, ostensibly packing luggage in the guest room, heard the ruckus and came down the stairs. Seeing the worried look on Rem's face, Subaru scratched his head, unsure how he ought to explain things.

"Er, I was thinking that maybe I could help out with something, but Ferris was saying I'd be in the way, and now I'm not even sure what he was trying to tell me."

"Subawu, you're just awful at putting things together. Sheesh, I tried to tell you... It's all because you tried to get in the way of everyone's work..."

"Don't call it 'getting in the way'! I wanna help. I mean, all this started because of me..."

"It's that!"

Ferris lifted his face, powerfully interrupting Subaru's meandering words. Then, the cat ears on his head made a little twitch as he poked a finger into Subaru's chest.

"Subawu, I hate how you say 'because of.' It's not 'because of,' it's 'thanks to.' That's why everyone's pulling an all-nighter and why Old Man Wil finally has a chance to fight the White Whale."

"Thanks to me…?"

Subaru quizzically tilted his head at words that didn't seem real to him. But Rem, standing close by, smiled at Subaru, agreeing with Ferris's satisfaction.

"Competing in the royal selection, fighting the White Whale… It's not really for Lady Crusch's own benefit. It's for *everyone*."

With Subaru cowed into silence, Ferris continued on.

"Hunting down the White Whale is Old Man Wil's fondest wish. Apparently, he wasn't able to be at his wife's side when the White Whale took her, the previous Sword Saint."

"The previous Sword Saint…"

"To take his revenge, Old Man Wil chased after the White Whale like he had a death wish. Without anything concrete to go on, it was a lot like trying to grab mist with your hand. He recorded the places the White Whale appeared, the time of day, the weather… For that, we went all over the place, testing different hypotheses, and finally, he figured out that there's something like an order to it."

Subaru wondered just how deep Wilhelm's vindictiveness ran.

Everyone knew of, and feared, the Demon Beast of Mist, a mighty foe in no small part due to how everything about the creature was shrouded in mystery—and yet, all alone, this elderly man continued to struggle against that being.

"But when he finally figured it out, no one would believe a word he said."

So the aged swordsman had spent night after night nursing his desire for vengeance as he pored over tomes with bloodshot eyes. Yet, when his fervor finally turned up a tangible lead, no one had the power to act on it—

"The kingdom's wounds from the Great Expedition still run deep. With the throne vacant, there wasn't anyone who could help Old

Man Wil. No one had the will to fight the White Whale, or the resources to spare… I think Old Man Wil was probably on the verge of despair when he couldn't find anyone to cooperate with him."

Wilhelm had yearned for vengeance, yet he could not even crawl to the foot of his hated foe.

Subaru knew the despair that came from crushing helplessness, for weakness was a sin that he himself couldn't escape.

"It seems like he thought about leaving behind everything and everyone he knew to fight the White Whale completely alone. I think his shame from not fighting it was outweighing the fact that he couldn't win—men really are idiots. His wife wouldn't have wanted him to do that, I'm sure of it."

"I suppose not…"

Yes, it was Rem, silent to that point, who agreed with Ferris.

Rem touched a hand to her own chest as she gently glanced at Subaru with her pale-blue eyes.

"I want the person I love to be happy forever. Even if I am gone, I want to be remembered with a smiling face."

"…It's way too soon to talk about remembrances, y'know."

Subaru couldn't help turning down Rem's sentimental words. He reached out with his hand and gave Rem's head a tiny poke, then gently touched her with his palm and caressed her.

Rem fondly narrowed her eyes at Subaru's open outburst of emotion.

"Then, it was Lady Crusch who approached Master Wilhelm?"

Ferris nodded, averting his face with a distant look in his eyes.

"That's because Lady Crusch is truly kind at heart. She'll reach out to someone drowning in grief and despair, or speak to a person everyone's turned their backs to, and she'll help anyone who wants to take care of someone precious to them— She'd say, 'That's what His Highness would do.'"

For a moment, Ferris closed his eyes; then, he lifted his face with a normal expression on it, sticking out his tongue.

"All right, weird talk over. It was a long talk, but the point is, Subawu, you don't need to brood over this one itsy bit! Besides, it's not like we're doing any of this for your sake, anyway! No one's as interested in you as much as you think they are!"

"Maybe you were trying to hide your embarrassment or something, but that was actually mean!"

"It is all right, Subaru. I am very interested in you. If this is what others think of you, then my feelings are ten times stronger."

"That's scary, too!"

After Ferris's harsh statement came Rem's very different follow-up. Buffeted by both, Subaru nonetheless tried to understand the core of what they were telling him.

"Man, that was a convoluted conversation..."

"That 'oh, now I understand' attitude really annoys me, *meow*. Hmph, that's Subawu for you."

"All that said...your tongue is somewhat too glib, Ferris."

"*Meow?!*"

Though he had adopted a blunt demeanor, Ferris jumped in surprise at the voice that suddenly came from behind. Anxiously, he looked back to see an aged gentleman standing behind him, arms folded.

Wilhelm's sharp stare seemed to make Ferris shrink.

"I cannot say it is a good hobby to speak excessively of a man's shame to others?"

"It's nothing to be ashamed of, *meow*. It's like a Ferri-style literary deconstruction of Old Man Wil's character?"

Ferris brought his fingers from both hands together and stuck his tongue out in a flirty pose. For all the world, he seemed like a pretty, adorable, cat-eared girl, but sadly, he was very much a guy.

Of course, that sex appeal was unlikely in the extreme to work on Wilhelm.

"At any rate, do not prattle so much about a person without his permission."

"Gooot it."

Curtly dressed down, Ferris's shoulders drooped as he meekly backed away. It was just like Ferris to bid them farewell, only to slip in a wink at the end.

But it was Subaru whose mental state was in chaos. Having unintentionally heard all the details about Wilhelm's past, he couldn't help feeling guilty.

He thought briefly about divulging his own past embarrassments to make up for it, but he could imagine what kind of scorched-earth landscape that would leave, so he firmly rejected the idea.

As a result, the silence continued unbroken, with a bead of sweat trickling down Subaru's brow.

"My apologies you had to hear that unpleasant tale. I do not wish to waste your time with an old man's trivial delusions. Please, forget them."

It was Wilhelm who broke the silence, trying to act like the conversation earlier had never happened. Seeing the painful smile on his face, Subaru silently resolved to respect his wishes. *Ask nothing*, said Wilhelm's silent wish. So he would ask nothing.

"You truly love your wife, don't you?"

—*Miss Rem?!*

Subaru's shock was palpable. Rem had walked directly into a veritable minefield.

Paying Subaru's nervousness no heed, Wilhelm raised an eyebrow for a moment before he replied.

"Yes, I love my wife. More than anything, more than anyone, no matter how much time may pass."

Wilhelm's age itself gave his statement that much more weight.

On several past occasions, Subaru had heard Wilhelm voice his feelings for his beloved wife. In those few moments, Wilhelm had conveyed just how dear his wife was to him, but now that he knew that these were Wilhelm's feelings for someone departed from this world, it stirred a different emotion deep within Subaru.

"If you will excuse me, preparations for tomorrow yet await. Please rest peacefully this evening."

With the pair falling silent, Wilhelm turned his back to them and gently headed off.

"Tomorrow—"

As Wilhelm excused himself, Subaru spoke to him spur-of-the-moment.

He stopped. But he did not look back when he started speaking.

"Tomorrow, Rem and I will be fighting with you."

"That is…"

"As if we can sit back and watch while our allies face a powerful enemy. Don't worry. Rem can fight…and I have things to do, too." Subaru piled onto his hastily spoken words, cutting off any rejection of his cooperation. Then he added, "Let's join our strength together and give that whale bastard a real beating! I'll help every way I can!"

"_____"

Subaru raised the thumb of his right hand as he swore that he and Wilhelm would be comrades in arms.

For a time, Wilhelm said nothing to his declaration. Then—

"—My wife was a woman who loved to admire flowers."

Haltingly, he replied to Subaru's oath in a very different tone.

"She did not care for the way of the sword, yet the sword loved her like none other. She was not permitted to live any life save one with the sword, and my wife came to accept that destiny."

Subaru had personally witnessed the might of Reinhard, the current Sword Saint. The blessing of Sword Saint granted the human body an absurd level of power—enough power to define a person's future and narrow one's possibilities without limit.

"It is I who robbed my wife of the sword and made her abandon the title of Sword Saint."

Once, Wilhelm had told Subaru that he was an aged swordsman with no talent—that his current state had been achieved after offering half of his life to the sword. What setbacks must he have suffered, what nails must have been driven into his heart until he arrived at that dear wish? And then—

"She abandoned the sword and became a woman—and my wife. All this she permitted so that she might live as Theresia instead of the Sword Saint— However, the sword did not forgive her."

If she had abandoned the sword, how had she ended up part of the White Whale expeditionary force?

However, Wilhelm's recollection did not touch upon that issue as he spoke.

"Sir Subaru, I thank you." After a breath, he added, "In tomorrow's battle, I shall find my answer with my own blade. I will be able to go where my wife rests. I shall finally be able to meet her."

Leaving those words behind, Wilhelm departed the room for good.

Subaru couldn't keep his entire body from trembling from the flood of emotions within him.

As a fellow man, Wilhelm's determination could not fail to inspire a deep reverence within him. Wilhelm was a man earnestly, sincerely beholden to love.

"Subaru..."

Suddenly, Rem's voice echoed across the now-silent room. Without a word, Subaru turned toward her, perfectly meeting Rem's gaze.

"...If I am gone, will you remember me just as long?"

"...I don't wanna answer that. It's bad luck."

Speaking with a voice of dismay, Subaru gave Rem's forehead a little poke.

When he touched Rem's forehead, she smiled with a happy expression, almost as if she'd received the reply she had been hoping for.

2

It was the following morning—seventeen hours before the appointed hour for subjugating the White Whale.

"Now then, it's Lady Crusch's orders, so go ahead, pick whichever one you like."

"Even if you put it like that..."

With a cool morning breeze blowing, Subaru was at the Crusch residence, utterly lost in front of a lineup of land dragons.

Ferris, wearing a white uniform of the Knights of the Royal Guard instead of his usual feminine clothing, was having Subaru examine the land dragons. With a snow-white cape on top, and a face full of zeal, Ferris's cheeks puffed up at Subaru's reply.

"What?! Lady Crusch went out of her way to be so kind, and you don't like them?!"

"It's not that. I'm really happy I can choose the land dragon I'll ride, but I don't have a clue how to figure out what's good or bad about each one. Do I look like a vet who's been handling 'em for decades?"

"Hmm...not even a little. So how about you pick based on intuition? Considering that it's who you'll trust with your life, and who you might end up dying beside, Ferri won't hold any choice against you, *meow*."

"Stop that! Don't raise weird event flags like that! I'm not planning to die here!"

Even with twelve-odd hours left before the decisive battle, Ferris didn't seem tense whatsoever. It was better than being oddly stressed out, but Subaru thought the mood was a little too slack.

At that moment, numerous land dragons were lined up in the front yard of the Crusch residence for the offensive against the White Whale. Many land dragons were for hauling freight, but a dragon mount to take into actual combat was an especially crucial decision. He'd heard that the House of Karsten had a fine selection, including famous dragons from excellent bloodlines, but...

"No matter how much I look, I can't really get past 'They seem really cool.' Rem, what do you think?"

Just like many knights setting out for battle with their favorite horse, Subaru had been given the privilege of choosing his mount. But at that rate, such a prized right would simply go to waste.

Rem, standing at Subaru's side while stroking the neck of the land dragon in front of her, responded to his prompt.

"I wonder. In my case, I can tell most land dragons which one of us is in charge, so I have had little reason to be concerned with the differences between individuals..."

"That figures. You really know how to crack the whip. Huh, what should I do...?"

The land dragon Rem was stroking sat on the ground, almost as if to display its submission. It probably did what came naturally after sensing that it stood lower on the food chain. Subaru couldn't really pull off the same thing, nor did he want to.

"If you spend too much time picking, we'll pay for it later, so pick quiiiick."

"You say it like this is none of your concern, sheesh."

"It actually isn't, but that's not the point. Seriously, they're all well bred, so you can't go wrong with any of these guys. Just pick on intuition."

"Well, that does make a certain amount of sense, but...mm?"

With Ferris urging him to hurry, Subaru walked around to examine the various land dragons, when he suddenly stopped. Rem had been walking beside him until he froze, which earned him a curious expression.

"Subaru, is something wrong?"

"Nah... This one just kinda caught my eye."

As Subaru stood still, there was a beautiful, pitch-black land dragon before him.

It had sharp facial features and yellow eyes. Resting atop the saddle on its back was a leather helmet for dragon riders. The variety of gear didn't differ from that of the other land dragons, but what struck Subaru were its eyes.

"_____"

The land dragon's quiet gaze gave Subaru a different impression compared to its peers. There was not even the tiniest smidgeon of the pride or fidelity that land dragons typically displayed. The pitch-black land dragon simply sat there, calmly waiting to be selected.

"Hey...you're the land dragon I met at the mansion a while back, aren't you?"

Subaru, suddenly recognizing the individual dragon, reached out toward it. At his side, Rem was a little startled and was instantly tempted to pull back Subaru's hand. But faster than Rem could stop him, the land dragon nuzzled its nose against Subaru's hand.

"...Looks like this one is number one."

"I am surprised. I believe this land dragon is from an especially proud breed... I was concerned it might eat your hand, Subaru."

"Okay, maybe I was a little careless just now!"

But he'd thought there was no need for such concern. Maybe he and the land dragon were on the same wavelength.

Subaru decided he'd bet his life on the black land dragon that had nuzzled him with the tip of its nose.

"Ferris, I'm picking this one. It's love at first sight."

"Yes, yes. Ohhh, nice pick. Subawu, you really are quite shameless... Also, don't say 'love at first sight'; you'll make Rem pout."

"I am not pouting. I will get along with it properly. I can do it."

Subaru was a little concerned at how she added extra words for emphasis, but with Rem's permission, Subaru's choice of mount was decided. Ferris, who had a few other things to take care of, remained behind while Subaru and Rem headed back into the mansion side by side.

There was little time remaining before they were due to set out.

The Crusch residence had been gathering manpower in bits and pieces, forming an expeditionary force with the goal of fighting the White Whale. Even among them, there was something in the hall that especially drew Subaru's attention...

"Wh-what are they doing here...?"

Subaru was beside himself, unwittingly staring right at them. A member of the group noticed his gaze and approached him with an audible patter.

"Guess you're part of the expeditionary force, too! Nice to meet-cha, bro!"

The voice Subaru heard had enough force to blow the crisp morning air away. The sound reached the far corners of the spacious mansion. Subaru could not help being struck by the forceful bellow.

Subaru put his hands on his ears and grimaced heavily, glaring back at the other party, but...

"I heard all about ya from the lady! You're the one who made today's whale hunt happen. Ain't that right?! From here on, I'm part of the hunt, too! Glad the weather's cooperating!"

"You're too loud! Can't those round eyes of yours read my reaction?!"

As a natural response to the booming words, Subaru ended up shouting, too.

His angry voice sent the dog-faced beast man into a laugh that was even more stupidly loud.

His entire body was covered in brown fur, with an oblong, dark-brown mane adorning his head like a Mahican hairstyle. However, he was almost six and a half feet tall, and the sight of his extremely muscular body clad in a leather outfit felt a lot like a truce coming after wildness and culture coming to blows. Subaru's eyes lingered on the steel epaulet protecting his otherwise exposed upper body, and the Hoshin Company logo engraved upon it.

"That logo on a beast man from Kararagi... That means you're Anastasia's Iron Fangs!"

"Wha—! Your voice is too quiet, bro! I can't hear what you're sayin'!"

"Oh, shut up for a second! What the hell did you eat to grow that big?! What race are you?!"

"I'm a kobold, can't you tell?! As if there could be a dog race besides kobolds?!"

"Huh, kobold... Wait, there's no way?!"

The beast man had called himself a kobold, but Subaru's image of a kobold was a little person with a dog face. The dog face and the humanoid body were in line with what he expected, but the body size was way, way off.

"They call me Ricardo. Nice to meet you, too, missy!"

"Yes, Master Ricardo. Thank you for your kind words. My name is Rem."

Emotionally prepared for Ricardo's hearty greeting, Rem politely introduced herself in turn.

When Subaru glanced, watching the exchange, he saw Anastasia with a grin coming over to the head of Ricardo's group—a band of beast people.

When her mischievous smile met Subaru's sour look, she teasingly tilted her head.

"Oh no, Natsuki. It would seem Ricardo isn't very agreeable with your ears. The best way to get along with him is to not wander too close, you see."

"It would've been useful to know about that before meeting him. You really are rough on people."

"Sorry, I couldn't help wondering how you'd react, you see..."

"Not just rough on people, a bad personality, too. Er, ow!"

As Anastasia giggled teasingly, Ricardo's huge beast-man hand gave Subaru's head a little push. He opened his big mouth wide to speak, which neatly displayed his fangs.

"Hey, bro! Watch your mouth when speaking with the lady! Be a little nicer to our employer, will ya! She almost never talks to anyone if it's not about profits and losses, so she has no friends! At this point, you can probably get in good with her with a little kindness!"

"Ricardo. If you're going to sweep something under the rug, best not to be insulting about it along the way, yes?"

"It's not an insult! I'm worried about you, miss! Ever since way back, you never got along with people too well, so comin' here from Kararagi without anyone you know has gotta been wearing you down, right?! But lookie right here! Heeeere ya go, friend number one!"

"Hey, don't butt in and babble when people are talking! And don't go grabbing a guy's head and shaking it around like that! That ridiculous strength of yours could tear my head off!"

Assailed by literally superhuman strength, Subaru tried to somehow shake his attacker off before his neck snapped first. In a hurry, he escaped from Ricardo and immediately began neck-stretching exercises, rotating his head around.

"M-man, that was close. Wouldn't be funny to get injured and sidelined during chitchat right before the big battle. I'm pretty worked up for this, so no way am I gonna accept that kind of foul-up..."

"What's with the big fuss! I'm just tellin' you guys to get along!"

"Maybe different cultures have different definitions of getting along. Are all Kararagi people like this?"

"Well, of course not. Ricardo's special. You see a vast difference in elegance and grace between him and me, don't you?"

Anastasia stood beside Ricardo and brazenly laid out her claim. Subaru deeply exhaled, pushing Rem forward as he countered.

"Now, look. If you wanna talk about real grace, talk about someone like Rem. See this elegance?"

"Oh no... Calling me cute like this... I'm blushing."

"Hmm, a strange girl, but she seems nice and has excellent future prospects. You've got quite the catch there, Natsuki."

Subaru almost wanted to say that it was more like they had caught each other, but Rem's reaction was already a little different from what Subaru expected, so it was hard for him to bring it up.

Then, Crusch emerged from below Subaru and the others at the head of a motley assembly.

"From the look of things, you have finished getting to know one another."

Crusch was not in her usual handsome dress uniform but rather, a light suit of unornamented armor. The build clearly focused on ease of movement; perhaps prioritizing mobility was in itself a feminine choice. To Subaru's eyes, it seemed questionable how much protection it would be able to provide the wearer.

"It is better to wear gear that is easy to move in. Do not be overly concerned. An earth blacksmith engraved this with the durability blessing. So long as my mana is not exhausted, it is far stouter than it appears," Crusch explained, realizing the doubts behind Subaru's gaze, and she touched a hand to her breastplate.

"There's a thing like that? As usual, magic and blessings are basically cheating... Maybe I have a convenient blessing like that sleeping inside of me and I just don't know yet?"

"No matter how long a person sleeps, it is not as if anyone ever forgets how to breathe, yes? That is what blessings are like for those who possess them. If you are not aware of one, it is best to abandon the notion."

Having experienced a similar put-down once before, Subaru pouted and discarded his faint hope.

Rem comforted Subaru as if she were consoling a sulking child. Meanwhile, Crusch noticed Ricardo gazing down at her, so she peered up at his huge frame and spoke again.

"I see. I had heard the stories, but you are an even greater warrior than rumored. So you are the captain of the Iron Fangs, the blade who stands by Anastasia Hoshin's side?"

"In the end, we're just being paid to do a job. You're Crusch Karsten, right? Besides the usual rumors, I've heard about you from the lady, but seeing you in the flesh is…"

With Crusch folding her arms and looking up at him, Ricardo audibly sniffed, using his canine sense of smell. Then, the folds of his nose crinkled and his throat rumbled in laughter.

"What a piece of work! This royal selection's gonna be pretty tough, miss!"

"Well, that's why we have to sell favors like this. The price tag I can put on it depends on how hard you work, so better work hard, Ricardo."

"Gah-ha-ha-ha! That's our lady! Whether it's people or dogs, she works them to the bone!"

Anastasia seemed to agree with Ricardo's assessment of Crusch. Maybe she and the stupidly laughing Ricardo had been working together for a long time, for Anastasia seemed like just a regular young girl when talking with him. She must have had a soft spot for him.

Loud voice aside, Subaru didn't sense any problems dealing with Ricardo, either. Maybe it was just his personality as a man, or perhaps he should say as a dog? However, Subaru did feel like he was just a bit too outspoken…

"Did you rest well last night?"

Crusch shifted her gaze away from Ricardo to show Subaru some consideration. Subaru was still massaging the neck Ricardo had twisted a short while ago as he responded.

"Yeah, thanks. It didn't seem like a good thing to be sleeping so easily while the rest of you were busy, though."

"There is a time and place for everything. Your job was assembling myself, Russel Fellow, and Anastasia Hoshin last night and accomplishing the formation of the White Whale expeditionary force. Indeed, from my perspective, your offering to assist in fighting the White Whale was unexpected."

After a faint smile, Crusch's lips became taut as she stared straight at Subaru. Seeing the complex emotions behind her amber eyes, Subaru wilted at what might be coming next.

"I am grateful for assistance in fighting the White Whale...but can you fight?"

"Not really? If you count me in, I'm like the cat's claws you borrow, because you're scraping the bottom of the barrel. A dog's claws can get pretty big, though."

"Hey, were you talkin' 'bout me just now?!"

"I was, but you don't need to butt in! Man, you've got convenient hearing!"

Subaru yelled at Ricardo for interrupting the conversation, but Crusch's eyes had gone wide when he openly declared that he was useless in combat. Subaru racked his brain over how to explain it to her.

"So as fighting goes, it's like that...but I think I'll be a help against the White Whale."

"Let's hear it, then. What do you mean?"

"I'm not all that happy about this, mind you...but it seems that I have a peculiar scent that attracts demon beasts."

The odd nuance of Subaru's statement once again pressed Crusch into silence. However, when Rem stated, "There is no mistake," in an odd agreement while standing beside him, Crusch displayed only a brief hint of concern before asking him to continue.

"I shall tentatively state that I understand. Please give us the details."

"Maybe *scent* isn't quite the right word, but it's a physical condition I have. In fact, when we had that demon beast incident back at the mansion we mentioned last night, I used it to lure the demon beasts."

"Is that so…? Then the fact that you possess a metia to warn you of the danger of demon beasts is connected to this?"

"Ah, that's some unexpected foreshadowing you— Er, I'm just talking to myself."

With suspicious gazes trained on Subaru, he shut his mouth before he said too much.

"Anyway, I think that characteristic of mine will probably work on the White Whale, too. If I'm there, we can predict to a decent degree where the White Whale goes. But when we do, the demon beast's danger level is off the charts, so expecting me to actually fight it is a little much."

An Urugarum was about as dangerous as a large dog. Even so, they had nearly killed him. Not that threats were proportional to body length, but the White Whale was thousands of times larger than an Urugarum. By himself, Subaru couldn't outrun the White Whale, let alone counterattack.

"That's why I'll take the land dragon you lent me and run around right under the White Whale's nose to draw its attention. While it's doing that, you'll go after it full force…or at least that's the tactic I'd recommend."

To be blunt, it was a plan he wasn't sure he could speak from his own lips. He was saying they couldn't count on him for fighting strength but that he'd be useful running around the battlefield as bait. It was a role that would make even those with a death wish turn pale.

"—I do not sense any deceit from you, which surprises me greatly."

Crusch put a hand to her chin, barely able to believe her eyes as she let out a sigh of resignation. She'd no doubt weighed Subaru's statement with the blessing of wind reading, considering how the truth or falsity affected its effectiveness for the operation.

"Many times in the half day since last night, I have wanted to doubt my own blessing. I do not claim it is infallible, but…"

"You've lost a little confidence in it?"

"No. I simply get tense when the world exceeds my expectations in various ways."

As she said those words, a smile came over Crusch that did not seem sore or bitter. It was the expression of a beautiful lioness, which she immediately hid under a gallant expression as she continued speaking.

"I heard from Ferris that you selected a fine land dragon even by my house's standards. If that is the role you desire, I have no objections. However, I require that you obey my commands."

"Also, I guess it goes without saying with that outfit, but you're planning on fighting, too, Crusch?"

"Do you think I can simply sit in a chair at my mansion and await good news?"

Crusch flicked a finger off a fitting on her armor, puffing out her chest as if the answer was obvious. Subaru, seeing her so valiant, politely lowered his head for having asked about something so self-evident.

"—It seems everyone has assembled."

Accepting Subaru's apology, Crusch closed one eye as she murmured. As if taking those words as a signal, people trod into the mansion's great hall one after another. All of them were clad in combat gear and possessed stern visages. Their various pieces of equipment seemed well worn, giving off the impression of seasoned veterans. But Subaru was struck more by their ages.

"Somehow, some of these members...don't look so young."

Subaru gave voice to what immediately came to mind.

The people passing before Subaru's eyes were probably participating in the expeditionary force. In one line, there were ten or so men with a rather high average age; it was probably that none of them were younger than fifty.

It was unlikely that anyone had heard Subaru's comment, but suddenly, one of the men turned to look his way. Before he knew it, Subaru froze as the man stepped toward him.

"Lady Crusch, we have arrived— Is this him?"

"Yes, it is."

The one posing the question to Crusch in a sober voice was a middle-aged man with both hair and beard graying. The man nodded to Crusch and faced Subaru once more, stretching a hand to his shoulder. Then, he spoke.

"Thank you, lad."

"Eh?"

"Thanks to you, our dearest wish has been granted. We have never been happier."

Subaru unwittingly lost his bearings as the hand grasping his shoulder conveyed the man's strong feelings.

"Thank you," said the man, patting a rocked Subaru on the shoulder before walking off.

From behind, Rem watched the men leave as she whispered into Subaru's ear, "All of them most likely have some connection to the White Whale."

"Connection to the White Whale... You mean, related to the old expeditionary force or something?"

"Though there were many who had already retired from fighting on the front lines, these are the warriors who answered Wilhelm's call to participate in the current expeditionary force. Their morale and level of training are in no way inferior to any currently serving as a royal knight."

"So it's some old men who are dying for a chance at vengeance, huh...? I'm getting all fired up."

Subaru felt something stir within him as he glanced over, watching Crusch examine the soldiers. It was Crusch who had set her sights to even exterminating the White Whale so that Wilhelm might realize his vengeance. The old men joining the battle must have felt the same gratitude toward her for giving them a chance to fulfill their greatest wish.

It was probably partly the "kindness" of Crusch that Ferris had spoken of the previous night, and the will of "His Highness" who had so greatly influenced her way of life.

"You're not telling me that those guys are all the forces we've got for this fight, right?"

"Those that arrived here are the principal members. The remainder should have already set out for the Great Flugel Tree to facilitate the force's deployment along the Liphas Highway."

In other words, with the appointed hour impending, those assembled were the VIPs of the expeditionary force. The participation of the old veterans really imparted the feeling that the decisive battle was finally drawing near. As he might have expected, the tension in Subaru's heart rose, along with the feeling that it was a must-win battle.

"The time is ripe. I want both of you in the hall as well."

Crusch looked up at the time crystal above the entrance, speaking curtly. She was surely to address the troops before departure, a kind of motivational speech to boost morale.

Just as Crusch set out, Subaru saw Wilhelm and Ferris entering from the hall. Ferris was dressed in the same outfit Subaru had already seen him in when encountering him in the courtyard earlier, but Wilhelm was not.

Gone was the usual black uniform; instead, he wore a light, minimalist suit of armor protecting only the most vital of organs. On both sides of his hips, he wore a total of six slender swords, and he seemed almost too ready to fight.

"Oh, so you're here, too, Russel. Maybe we can chat a bit?"

Following behind Wilhelm and Ferris was dark-blond-haired Russel. He looked like he had been working all night, but with the great battle before them, his eyes were overflowing with vitality.

"If you're making that face, then it's probably safe to say that you held up your end. How about you, Anastasia?"

"Did you really think I'd come up short?"

"Not really, but I just thought I'd ask."

When it came to who seemed the most meticulous out of all the royal selection candidates, Anastasia was second to none.

With preparations steadily completed and the appointed hour fast approaching, the hall was tense with fighting spirit. In moments, all would be set into motion toward the decisive battle.

"But before that..."

Subaru had one thing he had to do.

Rem, standing beside him, tilted her head and glanced sidelong at Subaru as he called out to Anastasia just as she turned to head off as well.

"Anastasia. Would you mind letting Russel join us for a little chitchat?"

"Heh..."

When Anastasia stopped and looked back, her face was all business. She was acutely sensitive to the fact that Subaru had something to offer. The girly attitude vanished from her eyes, replaced by the glint of a merchant flicking an abacus in her head.

In that moment, the transformation was reassuring.

Subaru headed for Russel, an impish Anastasia in tow. Noticing the pair's approach, life returned to Russel's tired face.

Truly, merchants were a reliable bunch.

"I have something to discuss with you, as two merchants who are successful and possess a sharp eye for the future. You might laugh this off as counting my chickens before they hatch, but this is about after the whale's taken out."

With that preamble, he proceeded to "prepare the battlefield" on the eve of the White Whale's extermination.

3

"—Four hundred years."

The appointed hour came, and with those words, she began to address the assembled troops.

Her voice was grave; the atmosphere, strained.

Amid sharp sensations akin to pain running up a spine being stretched, Crusch stood perfectly straight, chest thrust forward, as all eyes rested upon her.

Crusch stood upon the floor with a treasured sword bearing the mark of the House of Karsten, the Lion Rampant, and rested her hands upon its hilt as she slowly surveyed the faces of all present and said:

"Four centuries have passed since the Witch of Jealousy, the worst calamity in all of recorded history, threatened the world. During this time, the White Whale born of the Witch's hand has made the world its very own hunting ground, dominating and savaging those weaker than it."

The Witch of Jealousy was the one who had apparently swallowed half the world in ages past. Her very name had been synonymous with fear for as long as anyone could remember. Having lost its master, the Demon Beast of Mist danced to its own tune.

From the Great Expedition launched fourteen years prior on down, the monster had given rise to many casualties in every nation, swallowing one's very will to fight.

"The lives the White Whale has taken are beyond measure. Perhaps it is better to say, the mist's vile nature itself ensures that we will never know the true number of casualties. Over the course of four hundred years, the number of names on tombstones, and the graves that do not even have names, have only increased."

Crusch's words made some old men stare at the ground, gritting their teeth as they held back sobs. There were others whose chests contained fierce, inexhaustible emotion, quiet anger they had carried with them, waiting for a chance to let it explode.

Their regrets, their hatred piled up with every corpse, began to envelop the atmosphere of the hall in stagnant darkness.

However—

"But today, that time is over."

"_____"

"We shall bring it to an end. When we slay the White Whale, it will dispel so much sadness. Those who have never permitted themselves a moment shall finally be granted a proper chance to grieve."

"—!"

"We shall end this pathetic demon beast, unceasingly obeying the command of its dead master."

Subaru's chest was on fire.

Without saying a word, everyone conveyed the same heat that was burning inside him.

The old veterans were looking down; the warriors clenching their fists. The aged swordsman had closed his eyes—but now, all of them stared at Crusch, standing before them.

Accepting their gazes, Crusch thrust a hand out, speaking in a great voice.

"We march! To the Liphas Highway! To the Great Flugel Tree!"

"—Yes!!"

The stomping on the ground accompanying the roaring response seemed to make the very earth quake. Subaru realized that the hot fighting spirit surging within him had made him shout as well.

Among them all, Crusch stood stronger and taller as she raised her drawn treasured sword to the heavens and made a proclamation.

"This night, by our hand—the White Whale will fall!!"

The Battle of the White Whale, the largest operation since Subaru had been summoned to that world, had commenced.

CHAPTER 3

THE BATTLE OF THE WHITE WHALE

1

With Duchess Crusch Karsten at the head, the latest expedition to defeat the White Whale set forth.

It was the first operation of its kind since the Great Expedition of fourteen years prior, undertaken with the expectation of fierce combat few would ever see.

The expeditionary force assembled for the campaign was under Crusch's command—with Wilhelm van Astrea, member of the family of Sword Saints, appointed as captain.

The troops serving under Wilhelm were divided into fifteen platoons, with each headed by one of the old veterans who had attended Crusch's address in the great hall. Each platoon was composed of fifteen men, so the combined force under Crusch's command numbered roughly 220.

However, the total combat strength was not limited to that. A wagon train under Russel's command was apparently running ahead of them to the site of the decisive battle, the Great Flugel Tree, so they could begin transporting the supplies necessary for deployment.

On top of that, thirteen members of the beast-man mercenary

group Iron Fangs, on loan from Anastasia, had joined under Ricardo's command. Ricardo was in overall command with two lieutenants reporting to him.

And the "lieutenants" of the Iron Fangs were...

"I'm Mimi!"

"I'm Hetaro!"

With great energy, the two kitten-like beast people waved, then politely bowed.

They had orange fur, and their heads didn't even reach up to Subaru's hips. They had adorable faces, and really, the snow-white robes covering them up to their necks suited them very well, so if Subaru was to put his thoughts bluntly—

"They're so cute I wanna steal them for myself!"

"The miss says that a lot, too!"

"Th-there you go saying that again, Big Sis..."

The girl calling herself Mimi laughed vibrantly at Subaru's thought, with the young boy calling himself Hetaro appearing oddly ruffled as he rebuked her. Based on how he addressed her, they were siblings—probably twins. They looked like a tomboyish older sister with a straitlaced, docile younger brother following in her wake.

Subaru had no objection to the charm, but what mattered here wasn't appearance but ability. They weren't heading off to a picnic.

"So it's not that I'm doubting you, but...you're really lieutenants?"

"Mm? Mister, have you met Mimi somewhere before? Mmmm, I can't remember, but it really feels like it...!"

Mimi crossed her arms and cocked her head, but Subaru glossed it over with a strained smile.

It couldn't be helped that she didn't remember him. To Subaru, the first time he met Mimi was during the events of the last go-around. Furthermore, it wasn't an occasion he wanted to remember.

However, then and now, Mimi's bottomless cheer was completely unchanged...

"Don't worry about it. My name's Subaru Natsuki. So are you two good?"

"Okay, won't worry! And Mimi and Hetaro are the best! If TB's with us, we're even stronger! Super bestest! Ka-ching!"

"Errr, yes, that's right. Big Sis and I will both work hard."

The younger brother took the reins of his boastful older sister and somehow brought her under control. Watching the two, Subaru had to wonder if that world had any older sisters besides ones making the younger sibling follow in their footsteps.

"—? What is the matter, Subaru?"

When Subaru, harboring that question, looked at Rem, she tilted her head with a questioning expression and an adorable smile. At that point, Subaru cleared his throat, turning back to face Mimi as he said, "Well that is an awful lot of confidence. Lieutenant's not something you can be unless you're hot stuff."

"In place of the captain and Big Sis, I give orders out to everyone else."

"Ahh, I see... Tough job, huh."

Subaru imagined the older sister running alongside the belligerent giant, dashing across the battlefield with a hearty laugh. That would mean, lieutenant or not, Hetaro was the only one actually performing the appropriate duties. The cute older sister was like an image of naive recklessness drawn by a child.

"We will follow Lady Crusch's commands to the extent possible, but we have our own ways of fighting. I thought it was best to inform you of this to minimize chaos, Mr. Natsuki... Er, Mr. Natsuki?"

"No, I'm just impressed you're so sharp and serious. That attention to detail is comparable to Rem."

"Mm-hmm, he's just amazing!"

"Now you'll make Big Sis get carried away again... So cute."

For some reason, Mimi was the one to puff her chest out in pride when she saw Subaru's frank assessment of Hetaro. Hetaro had a constrained look on his face from Mimi's reaction, only to slip in what he really thought at the very end.

Subaru added the drawback of overly spoiled big sisters to the list of high-spec misgivings he had about twins of that world. Hetaro was in Rem's league on that point, too. Growing up with Mimi surely had no small amount of influence on Hetaro.

Having finished meeting the siblings, Subaru glanced at his cell phone to check the time.

—Twelve hours remained until the White Whale was scheduled to appear.

They had about half the distance left to their destination, likely giving them about five hours after arrival until the decisive battle.

"Once we get to the Great Tree, we'll have to go over the operation one last time... It seems like having me running around is gonna create a fair bit of chaos."

"This time, you will have me by your side, Subaru—I won't allow a repeat of what happened when we fought the Urugarum."

Rem replied to Subaru's comment with quiet resolve burning in her eyes.

"I really am opposed to this. I believe using the scent of the Witch to lure the White Whale is too dangerous...and in the first place, the fact that the scent comes from you is..."

"I'll use anything I can. If it adds a tenth of a percent to the win rate, that's a bet I'll take. I come up short on so many levels, if I don't do even this, I'll never make up for it."

"You are amazing, Subaru."

Even faced with Subaru's determination, this was one thing Rem stubbornly refused to let go of. The way she seemed to pout as she turned her face away was a rare display of a flood of emotions, making Subaru's smile not so much strained as very, very soft.

Subaru felt all too keenly the obvious change in Rem's demeanor in the last half day. Ever since the demon beast incident, he'd been convinced Rem had opened her heart to him, but it was only the previous day that their hearts had connected in a true sense.

Perhaps Rem had sensed that where time had stopped, it had begun to move once more. Truly, it was so.

That was why—

"I wanna win this."

Quietly, Subaru voiced that hope.

At present, things had proceeded apace to a degree he couldn't even have imagined during prior go-arounds. Where no one would listen to him no matter how much he pleaded, this time, they accepted his request. Relations with the Crusch camp, destined for rupture, were good. Setting aside the exposure of all the embarrassing things inside him, it was no boast to say his relationship with Rem was now a far stronger bond.

But on the other hand, it was a fact that things had developed in a way more perilous than ever before.

Even in that moment, the menace of the White Whale was seared into Subaru's mind, clear as day. Even Rem's might had proved completely unequal to the task against its huge, flying frame, able to send a dragon carriage flying in pieces with not even an attack but a flick of its tail. Its open maw swallowed a land dragon and the ground under it whole; its death cries, when those vile, millstone-like teeth ground its flesh, would never leave his ears.

Just the thought that he was heading to face that thing made his limbs tremble, but he couldn't stop running forward.

Yet, even as Subaru's mind backslid toward weakness...

"_____"

Rem, sitting beside him, peered at Subaru as if she could see straight into his mind.

A weak, helpless Subaru Natsuki could not be permitted before Rem's eyes.

"Even I know that resolve doesn't make everything okay, but..."

Even if he'd stopped being a pessimist, that didn't mean his fortunes had improved dramatically. The route he was on held even greater danger ahead, yet he absolutely couldn't say preparations were ideal.

All Subaru could do was what he thought best in the limited time available to him, calling on the girls and their allies for aid and leaving all the rest that lay ahead to the power of others. That said, Crusch and the others sought nothing further from Subaru, which was absolutely not because they were maltreating Subaru as a useless troublemaker.

But when the time came, he'd do whatever he could with everything he had.

Because the things Subaru could do occupied such a narrow range, he had to at least firmly grasp the range's breadth, thinking of what he could do within those limits.

"In other words, it's the same as usual. Guess that goes without saying, though."

"What's up, bro—? That's a determined-lookin' face you got there."

Abruptly, Ricardo, riding alongside the line of dragon carriages, observed Subaru, laughing as he spoke.

Glaring back at the dog-headed beast man, Subaru firmly twisted the corners of his lips.

"That's right. Took long enough, but it's rock solid. I'm really something when I've set my mind, okay? Whatever happens, I'm not givin' up on the future, even if it kills me."

"That's a man's words there! The lady's gonna be real happy to hear that! Like I figured, you're just the friend the lady needs!"

"I don't think shaking her hand away from the big stage is a bad thing, either… Ah, but if I get along nicely with Anastasia, there's a troublesome guy there, too…"

Remembering Anastasia made him remember the sight of a handsome man beside her as a package deal.

Even his beating at the parade grounds at Julius's hand seemed like a long time ago. He'd experienced time on the level of weeks, even though it had been only five days or so in actual time lapsed.

Then, Subaru's words brought a huge, irrepressible smile over Ricardo's big mouth.

From the reaction and the teasing look in his eyes, it seemed he'd heard all about Subaru's humiliation. Naturally, Subaru turned his face away in a visible sulk.

"If you're gonna laugh, laugh nice and hard. Even I can now appreciate just how little I read the mood back then."

"Hey, wait up! It's not that I'm findin' funny, it's somethin' else. Well, you'll figure it out on your own, so dumpin' it all out here would be just rude!"

Thus self-convinced, Ricardo stroked his own mane as he cut the topic off. The suggestive behavior tugged at Subaru, but even if he pressed the point, odds of a reply were slim.

"Incidentally, I've been meaning to ask you something since we set out..."

"What? Ask me anythin'. We're buds, bro! If it's not crazy stuff, I'll talk about whatever! And if it is, it depends on what nails I'm steppin' on!"

"That part sounds like the Kararagi in you talking... I was just thinking, those huge dogish creatures you guys are riding, they're really something else."

Subaru pointed below the enthused Ricardo's rump to the creature he was riding, unsure how best to broach the subject.

The beast mounts that Ricardo's Iron Fangs were riding were completely different creatures from land dragons. The closest comparison was to a huge dog, but the huge frames of the carnivores rivaled that of lions and tigers from his original world, and their speed and endurance were in no way inferior to that of land dragons.

Subaru's comment brought an understanding expression from Ricardo as he patted the beast mount on the back.

"You don't see 'em much in these parts. These critters are called ligers. They're as precious in Kararagi as land dragons are over here. They're real territorial, so it's tough to raise 'em, which is why there ain't many in Lugunica or other countries."

"Ligers..."

When he blinked and looked, Subaru thought he was seeing some kind of offshoot of the Urugarums he had a history with. Fortunately, there were no signs of horns on their heads, and compared with those demon beasts, their faces were clearly more adorable. If the demon beasts seemed more like wolves, he could say that the ligers definitely looked more like dogs.

But having Ricardo, a dog-type beast man, riding on top of that super-huge dog was a little—

"Somehow, it's a really weird feeling, like someone should paint this...but don't you feel awkward?"

"Sometimes people mention that, but not really. I mean, I'm a beast man, this is an animal, big difference between us... Ah, now that you mention it, some guys might get ticked off if you say that. I don't mind, though."

"Nah, I was wondering if I should say anything or not. Sorry, my bad."

"Gah-ha-ha, well ain't that honest of ya!"

Baring his teeth as he laughed, Ricardo gave the back of the liger's neck a good rub. The liger made no reaction to its master's action, but the way it silently indulged its owner certainly make it look like a good, loyal dog. Even with the size difference, it apparently hadn't lost any of its canine virtues.

"Ligers don't have the horsepower that land dragons do, but their agility's way up there. Just watch, a wild battle to send the whale packin' is right up our alley!"

"Horsepower, huh. Guess you still measure animal power like that, even with dragons and dogs all over the place... Not that I've actually seen a horse."

He'd heard straight from Emilia's mouth that they existed, but he hadn't actually seen one in that world yet. Apparently, their rate of use was fairly low.

After that, Subaru pointed to the expeditionary force on the march behind them.

"So less horsepower is why you have teams of dogs for pulling each carriage? Why not just have land dragons haul the freight? Don't want the dogs to get tired before the main event."

"Hey, we've gotta move our own stuff ourselves. Besides, don't worry, any liger haulin' freight is a liger properly trained for it. We don't spoil 'em, and no enemy's swinging 'em off their feet, White Whale or not."

With a gulp, Subaru somehow stopped his internal mental turmoil from coming out onto his face. On the other hand, Ricardo failed to notice Subaru's surprise as he spoke.

"You never know what you'll come across on the road, like bandits or whatever. If you take too much time, you'll be late, and that's the worst outcome of all. So we've gotta at least be able to carry stuff by ourselves."

"…No way there are any bandits who have the guts to attack a completely armed group like you guys. If they did, it wouldn't be brave—it'd be a death wish."

"Got a point there!"

Ricardo burst into laughter and, waving to Subaru, shifted away from the dragon carriage. He took up his post at the head of the beast mounts as other people around them looked over at the loud conversation.

"It would seem that Master Ricardo is going around speaking like that to alleviate everyone's tension before the battle."

"_____"

Watching Ricardo go off into the distance, Subaru heard Rem's soft whisper into his ear. A bitter smile crossed Subaru's face as he realized, suddenly, that the big beast man was looking out for him.

"And here I was thinking I'd hardened my resolve…"

Meaning, he still seemed awful green from his senior's perspective— even though the impending battle with the White Whale was but the first hurdle, with others waiting ahead.

"Geez, you can say, 'Set forth, hero,' but it sure is easier said than done."

Subaru murmured very quietly so that Rem might not hear, but his cheeks formed a smile.

The things he had to do and the things he wanted to do were one and the same, and he had someone at his back to urge him to do them—he supposed that made it all worth it.

Their morale was at its peak on the eve of the approaching battle.

"—Now, let's do this, Mr. Fate."

2

Fortunately, the expeditionary force safely arrived at its destination without any undue trouble.

· As scheduled, they arrived five hours early—the gleaming moon had just begun to rise on the night of the decisive battle.

The expeditionary force deployed, linked up with the vanguard, and proceeded to inspect arms and go over the operation one last time. Naturally, Subaru participated in the discussion, and when details of the operation were hammered out, how everyone would maneuver included, any time remaining before the fight was for free action.

And as he spent his time until the operation with various thoughts running through his head, Subaru—

"It...sure is huuuge."

"You seem very happy, Subaru."

Looking up to the point that his neck hurt, Subaru almost couldn't see the top of the tree because the trunk was so tall. With how it jutted up from the earth, its great roots spreading all around its base, Subaru couldn't keep his honest feelings of excitement off his lips.

"Men are creatures impressed by big, strong stuff by nature. I was pretty impressed the first time I saw a land dragon, but Mother Nature ain't half-bad! That Flugel guy did good work."

As he touched the tree trunk, Subaru praised the work of the sage said to have planted the tree. Apparently, he was hot stuff, but no one knew what he'd done besides planting the tree; but even if that was his one great feat recorded in history, that wasn't a problem. The name Flugel was cool, too.

"Ah, gotta carve someone's name into the trunk, though. We're not students on a field trip, so it's just, well, proper manners. Rem, lend me a carving knife."

"Even for you, Subaru, I will be upset if you do that, as shall others."

Rem gently and properly chided Subaru for his burning, rebellious desire to have his name carved. Then, as Subaru pouted, she gave him a little smile and looked up at the Great Tree.

"This is where the White Whale shall come?"

"Yeah, it'll come. When it's time, this cell pho...this *metia* will ring."

Subaru took the cell phone out of his pocket, fingering the strap to sway it left and right. The alarm had already been set to ring when the White Whale was due to emerge.

They were the same words he'd shared during the final meeting, and the explanation for Crusch he'd racked his brains to come up with. He felt guilty at not divulging the truth, feeling like he had to make up for it by getting results.

Of course, not exposing the truth to even Rem tugged at his heart-strings, but—

"So this metia will alert us to the presence of a demon beast…"

"Mm, that's right. Put bluntly, if it wasn't for this, my worth this time around would be right about…"

"—That is a lie, is it not?"

When Rem said that with narrowed eyes, Subaru was sure his heart had stopped. Letting out a voice that did not even amount to a gasp, his heartbeats belatedly restarted.

"_____"

What had Rem said to him just then?

I must have heard her wrong, Subaru vainly hoped, but the eyes with which Rem stared at him smashed that hope to pieces.

She had said it, and with conviction.

"Wh-what are you talkin' about? Ya know what they'd do to me if I was lyin' about somethin' like…"

"Resorting to Kararagi dialect does not suit you, Subaru."

"Er, fact is, even Crusch and the others accepted it, so it can't be a lie."

Glossing things over wasn't working on Rem. Even so, Subaru tried to see the lie through, for if the truth was revealed, there was no mistaking that it would herald a worsening of the situation. If the lie was exposed, Subaru would no longer be consistent with the circumstances known to Crusch and the others, for the only way to square those inconsistencies would be to explain Return by Death.

Of course, so long as he obeyed the taboo set in place by the Witch, he could not reveal Return by Death to anyone, all the more so because the pranks played by the Witch's hands had finally progressed to crushing Emilia's heart. If he had to guess who the next casualty would be, it was clear that it might very well be Rem.

—He absolutely couldn't let Rem know the truth.

And yet, Rem slowly shook her head at Subaru's excuses.

"Crusch and the others merely decided that it was not necessary for you to lie. If you risked that, you would make an enemy of not only Lady Crusch but Lady Anastasia and all the merchants in the guild, Master Russel included. That would be meaningless."

"That's..."

It was an undeniable truth.

Back at the negotiating table, Crusch surely could have offered any number of rebuttals to Subaru. Russel and Anastasia, seasoned negotiators both, could have done likewise. He could only conclude that the fact that they had closed their eyes to the inconsistencies and accepted negotiations regardless was not due to trust in Subaru but a judgment based on the circumstances.

Subaru had arranged the place and the people for negotiations. There was no necessity to Subaru deceiving them. Of course, the calculation that they would think that way was one of the pieces of insurance Subaru had employed.

But that was based on nothing more than the pros and cons of success aligning atop the thinnest of ice.

The type of "lie" Subaru was seeing through was based on a false initial impression. And it was the kind of lie that need never be exposed if it brought results...ever.

But it was different as far as Rem was concerned.

Then, as ever, Rem stood as Subaru's ally. Subaru was deeply aware that Rem was now the closest person to him in the other world.

To continue lying to Rem held a completely different meaning than maintaining the deception with Crusch and the others. Making her accept it after she had realized it was false left an entirely different impression: namely, that he didn't reveal the lie to Crusch and the others because the pros and cons aligned that way, but he didn't reveal it to Rem because he didn't trust her.

He couldn't help if it made her think that way, for whether she did or not, he absolutely could not reveal the truth to her...

"Rem, I..."

"It's fine, Subaru."

"Huh?"

Subaru planned to use words to somehow smooth things over and protect Rem. But Rem rejected that with a shake of the head, a thin smile coming over her lips.

With Subaru too surprised to close his mouth, Rem turned a sincere look toward him and spoke.

"I understand you enough to know when you are lying, Subaru. I have been watching you a great, great deal, after all."

With a bashful, blushing smile, Rem teasingly touched a finger to her lips. Then, she moved the finger in Subaru's direction and continued.

"I also know you won't tell me the reason for the lie. But the fact that you won't speak to me about it does not bother me that much, you know?"

"_____"

"After all, I believe in you, Subaru."

At the base of the Great Flugel Tree, a breeze passed between the two as they faced each other.

With Subaru stunned into silence, Rem gently put a hand to her breast and stated before him, "Subaru, if you say that you know where the White Whale shall appear, I believe you. If you say the Witch Cult is after Lady Emilia and the others, I believe you. Even should you say the moon shall fall and destroy this nation, I shall believe you, Subaru."

"...Well, I wouldn't go quite that far."

"Yes, I suppose not. But that is how serious I am."

The smile vanished, and Rem stared at Subaru with very serious eyes. Then, she silently lowered her hips, grasping the hem of her skirt with both hands as she curtsied.

"I adore you with all this body and all this heart, Subaru—furthermore, now and in the future, I shall never, ever doubt you, Subaru."

"_____"

"Therefore, it's not necessary whatsoever to push yourself into a corner to make me believe your lie."

Subaru barely managed to choke back the heat welling up from his throat.

He pressed down on the inner corners of his eyes, turned his face up, and opened his trembling mouth wide and exclaimed, "Ahh! Man, staring at this huge tree really raises the tension!"

"Yes, I suppose so."

"I won't be able to calm down unless I'm looking up at this tree! There's no other reason at all, but I won't be able to look down for a little while!"

"Yes, I suppose not."

Subaru put on a show to keep his face turned up so that tears might not fall. It was a frail bluff on his part, but Rem, enveloped by gentle benevolence, did not call him on it.

That moment, Subaru understood the true extent of his own idiocy all over again.

If only he could have divulged everything to Rem from the very beginning. He couldn't have just told her everything, but if he could have at least conveyed to her the tragedy yet to come, Subaru would no doubt have been spared having the tragedy repeated a second and a third time.

Subaru couldn't explain the reasons why, so he thought no one would believe him if he said anything. Thus, he decided he had to go it alone, leading to various failures over and over.

But Rem was different.

She wasn't asking for a reason. She'd believe Subaru, even if he didn't explain. Just like that moment, she forgave Subaru, in her gentle, affectionate way, for not speaking the truth.

"This is when, instead of sorry, you say thank you, huh?"

Having desperately held back the tears, Subaru somehow managed to face Rem once more. Rem made a beaming smile and nodded at his reply.

"To be honest, I feel like I'll only be able to return super-tiny little pieces of everything you've given me, Rem…"

"That is not so."

Rem lowered her head slightly as she denied Subaru's words.

"I really do understand that speaking like this will only bring you suffering, Subaru. That I have spoken regardless is my own selfishness."

"I don't think of it like that at all. I'm the bad one for hiding stuff."

"But it really is selfish of me even so. I am sorry."

The words were self-effacing, but when Rem lifted her face, her expression was sunny. Seeing Subaru happily falter from the inconsistent sight, Rem tilted her head.

"I thought…it would be nice if you passed on to others a tiny bit of the load you carry. As I am now, that you had no one to do so makes me….unbearably sad."

"I…"

In that moment, Rem conveyed her resolve, the firmness of her feelings.

Subaru leaned against the trunk of the Great Tree and took a deep breath.

"I…love Emilia."

"Yes."

He revisited the words he had once exchanged with Rem.

He knew that the words wounded her deeply, that they were words that made her suffer, yet Subaru spoke them once more.

However—

"But…"

"_____"

"But when you're with me, my heart trembles… Go ahead. You probably think I'm a terrible guy now."

He wondered if the word *terrible* even cut it.

But they were Subaru's honest feelings.

For even though he knew he could not answer Rem's hopes, only her words had warmed his heart so.

Somehow, the breath Rem let out seemed hot as she said:

"Truly, you are a terrible person, Subaru."

"…I know."

"That is a lie. I love you."

"I…I know that, geez."

Subaru's face turned beet red as she stated plainly how she felt all over again.

If it were not night, that redness would have surely stood out. Subaru turned his back, as if trying to conceal the red surface of his face, and began to walk away from the tree.

"Time to head back," he said. "We need to get mind and body ready right up to when the White Whale appears."

Before he passed in front of Rem, he grasped her dangling right hand.

When her hand was grasped, Rem raised her voice in a little *ah*, but immediately hurried to match Subaru's walking pace, staring at the side of the young man's face, one he did not wish her to see, with teasing eyes as she said:

"Subaru."

"…What?"

"I am fine with being your second wife."

They were words to make a man unwittingly halt in his tracks.

When Subaru, unable to resist, looked toward her, Rem made a face like that of an adorable puppy, seemingly wagging her tail as she awaited Subaru's reply.

Oh, good grief, just how far is this girl gonna—?

"If Emilia-tan's a very generous first wife…"

"Well then, when we get back you must convince Lady Emilia. I shall try hard as well."

Rem clenched the hand not grasped into a fist, very animated as she spoke with a smile.

Speaking jokingly like that broke all the tension, driving home to Subaru how weak he was. He truly couldn't hold a candle to the girl.

No man could hold a candle to a woman, be it Emilia or Rem, in that kind of situation.

Not that he really minded accepting that particular weakness, compared with the other ones he had known to date…

3

With the approaching hour growing nigh, the area around the Great Tree grew taut with the tension particular to the field of battle.

Having taken meals and sleep in shifts, the condition of the expeditionary force gathered in the battle zone was tip-top. The land dragons and ligers for the cavalry were breathing roughly through their noses, eagerly awaiting the signal.

Everyone lowered their breaths and calmed their hearts, continuing to wait for the time to come.

In the night sky of the Liphas Highway, the strong wind made the clouds flow quickly.

As the clouds obstructed the moonlight, not a moment passed without gazes raised, checking to see that it was not the White Whale's giant body swimming in the sky above. That was how much vigilance ruled the hearts of all present.

"It is a short time until the appointed hour."

When Crusch made that small murmur, Ferris, standing beside her, nodded briefly, glancing from the corner of his eye. In that moment, not even Ferris, having served Crusch for so many years without ever losing that witty nuance, could voice a single jest.

It was not that he'd been swallowed up by the strained tension. It was because Ferris knew his role—that of one of the expeditionary force's lifelines—and had wholly set his heart upon fulfilling that duty.

It was more than likely true that Ferris's actions would alter the final number of victors surviving the battle.

Crusch believed that her force would emerge victorious. But she was not so conceited as to think they could slay the White Whale without sacrifices. Nonetheless, she held self-confidence that she could mitigate the number of casualties required.

That self-confidence came from the trust she held in Ferris, her knight, so perhaps one could question if it ought to be called self-confidence.

"_____"

The sword-armed Wilhelm stood in front of her, on the very front line of the expeditionary force.

Of the six swords on the aged swordsman's belt, he wielded one in each hand, poised to rush out in an instant. The quiet antagonism wafting around the Sword Devil was in a polished realm, honed to a fine point as he faced the moment for which he had so yearned.

Crusch could not fail to be enveloped by an out-of-place sense of admiration at the Sword Devil's sheer purity—that a person could maintain a soul so pure, so unswerving.

Crusch thought from her heart that one day she, too, would arrive at the same realm.

"_____"

The faces of each brave warrior of the expeditionary force along-side Wilhelm had an expression of hardened resolve, their morale high.

They obeyed Crusch's command, but as they awaited the White Whale, surely their hearts harbored doubts of their own—both about Subaru, the primary source of information for the White Whale's emergence, and the fact that they had far too little time to develop bonds of trust between them.

And yet, they obeyed without a single contrary utterance, for they deeply valued Crusch's judgment. Crusch was strongly aware of her own duty to respond to the trust they placed in her.

"_____"

As the time limit approached, the brimming will to fight was reas-suring, but inside, Crusch was nervous.

Crusch touched the hilt of her treasured sword, ensuring by feel that the engraved crest of the lion was truly there. It was a habit from her youth, a little spell by which she poured resolve into herself.

They had to win.

She felt the presence of Ferris at her side and the legacy of the Lion King on her fingertips. However mighty the foe, it was all Crusch needed to fight.

And then—

"—!"

Abruptly, it rang across the Liphas Highway, subsumed by the darkness of night.

She was slow to realize that the series of light sounds making her eardrums tremble resembled music of some sort.

When she turned her eyes toward the source of the sound, she saw Subaru putting his hand on the shining metia. It was from the metia in his hand that the music was noisily flowing.

It was the signal Subaru had said would announce that the time had come.

"All hands, on alert—!"

At Crusch's shout, the expeditionary force poised as one.

According to Subaru, the White Whale would appear within tens of seconds after the metia alerted him. If he was to be believed, it would not be strange for the White Whale's giant body to be swimming in the sky that very moment. With the metia having alerted him, the place had to be correct as well.

She had plenty of room for doubts, but Subaru had given her no reason to doubt him. Crusch set her misgivings and apprehensions aside, honing her nerves as she awaited the demon beast.

"_____"

Amid the silence, she felt no sign of the enormous demon beast appearing.

The expression on her face was not disappointment, properly speaking, but after a minute had passed with no change on the field of battle, Crusch could not help herself from being, for one, unnerved.

Discrepancies in the information. Mistaken assumptions. Some kind of random accident.

There was no change in the silence that had descended over the Liphas Highway; there was no sight of the enemy in the landscape around her.

As before, the moonlight was obstructed by clouds, causing a large, dark shadow to fall over the plains, but—

"—!"

Looking up, Crusch instantly cursed her own shallowness.

The moonlight vanished as a shadow fell over the plains.

The altitude of the cloud intercepting the moonlight was gently descending, coming before their eyes.

—But a cloud, it was not.

'Twas a demon beast, floating in the sky in the form of a gargantuan fish.

As Crusch sucked in her breath, virtually everyone in the expeditionary force came to the same understanding. Then, as if their minds were one, they tossed their gazes toward Crusch.

—They were waiting for the command for a preemptive strike.

They had succeeded in taking the initiative, catching the White Whale at the moment of its appearance. All that remained was to launch a surprise attack as planned, seizing control of the front.

"_____"

Crusch breathed in, as if to settle her heart upon the first command to unleash.

The White Whale had yet to notice the puny beings arrayed against it. The way the White Whale was moving its enormous head was as if to check where it was. And as it acted thus, its guard was down, full of openings—

That settled it for Crusch.

"—All hands..."

Full-scale attack, she went to command when—

"—Nail it!!"

"—Al Hyuma!!"

As signal leaped ahead of Crusch, mana was simultaneously deployed via magical incantation.

The world made a sound as if it had frozen over, bringing forth enormous and incredibly dense pillars of ice. Each and every one of the icy pillars rivaled the central pillar of a mansion, with there being four in total. Launched at super-high speed, the pillars raced through the sky and scored a direct hit on the White Whale's torso;

with a slight delay, the demon beast's scream and spurting blood poured down to earth.

When Crusch hurriedly looked, the land dragon Subaru and Rem were both riding was galloping, cutting across the vanguard. As Subaru clung to Rem's hips, he raised a fist, and Rem, having succeeded in her own duty by launching the preemptive magical attack, wore a very satisfied expression.

How the two of them jumped the gun—rather, got the jump on the rest—rocked the expeditionary force.

At the sight of them galloping forth, Crusch could not keep her own mouth from twisting greatly.

Not in anger but in mirth.

"All hands, follow that pair of fools!!"

Crusch's order erased the unrest as the various members of the expeditionary force began the offensive. Dust kicked up in the process, and on the other side, the White Whale's cries grew loud once more, echoing across the night sky of the Liphas Highway.

After much waiting, the Battle of the White Whale had begun.

4

No matter how many times Subaru experienced the wind repel blessing, he could not help thinking of it as unnatural. Vibration, wind, posture—the impossible phenomenon blocked all those things from affecting them.

While Rem sat squarely on the land dragon as it ran, Subaru put a hand around her hip as he strained his eyes. He licked his lips, which had begun to dry, moistening them a bit as he sucked in his breath.

The cell phone alarm had rung as it was set to, and the White Whale had appeared in the twilight above the plains.

He could only describe the emergence of the giant body as splitting the sky and crawling out of the resulting shadow. Its massive body instilled primordial fear in Subaru, with all the memories of it having menaced his life surging back into his heart.

When he looked around, tension was running through the expeditionary force, noticing it just as Subaru had. As prearranged, they ought to be launching an all-out attack at Crusch's order.

But for a brief moment, the feeling of oppression had left even Crusch drawing a blank, her breath caught.

It could only be called a critical error, but such was the terror of combat the extreme situation had wrought.

Accordingly, Subaru patted Rem's shoulder.

"—Nail it!!"

"—Al Hyuma!!"

A half second before Crusch breathed out, that shout cut the covers of the gun barrels on the front.

Responding to Subaru's voice, Rem gave direction to the vast amount of mana she had woven together. This gave rise to four of those vile pillars of ice, with their sharply tapered tips mercilessly gouging holes in the White Whale's underbelly as it floated in the sky.

The ice collided with its stone skin, audibly shattering. However, just before the shattered pillars completely spread apart, the force of their stabs broke through the defense of the White Whale's thick hide—scattering its blood all over the plains.

The scream of the White Whale resounded across the plains. Even as the air shuddered enough to make one's eardrums go numb, the pitch-black land dragon Subaru and Rem rode advanced without fear.

—Subaru and Rem had not acted rashly.

The instant the White Whale emerged, a momentary lull occurred within the expeditionary force. Had they not acted during that time, the preemptive attack would have probably failed.

That pause was a watershed moment. And knowing that such momentary hesitation was a matter of life-and-death, even someone of such remarkable character as Crusch had her breath caught before the menace of the White Whale.

Even if she had been halfway confident the White Whale would appear, seeing the real thing created a ripple in the human heart. That ripple could create even tiny distortions in one's thought process, and distortion led to stagnation, and stagnation invited defeat.

If it had been so, the battle might have begun with their side at a disadvantage.

—If there was a difference between Subaru and Crusch that moment, he had to call it…love.

Crusch's split-second delay had been born from her inability to have absolute trust in Subaru and his metia. Even if her mind believed him, it could not force a statesman of her caliber to forget her misgivings.

But Rem had not even the tiniest smidgeon of doubt that the White Whale would appear the very instant Subaru said it would. Accordingly, Rem had prepared magic with the greatest firepower that she could muster, waiting for the moment Subaru had indicated, and slammed an attack into the White Whale the very moment it appeared.

If he could not call that Rem's love winning out, what could he call it?

"But that analysis is super-embarrassing—!!"

"Subaru, please hold on to me more diligently. You'll be thrown off!"

In contrast to Subaru, assessing his own starting of hostilities, Rem shouted as she gripped the land dragon's reins. She announced that they were shifting from phase one of the operation—the preemptive strike—to phase two.

"Everyone—follow that pair of fools!!"

A half second later, as Subaru and Rem galloped like the wind, the expeditionary force behind them obeyed Crusch's order, loading one cannon after another—or rather, stuffing things like cannons with magic crystals, with the magic crystal cannons firing them like cannonballs.

With a roar, that fusillade landed, its destructive power violating the White Whale's flesh.

The instant they hit squarely, the magic crystals embedding into it transformed into the magical power of their corresponding mana, be it fire, ice, or light, widening the wound Rem had created, causing soot-black blood to pour down onto the highway.

Amid the drizzle of blood, Subaru and Rem's land dragon employed agile movements to circle around to the White Whale's rear. The movement was just as arranged.

"I'll get the White Whale's attention, making it turn so that its back is to the expeditionary force...!"

"The sky! They are using Night Repel! Please close your eyes!"

Rem took in the state of the battle, looking up and gazing at the horn on the White Whale's brow as she shouted. Subaru hurried to follow her instructions, lowering his face and closing his eyes—and the next moment, the world became bright.

A white light exploded in the sky above, and that white glow instantly burned the night away. The light was so powerful that it permeated Subaru's optic nerves through his closed eyes, making his throat catch in surprise.

"Whoaaa! It's just as incredible as you said!"

All trace of night had completely vanished from the Liphas Highway. Whatever had happened during those several seconds, the worlds of night and day had swapped places, and a light as bright as midday shone onto the plains.

Above their heads, separate from the attacks on the White Whale, a special magical stone with an effect called Night Repel had been launched to shine in place of the purportedly sunken sun. Normally, it was simply a collection of light proportional to the mana infused into it, unable to shine with much more than a dull light, but...

"So when you abuse assets to put a mountain of 'em together, you've got a mini-sun on your hands?"

"It is difficult to track the White Whale in a dark sky, after all— Now, it has only just begun!"

Putting together two of the top merchants, even by the royal capital's standards, and having them run around gathering magic stones was playing to their strengths.

The effective range was the area around the Great Tree, and the time limit was a bit under an hour—more than enough time to end the decisive battle.

Having lost the twilight over the plains, the huge body was distinct as it floated overhead. That was—

"That's…!"

To that point, he had not been able to clearly make out the White Whale even once, but now, it was exposed under the light of day.

"_____!!"

The White Whale's enormous frame shuddered as it bellowed, seemingly enraged at having been dragged out of the night sky.

The roar it unleashed surpassed the level of noise, closer to an act of raw destruction. The atmosphere rumbled, frightening even the trained land dragons, causing them to roar violently.

Though it appeared to be bleeding from its entire body, its swimming showed no effects from the wounds. The White Whale's head traversed the sky over the plains, calmly gazing down at the puny humans daring to challenge it.

"What…size…?"

Subaru's voice shook as it trickled out, unable to stop the feeling that his limbs were going numb, unable to move.

To that point, Subaru had seen, brushed against, and come to hate the menace of the White Whale, but faced with the full sight of it, he understood for the first time that he had seen only a fraction of the being.

The White Whale: Just as its name suggested, the demon beast's figure was covered all in white. Countless body hairs sprouted from hide that resembled finely chiseled bedrock. The pectoral fins extended from the underbelly like grim reapers' scythes, with the smaller dorsal and caudal fins shaped similarly.

Setting aside the disparity in savagery, the shape of the White Whale very much resembled that of the whales Subaru knew—but its size betrayed his expectations twice over.

As far as Subaru knew, the blue whale, the world's largest whale, was almost one hundred feet long, give or take, making it literally the largest mammal on Earth. However, the enormous body of the whale he saw in the distance easily surpassed one hundred feet, probably large enough to be close to one hundred sixty-five. Its giant frame was closer to a mountain than a living creature.

By some cosmic joke, a white mountain was leisurely swimming in the sky above.

"Subaru."

With Subaru trembling even then, unable to align his teeth as he bit down, a voice called out to him. It was the voice of Rem, her back facing him as Subaru clung to the hips of her small figure. She was already right in front of him, close enough for him to hear her breathe, so she didn't look back at Subaru when she asked the question.

"Are you scared?"

It was not a taunt but a call for trust.

Firmly, Subaru clenched his teeth and twisted his mouth as he answered.

"Yeah, I'm scared—of my shining future, and the praise I'll get for bringing that thing down!"

Subaru met Rem's expectations by cracking a joke, patting her shoulder from behind.

"I'm putting my whole life in your hands! Now, let's make a run for it!"

"My life is yours as well, Subaru—now then, let's go."

When Subaru, his resolve hardened, declared they would run away in manly fashion, Rem softly made a little smile as she sternly cracked the reins. The pitch-black land dragon neighed, running across the ground, undaunted by even the fantastical White Whale.

The White Whale turned toward them as they galloped low and to the right of it, aiming to circle around to its tail. They dashed away from the expeditionary force, and the White Whale's giant eyes turned toward Subaru and Rem as they approached. The maw that could swallow a large dragon carriage whole opened wide, poising its mouth, lined with millstone-like teeth, for a roar.

Subaru, sensing baptism by destructive sound, braced himself against the land dragon he was riding.

And above their heads—

"To turn away, you must have greatly underestimated me—!!"

A moment after the valiant heroine's voice, the White Whale's head was shallowly cut by a single, horizontal slice. The invisible slash, grazing the solid, stone-like hide, drew blood from the White Whale's enormous frame once more.

When Subaru looked back toward the source of the attack, he saw a white land dragon running after him at the front of the vanguard—and Crusch, standing tall, with her arm out after following through the swing. But in her hand…

"She's not holding anything…?!"

"A formless sword that ignores range—Lady Crusch's famous swordsmanship is able to fell a hundred men in a single blow."

Rem replied in a low voice as Subaru gawked.

The anecdote Rem spoke concerning Crusch was news to Subaru, but the display was equal to the words. Though she appeared unarmed, such a statement was fitting for Crusch's skill and combat strength.

The invisible slash stopped the White Whale's initial response; with its movement halted, more attacks followed. The magic crystal cannons went to work once more, concentrating firepower on the White Whale and landing hit after hit, causing its altitude in the sky to drop as the damage and agony to the demon beast piled up.

The White Whale was at the same height as a cloud, but so long as its head was not pointed straight up, it was—

"Within…blade distance."

A single land dragon ran across the ground and leaped, displaying agility that clashed with its large frame as it launched into the air.

Even so, compared with the White Whale, it had little size to boast. The land dragon soaring before its nose must have seemed little more than a fly to the White Whale.

—The vertical sword flash running straight ahead cut deeply up the White Whale's nose.

The sight of the flash of metal rending the white, stony hide with such ease made the sound of cannons, echoing across the battlefield, vanish.

This was no spell, no magic crystal cannon, nor even the slash of an invisible blade, but human training, proof that steel swung by man could reach even the demon beast.

Proof that human willpower, expended over the course of many years, had indeed reached the Demon Beast of Mist.

"—Fourteen years."

The figure crouched as he thrust a sword into the split tip of its nose.

He maintained his posture, poising the cutting blade as the other sword thrust deep, and he waved off the demon beast's blood from his blade. Behind him, the hostility he gave off was enough to warp the very air.

"For all that time, I dreamed only of this day."

As the figure straightened his back, the White Whale twisted its body, trying to fling off the figure that had embarked upon the tip of its head. The White Whale let out a groan as it barrel-rolled in midair.

But...

"—!!"

The White Whale arched as it screamed in pain, its tail dancing wildly in the sky.

A single, horizontal cut was added to the vertical one from before, carving a cross-shaped wound into the White Whale's brow; the figure stomped on the White Whale's back with a light sound of his foot.

Malevolent laughter came over the Sword Devil as bloodlust glimmered in his blue eyes.

"Here you shall fall, and your corpse shall rot—filthy monster!"

Spitting those words out, Wilhelm poised his swords in both hands as his body became the wind.

He ran across the back of the White Whale from its head to its tail, slashing the demon beast's stone hide left and right with the blades in both hands. As he rent the purportedly hard, resistant hide with ease, sprinting as soot-black blood smeared the sky, he truly looked like a Sword Devil.

With Wilhelm clinging to the White Whale's body, it had no good method of shaking him off. Unable to dislodge the aged swordsman, even as it moved to somersault in midair with the force of a whirlwind, he proclaimed:

"Good of you to help me slice you more!"

A moment before the White Whale turned its body, Wilhelm made a short leap and stabbed his sword right under him. When the White Whale whirled its body, the thrust blade created a vivid slash down it, using the White Whale's own body in service of the blade.

Amid a scream and a mist of blood that mottled his own torso, the Sword Devil laughed. Laughing, his old bones continued swinging both swords as he headed for the giant frame's flank. With a swing, his blades carved a V shape into the flesh, leaving a reddish-black laceration behind.

A bellow tore through the sky as the White Whale aimed to slap the falling Sword Devil with its tail. But a moment before the tail was to strike him, a leaping land dragon snatched Wilhelm's body away. He had slipped away from the menace of certain death.

Upon landing, the land dragon instantly broke into a run. The White Whale gave into anger and chased after the elusive Sword Devil.

"Hey, don't look away, moron! Yer facin' the lot of us, too!!"

The single swing of the huge cleaver struck the White Whale squarely on the jaw with enough force to knock out several of the White Whale's enormous teeth, making a dull sound as yellow molars were sent flying.

It was Ricardo, riding a liger, who bellowed as they galloped onto the White Whale's face at an angle. Just as he'd said, the ferocious dog had greater agility than a land dragon, and it was using that nimbleness to the fullest extent, master in tow, traversing the White Whale as its body rose into the sky.

"Hey now, we ain't done with you yet!!"

Atop the sprinting liger, Ricardo gave a cry more bestial than a beast's as he swung the massive cleaver. The outer hide shattered and flesh was gouged, all in a single charge. And following after Ricardo...

"All riiiight, let's goooo!"

"Big Sis, you are too far out in front! Everyone, now!"

The lieutenant twins, both on the backs of small ligers, split apart, issuing commands to the mercenary band behind them. With ferocious leaps, a pack of ligers grappled onto the White Whale and began to run rampant with its giant body as their foothold. They swung sword and spear, inflicting damage to the White Whale like a swarm of wasps.

Save for making its enormous frame dance, the White Whale had no countermeasure for shaking off the interlopers clinging to it. Its very size made small movements difficult, a weakness that was being exposed. Furthermore, at that point—

"All hands, move away!!"

When Crusch's order cracked across the field of battle, the Iron Fangs clinging to the White Whale leaped off its body as one. All the ligers landed agilely, and the White Whale, now freed of them, made a large turn, believing it was finally time to counterattack—but it was mistaken in that judgment.

"So you've exposed your flank—!"

Crusch's second attack struck far overhead, her diagonal slash running along the White Whale's side at an angle, and that stroke of her sword was the prelude to yet a third attack—this time, from the magic squad, which had not attacked until that moment, devoting themselves solely to concentrating on chanting.

"—Al Goa!!"

From the compounded chants from multiple squad members came a red-hot aurora. In that world, with both a sun and a moon floating in the sky, a new, second sun was born, low in the sky and clad in incandescent flames.

Even knowing that it was the power of fire magic bundled together, Subaru could not turn his eyes away, gawking at the conflagration scorching the world before him. The waves of heat given off by the huge fireball, over thirty feet in diameter, could burn the skin even at a distance well removed, burning with enough heat to rob the moisture of his eyes, even with his eyelids protecting them.

That great fireball wavered, then it gained velocity.

"Uoooo!"

Velocity gave way to acceleration, and acceleration, to high speed. The fireball headed for the White Whale's side, then slammed it right in the belly. Through its accumulated wounds, the fire burned inside its body, and the White Whale screamed while its internal organs boiled.

Mercenaries hurriedly evacuated so as not to be caught up in the fragments of flame scattering over the plains. Subaru and Rem took part in that evacuation, even as their eyes continued to track the burning White Whale.

That overwhelming, even one-sided, circumstance meant nothing less than that the surprise attack had borne fruit. At that rate, might not the demon beast be subjugated without it being able to do a thing?

"Feels like that hit it pretty hard! Maybe it'll all go like this?!"

At a distance beyond the flames' reach, Subaru watched the White Whale from the back of the land dragon, shaking a closed fist.

Until that point, they'd completely overwhelmed the White Whale, surely inflicting no small amount of damage. With the failure of the Great Expedition fourteen years prior as precedent, he'd been on his guard, but this put him into an easy-win mood. It had bitten on the prearranged plan hook, line, and sinker, making him feel exhilarated that a quick victory was just before his eyes.

However, with regret, Rem shook her head at Subaru's optimistic viewpoint, glaring up at the flame-engulfed demon beast.

"No—were that the case, the surprise attack would have caused it to crash to the ground."

Her words made Subaru's eyes go wide. He turned his eyes to the White Whale, wondering what she meant.

Even then, half of the demon beast's body was being burned by the great magic, with no sense that the flames, spreading over its body hair, were dying out. The magic crystal cannons' direct attacks had inflicted many wounds, and the sight of blood trickling from them was downright painful.

But—

"The altitude...ain't dropping."

Looking up, he saw the White Whale calmly remaining in the sky.

It was not up so high that the cavalry could not leap up to it, but it would be very difficult for men to challenge it on foot. More importantly, without the demon beast falling to the ground, they could not shift to the next phase of the operation.

Ricardo pulled alongside, carrying his huge cleaver as blood spatter drenched the fur on his face.

"We played all our good cards right at the start. That it didn't go down means that thing was just tougher, huh." He snorted out of his canine snout, his pointy ears twitching as he said, "Feels like we scored a point, but it ain't easy breakin' through that thick hide underneath. 'Cept for a weapon like mine with brute force, or Mr. Wil's skills, it's a drop in the ol' bucket."

"Maybe that goes for physical attacks, but it looked like magic attacks worked, yeah?"

"I am quite doubtful that is the case. At first glance, they appeared to be spectacular strikes, but that white hair scatters the mana, dulling the force. My magic did not do as much damage as it appeared, either."

Rem voiced with regret that the magic representing her own greatest firepower had been ineffective.

When her words drew Subaru's attention, he saw that there certainly were numerous shallow wounds in the White Whale's flesh, but none amounted to deep wounds that diminished its fighting ability. But at the very least...

"Looks like the fire spells from earlier are burning its hair off pretty well, though."

"It's simple—burn the magic-scatterin' hair off and we can have that fried whale flesh under it for dinner."

Ricardo ferociously bared his fangs as he concurred with Subaru's guess. With the massive cleaver in hand, he gave the liger's back a pat, hurtling toward the front line once more.

"All riiight, let's bring what we've got left in the sack just like earlier! Crusch, give the big guy one more slug in the gut, will ya?"

Drawing up his own laundry list, he slipped under the White Whale and leaped onto its body once more.

When Subaru looked, Wilhelm, who he was sure had moved some distance off, was also aiming to get back on the White Whale, this time from the tail end. The expeditionary force had apparently come to the same conclusion as Subaru and Ricardo and was shifting to its next move—in other words, a second all-out attack.

"In this case, they'll be pouring firepower on the White Whale, so we'd just be in the way if we got close. Rem, can you slam magic into it like you did earlier?"

"It would take time for an incantation of identical strength, and water element mana cannot do damage when it is scattered. Anything of lesser might would have insufficient firepower to begin with, so…"

If he went by Ricardo's earlier conclusion, the right thing to do was to have Rem join the front line, morning star in one hand, and add to the blunt-force attacks against the White Whale. However, if Subaru made her do that, he'd turn into her ball and chain. It was pathetic, but using his physical condition to implement a decoy operation meant Subaru couldn't send Rem off alone.

"It sucks, but I've gotta watch until there's a move I can make…"

As Subaru spoke, their land dragon eased away from the battlefield at a slow pace, and a different land dragon pulled alongside.

"That annoying feeling's the same for me as it is for you, *meow*."

It was Ferris, riding a land dragon clad in heavily armored plates.

"Ferri doesn't have any ways to attack, so watching is pretty much all I can do. I'm kinda, sorta used to it, but it always bums me out, *meow*."

"Maybe so, but your healing is the expeditionary force's lifeline. Can't be havin' you go out in front. I'm begging you, focus on that job, okay?"

Subaru bluntly emphasized that to Ferris, taking that moment to approach in his normal demeanor. The reply made Ferris close one eye with a *hmm*.

"You really have changed in one day, *meow*. What happened to you?"

"If I've gotta put it in words, I became a bit more of a man."

As his eyes ran across the shifting battlefield, Subaru replied with a reflective expression, biting on bitter thoughts.

Subaru's behavior sent Ferris suggestively poking a finger into a cheek as he said, "Subawu, don't tell me Rem made a man out of you, *meow*?"

The answer was both yes and a definite no.

Subaru was about to level an angry shout to shut Ferris up for the out-of-place vulgarity.

"Master Wilhelm is—!"

But he was interrupted by Rem's urgent shout.

When he hurriedly sent his gaze in the direction Rem was looking, he saw the aged swordsman running on the White Whale's back.

With a sword, he stabbed the White Whale's backside, ripping the White Whale's body lengthwise as he ran. As Wilhelm ran from tail to back, the delayed spurting of whale blood made it look like he was being chased by geysers.

That moment, Wilhelm's works were truly those of an angry god.

The expeditionary force lifted their faces, with morale exploding higher at the Sword Devil's abnormal skill with the blade. The firing pace of the magic crystal cannons and the vigor of the mercenaries and cavalry unit's organized attacks grew greater still.

Unable to withstand the agony, the White Whale writhed in midair, completely unable to respond to the expeditionary force's attack.

Seeing the Demon Beast of Mist, the calamity that had caused continued suffering across four centuries, in such a pathetic state, Subaru firmly believed the tide was completely going their way.

"Cheeeeeiiiiii!"

With an energetic outburst, Wilhelm drew his sword in a line all the way to the White Whale's head, maintaining his momentum as his old bones leaped off from the tip of the enormous body. As the old man twisted and inverted in midair—

"There ya go!"

Ricardo's cleaver matched Wilhelm's timing, rising up to greet him from below. Wilhelm descended, aiming for the cleaver as it rose toward its zenith, the soles of the Sword Devil's feet meeting the cleaver's blunt, impending blow.

"Shii—!!"

Ricardo's brawn added to Wilhelm's leaping ability, sending the Sword Devil flying like a bullet.

Shot out, Wilhelm's dual blades whirled around, savagely slicing the White Whale's face. It was cruelly shredded from the tip of its nose up its cheek, with Wilhelm unleashing a stab toward its gigantic eye.

"_____!!"

The twin swords sank their hilts into the White Whale's left eye, and clear fluid flowed out of the ravaged eyeball.

Wilhelm instantly abandoned the two sunken swords, drawing two new swords in a flash—from right and left, his slashes cut above and below the eye; flipping the blades, he added vertical cuts to its left and right.

As a result, the White Whale's left eyeball was cut from four directions when—

"The eye's falling!"

Gouged out by four slices, the White Whale's left eye fell freely, and Wilhelm along with it—

The shout, from whatever source, became truth, and the eyeball, spewing blood and fluid, collided with the ground, squishing and splattering.

Wilhelm landed right beside it, the Sword Devil driving a sword into the eyeball, threatening to lose all coherence, and raised it high so that the White Whale's right eye could see it.

"—Pathetic."

Then, the corners of his lips turned up in a ghastly, triumphant smile.

The White Whale had been rendered helpless as the Sword Devil's sublime combat techniques made sport of it.

It was clear to all that their fighting strength was not determined by the overwhelming difference in the sizes of their bodies.

Perhaps it took the loss of its left eye for the White Whale to finally accept that fact...

"The color of the White Whale's eye is...!"

"It's coming!!"

"Subaru, please keep your head down—!!"

The instant Subaru noticed the change, Ferris shouted, and Rem accelerated the land dragon.

Because they had stopped, the wind repel blessing was not in effect. Subaru, clinging to Rem as he endured the ferocious wind and shaking, somehow managed to turn his eyes to the White Whale overhead.

Within Subaru's field of vision, the White Whale's state changed at once.

"_____!!"

The White Whale, angry at having an eye gouged out, let up a roar as its one intact eye was dyed deep red.

The eyeball, now the color of blood, shot like a dagger through the expeditionary force, pulling back to put distance between it and the beast. Immediately after, the White Whale's body quaked in hatred and rage as a change came over its flesh.

...the instant that change began, Subaru was unable to repress a sense of disgust that defied words.

The White Whale opened its mouth.

No, those words were both correct and incorrect. To more accurately express the truth...

—The mouths of countless cavities over the White Whale's entire body opened and began to raise their voices.

"_____!!"

Reverberations like shrieking voices poured out of the countless mouths created all over the demon beast's flesh.

The discordant sound one would not think existed in that world seemed to claw away directly at the listeners' spirits, coursing from their hearing to violate their cranial nerves.

The damage did not stop at human beings alone. The land dragons and ligers employed as mounts stopped in their tracks, seized by instinctive, primordial fear.

The expeditionary force was overcome by its worst instance of defenselessness since the start of the battle to bring down the White Whale.

And then...

"...Ah..."

Raising a chorus, the countless mouths spewed an immense amount of mist.

In the blink of an eye, the mist poured onto the plains, and the world illuminated by the effect of Night Repel was blotted out in white.

His vision obstructed, his entire body cowering, Subaru understood that the White Whale had acknowledged them as its enemies.

It was the Demon Beast of Mist raising its war cry that announced the true commencement of hostilities.

5

Loud laughter echoed across the Liphas Highway.

Discordant sounds trickled from the small mouths open across the giant body of the White Whale as it swam leisurely in the sky.

When it roared from its proper mouth, it came with such destruction that it made the earth shudder. But the sound given off by many mouths out of sync was twisted and repulsive, like being clawed by the very wind.

The unpleasant feeling was not a blow to the eardrums but rather, like having one's brain poked at by slender needles.

With that ghoulish change in the White Whale, Subaru sensed that the tide had turned.

They'd pounded that immense preemptive strike into it with the expeditionary force, from Wilhelm on down, adding their own concentrated attacks. The damage inflicted on the White Whale was by no means minimal. After all, the combined firepower was enough to kill Subaru a hundred times over; if comparing with other demon beasts, it was attack power sufficient to wipe out an entire Urugarum pack ten times over.

The beast, bathed in all that, had taken enough damage to lose one eye. If it was not enough to settle the battle, Subaru had hoped it would at least result in bringing the beast down to earth, but—

"Crap, the mist…!"

Continuing to raise a shrill cry, the White Whale spread mist from its countless mouths.

The mist spread in a wide range across the highway, its encroachment progressing as it fell thickly from the sky. Subaru's field of vision became progressively whiter, and the effect of the Night Repel magic crystal waned.

—The Demon Beast of Mist had come into its own.

With visibility worsening, the expeditionary force was unable to maintain tight cohesion over the mist-shrouded plains. Moreover, didn't it look like even the White Whale was melting into the mist, vanishing from sight…?

"You're kidding me…?!"

"—Subaru, please entrust me with your life!!"

Rem leaned forward and shouted to Subaru, shaken by the vanishing of the White Whale. Subaru responded to her shout by deepening his arms' embrace of Rem's body.

Obeying Rem's snap of the reins, the land dragon whirled around, splitting the ground as it began to sprint.

Ferris, beside them until just earlier, similarly turned the head of his land dragon toward the interior of the mist. With the White Whale entering a state of combat, the counterattack would grow desperate. Naturally, casualties could not be avoided. That being the case, this was where his duty lay as he was called The Blue Knight, the greatest of healers.

Yet, in spite of that…

"All hands, retreat—!!"

...a bellow from inside the mist resounded, halting them before they leaped into the sea of white.

It was Crusch's voice they heard.

What is she doing? was the look on the face Subaru lifted up, but the next moment—

"Whoa?!"

Subaru's body was shaken by centrifugal force as the land dragon veered left in a spur-of-the-moment decision. In front, Ferris's land dragon was making its own emergency right turn, resulting in them going separate ways.

And white came violently surging into the corners of Subaru's tilted vision.

"—Hey now, hold on?!"

The middle of the path that had opened up by their splitting apart was blown away in a single gust of very dense mist.

The force of the tall wave of mist shooting through would have surely swallowed up the land dragons had they evaded even a second slower.

Without having seen the real thing in action, one might laugh it off as making a big deal about mere mist. But no one seeing the nature of that mist up close with their own eyes would ever dismiss it so lightly.

The surface of the plains grazed by the mist was gouged out as if melted away, with the highway surface vanishing all the way down to the foundation.

A human body fully bathed in that mist would invariably share the same fate.

"If we got hit by that...!"

Subaru thought he'd fully taken to heart the briefing beforehand concerning the threat of the White Whale's mist. But the real thing was beyond even his expectations.

"So this is the serious mist...!"

The White Whale, called the Demon Beast of Mist, had mist that broadly fell into two varieties.

The first was the wide-area mist it scattered to expand its own swimming area, such as what it had used to cover the highway. And the second was the annihilating mist, which had erased a good chunk of the ground before his eyes just then.

He hadn't seen the means of attack until then, but it was the latter, the annihilating mist, that wrought destruction. And though a single glance was sufficient to understand its destructive power, there was even more to it than that.

Namely—

"Yaaa!!"

In a vigorous flash, a gallant voice cut through the mist as something suddenly sliced open the white scene before Subaru's eyes.

It was a white land dragon with Crusch on its back that leaped out of the mist. She'd probably used the super-long-range invisible slicing attack to disperse the mist and secure her vision.

Crusch brusquely wiped off the sweat on her brow, panting atop the land dragon. Using her as a marker at the center of the cleared mist, the scattered elements of the expeditionary force began to hastily regroup.

Crusch looked across her subordinates from each of the assembled squads and asked, "—How many people were hit?"

"Our squad has twelve people—we're three short."

"...Who are you missing?"

"We don't know...!"

Faced with Crusch's impatience, a man in his prime seemed to wring out his reply as he shook his head.

Under normal circumstances, such an exchange would be incomprehensible. The squad leader, cognizant of the number of people in his squad, was reporting that he could not remember the names of the lost members. Surely such a crazy thing was not possible, yet...

"We have fourteen and have lost one."

"Two men in my squad. Similarly unclear."

"Six men... I am very sorry! Our position was deep, and we were unable to avoid the mist...!"

Similar reports came in one after another, with none able to remember the names of their vanished comrades.

It was that bizarre circumstance that was the true menace of the White Whale's mist.

"The annihilating...mist...!!"

In shock, Subaru's molars clattered as the murmur came running up his throat.

Those literally annihilated by the mist had even the memories of their existence erased from the world. Even if proof remained of those erased, no memories of their existence remained.

That was the true meaning behind Crusch organizing the expeditionary force in squads of fifteen men each. If the squads were to lose men due to the mist, they would be unable to even discern who had been hit. Even so, by having a set number in each squad, they could at least grasp the fact that they had lost people.

—Subaru knew that eerie fear for himself, for he had tasted it the previous go-around.

For Otto, the traveling merchant accompanying him on the highway, the existence of a fellow merchant fallen prey to the White Whale, and the existence of Rem, who'd stayed behind to slow the White Whale down, had been completely consigned to oblivion.

At the time, Subaru was of the thought that Otto had forgotten those inconvenient memories out of fear, but it made more sense that he was under the effect of the White Whale's mist. All memory of his fellow merchant, and Rem, was erased from that world—just like when, back at the mansion, even Rem's older twin sister, Ram, had forgotten her.

Now, the same thing had happened again. Yet, even in spite of that—

"I'm the only one...who remembers..."

In a daze, Subaru voiced the undeniable fact.

Just like in the last go-around, when Subaru never forgot the erased merchant or Rem, sacrificing herself so that Subaru could escape, he alone remembered.

Two of the squad leaders gathered under Crusch…had become different people.

Bathed by the annihilating mist, the original squad leaders had been erased. Everyone accepted the next in line as the squad leaders in their place, with no one noticing the sudden change in rank.

Faced with that abnormality, Subaru knew that the Witch and the White Whale really were cut from the same cloth.

Subaru Natsuki continuing to remember the things everyone else had forgotten—surely this was not unrelated to Return by Death, a trait possessed by Subaru alone.

Crusch looked over the faces of the expeditionary force and cut the conversation short.

"Now that it has submerged into the mist, we cannot know from whence it attacks. Crowding together is a poor plan—we shall disperse, and employ mana repulsion crystals."

Seeing everyone nod at the order in his peripheral vision, Subaru's eyes widened when he realized he didn't see Wilhelm or Ricardo among them. Surely even those two were not erased by the mist…?

"So you have returned, Wilhelm."

But Subaru's nervousness was belied by a figure's timely return from the mist.

Having sliced through the dense fog, the Sword Devil seemed ghastly, his entire body bathed in blood. Wilhelm wiped off his blood-sullied swords, tersely smearing the blood from his cheeks as an afterthought.

"I ran too far ahead—our losses?" Wilhelm asked.

"A total of twenty-one… Essentially one squad was annihilated. We can no longer hope even to properly honor the memory of the fallen."

Being erased by the mist literally meant one's existence was wiped clean. With no traces left of them, even in people's memories, there was a complete blank where they had once existed in the world.

Subaru wondered if the bonds and feelings, even love, that had been so certain until then, vanished someplace.

When he looked closer, Subaru saw a pack of ligers behind Wilhelm, and among them were Ricardo, straddling his extra-large liger, and the two lieutenants. Apparently, just like Wilhelm, those fighting right up against the White Whale had endured minimal damage.

"The mist comin' out makes this rough. Mana repulsion crystals are scarce, and we've less than I'd like… If we use 'em in the wrong place, we're done."

"If we strike it with one more concentrated attack, it shall surely fall to the ground. Having lost sight of it, this is the right time to employ them, averting a surprise attack among other things. Objections?"

When everyone endorsed Crusch's judgment, her gaze turned to the support unit under Ferris's command.

"Ferris, launch anti-magic crystals from the magic crystal cannons. Twice only. We must employ them with care."

"Preparations are already complete~. Anytime, at your command."

When Ferris tapped his chest, Crusch drew in her chin, looking over everyone before the battle recommenced.

"From here on is the real battle! The response remaining in your own hands shall prove that our attacks are effective upon the White Whale! Certainly, our opponent is mighty and unfathomable. Worst case, there may be none who shall remember our deaths. However!"

Crusch, able to launch cutting blows with her bare hand, drew from her hip the treasured sword of the House of Karsten—a sword no doubt long bereft of use—and raised it to the sky, declaring in a loud voice:

"For the sake of the dead with no name left on their tombstones, for the sake of the weak who would be menaced by the mist in the world ahead, we shall slay it, whatever it takes! —Come with me!!"

Every manner of weapon was raised to the sky, everyone shouting in exultation as one.

The mist shuddered from the incredible surge of morale, ferociously setting their dampened fighting spirit alight.

"Launch the anti-magic crystal!!"

At Crusch's order, the individuals under Ferris's command fired magic crystal cannons in a salvo—the next moment, with a great roar, the magic crystals soared high into the misty sky when…

"The mist…is clearing—!"

…the glow of the magic crystals shattering in the heavens erased the white mist obstructing their sight all at once.

Properly speaking, all the mist covering the four corners of the plains had not been swept away. In the end, all that had changed was the density of the mist, which had thinned so that it was no longer difficult to maintain a clear view.

But one could call even that result sufficient.

—The White Whale's mist was apparently a calamity wrought from the vast mana it possessed. In other words, the White Whale scattered its mana in the direction of its choosing, and this became the mist visible to others.

The anti-magic crystals—by rights, crystals with the effect of forcing the mana in an area back into a colorless state, thus neutralizing it—had used their power to nullify the mana of the mist, blowing it away.

It was a dangerous gamble, for if the anti-magic crystals worked too well, it would also diminish the strength of their own magic attacks, but it seemed there was no need for concern so long as they could see remnants of the mist.

"Not enough to clear away all the mist, huh?"

"In turn, there is no effect on our own magic. I, too, am in peak condition."

Rem gave a little nod, but it was the glow of the horn on her forehead that offered the real answer. The fact that it sensed mana swirling around the area and had begun building Rem's magical energy once more was the proof.

"—All right! I can't get cold feet now. I've come too far to be useless now. It's time for us to take the stage!"

"Yes! Let us go!"

Rem handled the land dragon's reins, and its neigh matched the bounce of Subaru's rump. He grabbed hold of Rem's hips atop the dashing land dragon, searching for sight of the White Whale in the thin mist above their heads.

With Crusch at the head, the expeditionary force set out as well, dispersing as its various parts searched for the White Whale. With the battle resuming at possibly any moment, Subaru felt the tension drying his throat out in a hurry.

No one saw the White Whale come out yet. It felt like before the start of the battle, when they waited for the White Whale to appear in the night sky, when…

"—Mist."

Suddenly, a bad premonition popped up in the back of Subaru's mind.

He had no special kind of proof of it.

They were still able to use magic within the effect of the anti-magic crystals. When he remembered the various things spoken before the operation, and his experience meeting the White Whale on the previous go-around, that anxiety suddenly bubbled to the surface.

There were remnants of widely scattered mist in the atmosphere.

The White Whale had expanded its own turf and obstructed their fields of vision, the oldest trick in the Demon Beast of Mist's book. That was all the prior information he had, but could he really say that it was the only reason he was afraid?

But before the doubt in his head could take form…

"_____!!"

…the squeaking chorus that echoed across the slightly misty Liphas Highway came quicker.

"What the hell was that?!"

The high-pitched echo was like a woman's shriek, instilling a sense of disgust that made Subaru want to cover his ears. It was both roar and laughter, yet repulsive on a whole other level, traversing the mist to mock them across the plains.

"Just now…!"

Subaru tried to put the question into words when he noticed it—that the mist coiled around his entire body seemed to melt into him, as if trying to permeate his flesh.

And then—

"Aaa, aaa, aaa—?!"

The first shift came in the mounted dragon unit running alongside. Subaru's shoulders jumped at the strange voices, sounding nothing like ones coming from sane human beings. Guessing that something had changed, he looked over to see cavalrymen racing beside him, tumbling from their land dragons one after another.

"Hey! What's wrong?!"

Following the shouting Subaru's intentions, his own land dragon did a U-turn and headed toward them. He passed between the land dragons, confused by the loss of their riders, and called out to the tumbled men.

"You all right?! Falling from a horse can get you hurt pretty b..."

Subaru, concerned about such injuries, unwittingly let his voice die off midway. Having fallen from their land dragons, the knights were writhing around—but their state was far more precarious than mere physical wounds.

"Uu, uu, uu, aa—"

The strange voices they raised were not like those of human beings; they were closer to the noises of beasts.

One man was frothing at the mouth, convulsing on the ground with his eyes rolled up. Another man let out a moan as he desperately scratched at his own arms. Yet another clenched down on his molars until they broke, pounding his head against the ground.

There was no single set of symptoms, but even so, he *knew*: It was madness, using the mist as a medium to spread.

"This is..."

"The voice just now directly affected their minds through the mist... It is like mana poisoning, but this is terrible...!"

With Subaru restraining his voice, Rem put a hand to her forehead, making an anguished face as she replied.

"Mana poisoning...? So this really isn't normal mist after all?!"

Judging from Rem's state and the feel of the mist coiled around his body, Subaru realized that this was the real function of the mist.

The wide-area mist was an unavoidable trap inflicting abnormal status on the beings within its broad reach. The vastness of the effect, and the damage it inflicted, was in plain sight.

Subaru didn't think the effects of the mist were limited to the squads around him and Rem, either. In fact, even as far as his eyes could see, he saw multiple squads stopped in their tracks, trying to deal with the abnormal state of their allies.

"So some people are resistant to the mist, and some aren't...? I don't feel a thing...!"

"I only feel a little from...my head... I am calm...now."

Breathing deeply several times, Rem touched the horn on her forehead as she calmed herself.

In the meantime, Subaru dropped from his land dragon, rushing to stop those attempting to hurt themselves.

"Hey, cut that out! Your wounds'll... Whoa!"

"Yeah, yeah, yeah! Stay baaaaack!"

One of the confused men slapped his arm aside, scratching his arm without mercy. When the sharp pain sent Subaru into retreat, the man resumed his self-harming behavior, scraping his face enough that it began to bleed.

"That hurt, but ain't this pretty bad? They might not stop till they're dead!"

"Subaru! You're hurt?!"

"It hurts and I feel like cryin' a little, but it's nothin'! More importantly, everyone'll tear themselves apart if we don't do something! Isn't there anything we can do?"

As Rem rushed over, she had a grim look on her face as she shook her head to his reply.

"Unfortunately, I do not know how much effect my healing magic would have. This is not simply interfering with the body but the Odo directly through their gates. Only Master Ferris can deal with such powerful mana contamination..."

"In the first place, how long can he hold up against mental contamination? Besides the two of us, we're pretty much wiped out here!"

The squad running alongside Subaru and Rem was virtually routed—and the few unharmed souls were trying to stop their comrades from hurting themselves like Subaru had.

"If Ferris gets contaminated, we're totally done for. What do we do...?"

This was only as far as Subaru could see. He could only despair that it was like that everywhere else, too.

Along with Crusch and Wilhelm, if Ferris, their pillar of support, were to fall, that would be it for them. It would be difficult to even maintain the fight at all.

"Everyone who can move, get the wounded to the Great Tree! Use whatever force you have to!"

But he heard Crusch's voice from the other side of the mist. A series of voices responded, and apparently, Crusch had escaped the effect of the mist. She was conveying how they would deal with that same menace.

Immediately after ordering the entire force to attack, she was instantly changing policies. Crusch's voice was chagrined, and Subaru, too, felt anger as he vented abuse at the White Whale.

"Strength-wise, fighting with people wounded is tougher than fighting with the dead, but do monsters even think to do that...?!"

"It seems Master Felix is safe. With him going around healing, the effects of the contamination should at least be diminished, but..."

Rem hesitated, but Subaru knew what she was trying to say.

With this much damage sustained, Ferris would have his hands completely full. With manpower split to gather the wounded, that made their fighting strength that much less. And more importantly—

"There's not enough time. We can't just be defenseless like this till Ferris heals everyone."

"Worst case, with the expeditionary force grouped up together like this, the White Whale's mist could swallow it whole. I do not wish to think it is that intelligent, but...given it has created this situation, that is optimistic."

"It's possible it's doing all this out of instinct, but...no, we can't underestimate it either way."

Resigning herself to the danger, Crusch meant to entrust the wounded expeditionary force members to Ferris. Naturally, it was necessary to do something to buy time so that the White Whale did not approach the wounded.

They needed to tender an attractive piece of bait to distract it from thoroughly pounding its enemy.

"—Whew."

Deeply breathing out, Subaru emptied his lungs.

Wringing oxygen out of his body to his limit, he naturally felt stifled inside his chest—his heartbeats slowed, and he knew that its rhythm was growing surer.

Subaru spontaneously made a strained smile at how unexpectedly calm he was.

He'd always been swept around by circumstances, toyed with by the events before his eyes, and Subaru's heart had reflected his emotions, running wild over and over.

So why was it he was so calm, then, on the precipice of his decision?

"…Borrowed or not, courage is courage, I guess?"

Subaru thumped his chest and breathed in deeply. He paused once, closed his eyes, and then breathed out and opened his eyes. He turned forward. Before Subaru, Rem, riding the land dragon, was looking down at him.

What was Subaru going to say? What did he desire? That was what she was waiting to hear.

"Rem, stick with me through the most dangerous part."

"Yes—no matter where it may lead."

Without hesitation, Rem accepted Subaru's request, a smile appearing on her face.

With that accepted, Subaru ran over to the land dragon. Rem lent her hand, and he virtually flew onto the land dragon's back, straddling it as he headed toward the knights restraining their comrades struggling on the ground.

"Rem and I will draw off the White Whale! In the meantime, get them treatment from Ferris. After you hand them to Ferris, anyone who seems all right, hook up with Crusch!"

"Draw them off?! How in the world will you…?"

"Like this."

Subaru smiled at the aged soldier raising a voice of doubt, drawing his breath and clearing his throat, then announced, "—Everyone who can hear this, cover your ears!! And if you can't, stay right there!!"

Subaru's full-force voice echoed across the misty plain.

Rem listened comfortably to Subaru's loud voice, and then touched her hands to her ears. The nearby knights also rushed to cover their ears; other expeditionary force members within earshot had surely done the same—just as Subaru had asked of them at the briefing before the operation.

And then, Subaru willingly invoked the taboo—

"I've Returned by Death—"

The instant he spoke it, Subaru's heart was wrenched by a rising fear—that, in spite of his intentions, those black hands would stretch toward his comrades, toward Rem.

But he forced that fear down, raising his voice so that the Witch might hear.

—*You can have my heart, so gimme a hand here!!*

Subaru opened his eyes wide, suppressed his weakness, and shouted in his heart—and a moment later, *it* came to visit.

"I love you."

It was a frail, delicate voice that seemed to whisper into his ears.

However, what was the ardor infused within that made his breast tremble?

Unwittingly, tears welled in the corners of his eyes, and Subaru's breath caught as he was struck by the urge to chase after the receding voice to embrace the speaker that very moment.

His entire body was governed by the heat of love, burning white-hot in his mind—

"...I'm back."

After a brief sojourn, Subaru's mind woke to reality.

The fervor that had ruled Subaru until the moment before grew distant, and he became unable to remember the deep feelings he'd had until then. But he did feel unease at the fierce pain he'd supposedly resigned himself to having miraculously failed to arrive. Yet, even so...

"Rem, how is it? The Witch's scent on me..."

"You stink!"

"That was the idea, but isn't that a bit harsh?!"

Though not thrilled to receive a black mark from Rem, he'd accomplished his objective.

His body shrouded in the Witch's miasma, Subaru looked back and raised his voice to the knights all around.

"Get away from us right now! Get as close to the big tree as you can and link up with Crusch as best as you can manage!"

"U-understood! Good fighting!"

"You too!"

Sending off the knights, Subaru's pat of Rem's shoulder was the signal for the land dragon to start running.

At present, Subaru's body was giving off the fresh, lingering scent of the Witch—setting aside the contradiction in those words, the scent had to be wafting all around him. The problem was how much effect it would have on the White Whale.

"With the Urugarums, the effect was enough to cover the entire forest, but how 'bout this time...? To be honest, there's no way to measure it, but..."

When he'd encountered the White Whale in the previous world, the White Whale had tenaciously pursued Otto's dragon carriage after Subaru shifted over to it. At the time, he'd said nothing in relation to the Witch. So if Subaru gave off an even stronger scent than before, he ought to be prime bait for the White Whale—

Just after he had that thought—

"—?!"

The land dragon, charging straight ahead, sensed something and turned abruptly on its own judgment—with centrifugal force drawing an "Ugeh!!" out of Subaru as he hastily hugged Rem, right before his eyes, seemingly clinging for dear life.

"What's...?!"

"The White Whale!!"

As Rem, pressed against him, shouted, a gargantuan maw suddenly emerged from the side, breaking through the mist.

By a hair's breadth, Subaru and Rem diverged from their path and escaped, with the White Whale's huge mouth seeming to slide past them a little to the left, biting into the ground, swallowing grass and topsoil whole.

Its stony outer hide seemed to be grazed as the demon beast rushed past, and from nearby, they heard the sound of its maw biting the ground apart.

Then, with a roar, it chased after the pair.

"Whoaaaaa—?!"

There was an overwhelming amount of pressure as it chased them from the rear.

With the overpowering sense chasing his back that they would be squished, the land dragon that the shouting Subaru rode earnestly kicked the earth. However, the swimming speed of the pursuing White Whale was extraordinary. With an enormous body like a mountain, it swam with such force that it surpassed the wind, closing the distance quickly.

Steadily, the maw pressed close, drinking up the world around it.

When the tip of its nose was right at their backs, close enough to bathe them in the raw stench of its breath…

"Rem!"

"*Ul Hyuma!!*"

…Rem responded with an incantation, sending three pillars of ice thrusting out of the ground as one.

Her aim was true, punching into the White Whale pursuing the pair from right below it, impaling its belly in an attempt to halt its movements. Yet—

"It won't stop—!"

The icy spears, each as thick as a hundred spears bundled together, were snapped off at the base, giving off a high-pitched sound as the ice shattered. The destroyed spears of ice instantly returned to the mana from whence they came, and though the White Whale, having lost what was sealing its wounds, bled from them, there was no effect on its movement.

That it had been wounded and bled so much seemed only to bring into sharper relief the extent of its endurance. Subaru was aghast all over again at just how high a hurdle bringing down the White Whale was.

"This ain't like with the Urugarum when it was one-on-one!"

"_____!!"

As Subaru moved farther from the White Whale, he raised his middle finger, taunting it. Enraged at the gesture, the White Whale's roar thundered across the plains. But from the side of its torso…

"Ryaaaaa—!"

…Wilhelm intervened, flying in with a vertical slash.

Driving his blade in, Wilhelm ran up the White Whale's flank. As Wilhelm cut through the bloody mist, the kitten siblings appeared alongside, straddling their ligers and looking at each other's faces.

"Big Sis, join with me!" "Let's do this, Hetaro!!"

As the ligers crossed, Mimi and Hetaro leaped off and joined hands. The two stood before the gaping wound Wilhelm had carved as they yelled:

"Wa—!" "Ha—!"

The pair's voices overlapped; the sound waves broadened with incredibly destructive might.

The shock wave coursed in through the open wound, making every injury on the White Whale's body bleed once more. The enormous body shuddered, and the White Whale's altitude dropped precipitously against its will. The White Whale groaned in agony, raising its voice as it endured the pain, and barely managed to avoid crashing as the twins, riding their ligers, leaped off its back.

"Trump card compleeete!" "Captain, please!"

"Oh yeah, leave it to me! If the runts are tryin' hard, then I've gotta, too!!"

In place of the landing twins, a large liger climbed onto the White Whale from the tail end.

Swinging his cleaver upward, Ricardo went around smacking the countless mouths that spawned mist. Wilhelm did the same, jamming slashes into the annoying mouths, silencing them one by one.

But the White Whale didn't let them smash its means of attack without a response. From the mouths, seemingly infinite no matter how many they smashed, a literal barrage of annihilating mist spewed out.

Ricardo, relying on his liger's mobility, and Wilhelm, pushing his body past normal human limits, continued to dodge, dodge, and dodge that mist some more.

The expeditionary force and the Iron Fangs had both reorganized, and they began firing magic crystal cannons once more to assist Wilhelm and Ricardo in their precarious position. With the White Whale's own attacks unable to hit, and apparently losing patience from the increasing damage from the pesky attackers, it twisted its massive body, opening its mouth fully to spread mist far and wide.

"Rem—!!"

Faster than Subaru could shout, Rem had their land dragon leap up onto the White Whale's nose. The approach of Subaru, with the scent of the Witch wafting around him, made the White Whale reflexively stare at them, throwing off its concentration; it was looking to send them flying when a slash interrupted that plan.

"_____!!"

"That's very rude of you. Here I am, after nothing but your head for fourteen years, and you look away."

With a stab, Wilhelm thrust deep into the White Whale's brow, his movement halting when his blade sank into the skull. But the aged swordsman instantly abandoned his third sword, leaping in and kicking full force the hilt of the sword he had let go of, and withdrew his fourth and fifth swords, both blades dancing wildly across the White Whale's back.

Also atop the White Whale's back, Ricardo linked up with Wilhelm, opening his large mouth and laughing.

"This is gettin' fun! It's tougher than I thought, but it's not all that strong, now, is it!"

"No...the response is a little too weak."

While Ricardo exulted, Wilhelm knitted his brows and murmured. Biting his lip, Wilhelm sliced into the White Whale's tail fin as he said, "I cannot easily believe my wife...the Sword Saint...

could be defeated by this level of demon beast. Even considering that it did not take the initiative and split us apart with mist at the beginning..."

As Wilhelm swung his blades, his thought process was interrupted by the White Whale whirling its body about.

"Do—? Waaaah?!"

The demon beast's action, differing from all those before it, sent the White Whale's head suddenly rising up, with the force sending Ricardo and his liger flying off.

Then Wilhelm, still atop the White Whale, said, "I'll take one more before I take my leave!"

With the demon beast wriggling its body as it swam in the air, Wilhelm ran down it with nimble movements. The White Whale's body was climbing, with Wilhelm leaping down in the opposite direction. Finely adjusting his center of gravity and using the stabs of his blades to control his posture by force, the highly experienced old swordsman exercised his body to the fullest, chopping off at the base one of the dorsal fins at the extreme edge of the enormous body.

"_____!!"

Listening to the White Whale's scream, Wilhelm rode the fin he'd sent flying onto the ground below. Normally, you would think a fall from such a great altitude would result in instant death, but the soles of Wilhelm's feet kicked off the fin just before impact, and his land dragon caught him, softening the blow.

"Wilhelm!"

"_____"

Subaru tried to make sure he was all right, but Wilhelm did not respond, for his eyes were on the White Whale, still rapidly ascending.

Drawn in, Subaru looked up, and his vision was caught by the White Whale's tail as it swam in the sky high above.

Blood dripped from the fin that had been sliced off, pouring downward with violent force. The grassy plain was dyed scarlet, and Wilhelm was bathed in red rain, his will to fight undiminished.

Subaru didn't think the White Whale was going to just turn tail and run, either, but the demon beast's goal in heading up into the sky was unclear. The Iron Fangs and the expeditionary force uneasily looked up at the sky, and Subaru grew concerned for the wounded gathered at the roots of the Great Tree.

"It's coming."

Wilhelm made a small murmur as he turned his gaze upward.

Seeing the aged swordsman narrow his eyes and return both hands to his sword hilts put everyone on guard.

And then, as they held their breaths—they regretted it. Too late, they knew they should have deployed instantly without waiting for the White Whale, floating above their heads, to act.

"—Mist, incoming!!"

Subaru shouted as loudly as he could. Rem made the land dragon whirl about and move away from the front.

The land dragons and ligers all around them started running all at once, but there was no longer any leeway for Subaru to raise his head and see if the others were safe.

—Billowing, annihilating mist came falling to earth with such force that it seemed to blot out the sky.

The mist was like the clouds themselves were falling. There was no way to avoid it save escaping the area. Sheltering behind rocks or trees was meaningless resistance before destruction that would swallow all obstacles whole.

There was nothing they could do but start running and pray that they were in time.

Too afraid to look up, Subaru merely felt the oppression of the soundless apocalypse hurtling from above. He earnestly squatted against the land dragon's back, lowering his posture as far as he could as they ran—

"We got through?!"

Having apparently slipped out from under the thick mist and entered a clearer area, Subaru turned his head around and looked back.

There were several figures on the ground behind them that hadn't made it out in time, swallowed up as the mist pressed down upon them. With expressions of fear and anger chiseled on the human beings' faces, they earnestly fled, but they were engulfed by the mist from the head down and vanished.

The land dragons were obliterated with them. With the mist falling and scattering to the ground, no trace of their destruction remained. Not even their names would remain in anyone's memories. None save Subaru, the only one who would remember their deaths.

"U...aa..."

There were little moans in front of Subaru from distant figures scattered about the mists. It was clear that their numbers had greatly diminished since they had regrouped. That of course went for the expeditionary force's knights, but the Iron Fangs had not escaped unscathed, either.

If we at least have our big guns, thought Subaru, shifting his gaze. "Wil..."

He spotted Wilhelm, barely keeping one hand on his land dragon's back as he escaped the mist's area of effect. It was when Subaru called out to him from behind that he realized.

—That from the other side of the dense mist, the demon beast was chasing Wilhelm, opening its huge mouth.

"—Run!"

"Nn—?!"

Wilhelm noticed the impending menace at his back at about the same time Subaru shouted. But both came too late for him to react in time.

Approaching without a sound, the maw of the White Whale swallowed the ground, the land dragon, and Wilhelm whole.

Scraping the ground, everything on the surface around Wilhelm was gouged out, entering the White Whale's mouth.

"Aaah...!"

Faced with the shock of that spectacle, it was not only Subaru who shouted but Rem as well.

Knowing the grudge the old man bore, the sense of loss was all that much greater. More importantly, losing their main fighting strength would make their situation most dire, but...

"Oh no, ya don't!!"

This time, someone else raised his voice from right beside them.

Before they could react, a liger came in from the side, bumping their land dragon and sending Subaru and Rem flying.

"Whoaa?!"

Tumbling from the staggered land dragon, Subaru grimaced from the pain of getting smacked all over. From the voice, he knew that it was Ricardo who had committed the sudden act of violence, but before he could ask what the big idea was...

"—Gaa!"

...Subaru gasped as he saw crimson flowers bloom before his eyes.

"Huh?"

The liger was sliced apart, pieces of its flesh sent flying as its corpse cruelly rolled onto the grassland. The large-statured beast man who should have been straddling it had vanished, with a vast pool of fresh blood left behind in his place.

The White Whale swam at low altitude, swaying its enormous body and waving the tail that was covered in Ricardo's blood.

He...shielded us?

Then what...happened to Ricardo?

There were various questions coming to mind, but Subaru set them aside when he realized something he could not ignore.

Before him was a White Whale, which had mowed down Ricardo with its tail.

And...

"No...way..."

When he looked back, he saw the White Whale that had swallowed Wilhelm and the ground around him beginning to bite down.

In front, behind and up above, he saw yet another whale-shaped figure high in the sky, scattering mist all around.

—The infinite mouths of the three White Whales laughed together, drawing out the despair of men.

Bit by bit, Subaru once again felt hope being blotted out by a nightmare.

CHAPTER 4

A GAMBLE TO RESIST DESPAIR

1

The chorus grew higher and farther, echoing as they overlapped.

In a world thick with mist, there were three fish-shaped figures, their enormous bodies swaying as they swam.

The twisted mouths stretching from one side to the other of their huge frames were bizarre, continuing to emit a sound like fingernails on glass.

It was a malevolent monster that had swallowed people of many races, extinguishing innumerable lives.

That single monster had wielded enough power on its own to inspire despair within the hearts of all people, and now there were three, mocking those who dared to defy them.

As Subaru looked up at the White Whale floating above his head, he heard the small sound of someone falling to his knees. A string of similar sounds followed, joined by a chain of high-pitched clatters—weapons falling from their wielders' grasps.

He saw the shoulders of one of the knights participating in the expeditionary force had fallen, and the man stared at the ground as he crouched low. His shoulders trembled, and none could hold back the weep rushing up into his throat.

When Subaru gazed at the man's fellow knights around him, not one had a single word to say.

They'd come fully equipped with all the numbers they could muster, seized the initiative and slammed their firepower into it, yet having taken the offensive to that extent—they'd come to this senseless situation.

Their numbers had already been halved by the depth of the mental contamination, and their remaining main fighting strength had been pulverized in a surprise attack by the newly emerged White Whales. Even if they gathered all their remaining strength together, it would still amount to less than half the fighting strength they had started with. On top of that, the demon beasts they had to fell numbered three—surely there was no chance of victory.

Everyone grasped it in a single second. They realized that their objective, and their lives, would be ruined in that place.

The terror of the demon beast was great. And the bonds that the demon beast had robbed them of weighed heavily. And yet, they were powerless, unable to make it pay for the loss of precious life it had stolen from them.

When the weight of all that crashing down, and the hearts that had supported them until that moment had broken, who could blame them for falling to their knees on the spot?

In the face of such a senseless, unchangeable reality, could anyone deny that they should give up?

"—Don't let it swallow him!!"

Abruptly, an angry bellow reverberated far across the silence that had befallen the plain.

Hearing that voice, Subaru unwittingly lifted his face and he saw a lone figure kicking off the ground, leaping toward the White Whale—a girl, with a flutter of her maid uniform and wielding a vile, spiked iron ball with her hand.

With a gale entwined around it, the roaring iron ball came to a halt when it slammed straight into the White Whale's nose, easily smashing the hard outer hide, continuing on to gouge out exposed flesh and bone, widening the destructive wound further.

The White Whale let out a scream and tried to lift its head up to the sky. But a blade of ice stretched up from the ground to impale its tail, and as it twisted its body around, the small-statured girl whirled her iron ball around, scoring a merciless hit that made the White Whale's enormous frame shudder as blood was scattered all about.

"We can still save him if we get him out before he's in its belly—!"

There was a young man shouting, holding a rent shoulder as blood flowed from his brow.

He walked out in front, giving orders to the girl swinging the iron ball. He grimaced, bitterly feeling the powerlessness that kept him from joining the battle himself, but even so, he stepped forward.

A land dragon stood at the young man's side. He slowly climbed onto its back, his clumsy posture clearly from not being accustomed to riding, but still, he strongly gripped the reins and shouted, "We're not done yet! None of this is over!!"

Before the knights seized by surrender, the young man lifted his face as if he was bolstering his own spirits, bared his teeth, opened his eyes wide, glared at the White Whale, and yelled.

"—Don't think this is enough despair to stop me!!"

2

Subaru keenly felt the sound of despair's footsteps approaching.

One was above his head, one was behind him, and one was right in front of him—three in total.

This ain't funny.

How much fighting strength had they poured to confront just one of them, and how much did they actually wound it? Because things weren't going so well, it called out two of its buddies to start the real fight. It was all a bad joke.

Just how many senseless hardships would it take until Fate was satisfied?

Shielded by Ricardo, Subaru had been tossed to the ground and remained there as he grit his teeth. Had he not clamped his molars shut, he would have let out sounds of weakness, or even sobs.

Gently, he felt everything before his eyes go dark. His brain was unable to bear the strain of accepting the bitter circumstances; his mind seemed ready to give out from hopelessness at any moment.

Suddenly, he realized that the familiar despair was mocking him, chummily wrapping an arm around his shoulders.

"—Whaaaat, is it not about time you gave up once more?"

He could not see the face of the faint shadow, but someone was chuckling, the familiar voice suggesting he surrender.

With those words, Subaru vividly accepted the weight of the circumstances before him that barred his path.

Around him, Subaru saw the knights falling to their knees and giving up, just like him. They, too, comprehended that the situation before their eyes was beyond their means. Robbed even of the ardor to begin to resist, strength drained from everyone's eyes, and the willpower to even hold a weapon evaporated.

When that sight broke his spirit, and he gave in to the futility wrapped around his shoulders, he realized something.

Right at his side was Rem, thrown from the land dragon at the same time he had been. Having fallen on her side, she sat up, and he saw sadness on the side of her comely face.

Her cheeks were taut, her lips blue, and her eyelids shaking.

When he stared at her like that, he thought rather casually, *Her eyelashes are long, huh.* And he believed...

—A smile suits her so much better.

That was why—

"You're not getting any more stage time, ever!"

He brusquely shook off the chummy arm wrapped around his shoulders.

With the shadow's mouth twisting in visible surprise, Subaru's next action was to turn a smiling face toward it and deliver a straight right punch—smashing the black shadow to pieces and halting the shaking of his body.

Stupid. Pathetic. He didn't have the time for doubts or stopping in place.

So there were two more whales. So what?

His limbs could move. He could lift his face. His eyes could see. His voice came out. It reached her. Rem was there. Rem was alive. There was nothing there, nothing at all, that warranted giving up.

—Stand up.

Over and over, again and again, his heart had been broken.

—Stand up.

A senseless fate had buffeted him, with despair being the conclusion forced upon him.

—Stand up.

When he thought all was lost, he threw everything to the wind, trying to abandon all as he ran, and when even that was not permitted, he faced his own heart.

—Stand up.

*　　*　　*

What for?

"For a time...like this, damn it!!"

He rammed a fist into the ground, pushing his torso upright.
When Subaru howled, lifting his face, Rem looked at him in surprise.
Subaru turned to her, extended his hand, and glared at the White Whale in front of him.
"It ain't over yet—it won't end like this."
"...Subaru."
"Let's do it, Rem. It's our big scene."
Meekly, she slowly grasped the outstretched hand that then pulled her to her feet. As she rose, Subaru hugged her around her chest, drawing her face close.

"Giving up ain't our style. Not me, not you—not one of us!"

3

With a howl, Rem ferociously leaped at the White Whale, twisting her body and ramming her fist into its stony hide. Her left arm swung around the iron ball, which crashed into its target with a tremendous sound, causing the White Whale to groan in agony as blood frothed forth.

Rem was attacking the one that had swallowed Wilhelm from behind. The maw looked like it was biting down, but it was hard to believe that Sword Devil would be chewed so easily.

"As long as the head ain't smashed, we'll drag him out somehow—!"

Pulling the reins, Subaru didn't feel particularly secure, but he entrusted his body weight to the land dragon.

For Subaru to handle the reins himself, rather than Rem, was troubling; he had basically zero training. He only had the time on the road before arriving at the Great Flugel Tree and the free time after arrival to practice using a dragon mount.

There was no way Subaru, lacking any experience whatsoever with horses from his old world, could master land dragons with only a few hours of practice. It was all he could do to set direction and speed, and to cling so as not to fall off.

Even so, the highly intelligent land dragon perfectly grasped both Subaru's intentions and his capabilities. The pitch-black land dragon Subaru had chosen as his very own mount was being considerate so as not to let its inexperienced rider fall.

Good land dragon. Nimble on your feet, sturdy, and more than anything, very quick on the uptake. From this moment on, your name is Patlash. That's the only name I could think of for such a loyal partner.

"Let's go, Patlash! Circle around the tip of the whale's nose!"

The loud shout and a crack of the reins spurred the land dragon into a run. Patlash responded with a gallop at a forward angle, knowing no fear as it charged toward the mighty White Whale.

With Rem clinging to its body, the White Whale was twisting to try to throw her off, but it sensed Subaru's approach and instinctively turned its head in his direction.

"Sniffing Subaru's scent is a privilege for me alone—!"

Rem leaped to the side of its face, delivering a kick with the force of a cannonball.

The enormous face was greatly dented, and there, the iron ball scored an additional direct hit. The whirling iron ball broke through the White Whale's cheek, snapping molars and sullying the grassy ground reddish black from blood and saliva.

A yellow liquid dribbled out of the wound as the White Whale screeched. Its body crashed to the ground and began to writhe upon it like a fish out of water.

The earth was gouged in the process, with clods of soil violently scattered about. The wildly waving tail split the surface of the ground, mowing the wind and flying toward Subaru from the side with him seemingly unaware—and just when he was in danger of a square hit...

"Ta-daa, Mimi is here!!"

...the little feline beast person intervened a moment prior to the blow, the staff in her hand swinging to deploy a magical wall. With a yellow glow, the blow bounced off, and liger and land dragon rushed through the resulting gap at once.

Taking a breath, Subaru turned back to look at Mimi—the kitten that had saved him—and said, "Thanks a bunch! I'd have bought it right after starting the counterattack all cool and stuff!"

"Hu-huu, you can praise Mimi more! But for today I'll praise you for working so haaard, mister!"

"Working...?"

Mimi puffed her chest out, then when Subaru crooked his neck, she laughed at him. As she did so, she gave an orange pigtail a flick of her finger before she responded.

"Everyone was all blue and couldn't even stand, but you bounced back first, didn't you? Good boy! You're amazing! Not as good as Mimi, though!"

"It's no big deal. I'm not about to let despair get the better of me."

With Mimi extolling him in a loud voice, Subaru bit his lip and grimaced.

That's right. It wasn't anything to be praised for.

Just how much bitterness had Subaru tasted along the way?

Compared with the impossible horrors he'd faced, how did a situation where he could still fight afford him the leeway to immerse himself in surrender...?

If he had time to wallow in surrender, he might as well cough his blood out and go searching for hope, for defiance was far, far, far more comforting than surrender.

"_____!!"

As Patlash bounded, rushing straight forward, a fish silhouette suddenly appeared right in front, opening its huge mouth.

Seeing the inside of the grotesque throat at point-blank range, Subaru instantly leaned forward as they took evasive action. But the mist filling the mouth dispersed a little faster than he could evade it—

"Close your mouth—!"

From far overhead, an invisible blade swung down, vertically slashing the open maw.

The power of the blow closed the mouth by force, and the White Whale writhed on the ground as it passed Subaru and Mimi. When Subaru lifted his head after just barely escaping, he saw Crusch was galloping over from the other side of the battlefield.

She ran until she pulled alongside Subaru's land dragon, vilely glaring at the White Whale as she spoke.

"From a glance, this seems to be the worst possible case. What happened to Wilhelm?"

"If you remember him, that means at least he wasn't wiped out by the mist… It's up to Rem now."

Shifting his head, Subaru replied while keeping his eyes on the White Whale turning around and locking its sights on them. Receiving his answer, Crusch looked toward Rem, still in fierce combat. As the iron ball smashed downward, fresh blood spewed forth, and that White Whale made the ground quake as it thrashed in a sea of its own blood.

"What do you see, Subaru Natsuki?"

"What do you mean by 'what do you see'? If you're suggesting in the sense of winning, I could say something self-serving, like, 'I see various things separating my life and my death,' but…"

"Not that. Do you not find it strange?"

Crusch sent an invisible blade after the bridge of the nose of the White Whale pursuing from behind. The White Whale groaned, its pursuit crushed at the outset, while Subaru commented, "Strange?" as he looked at Crusch.

"The White Whales have multiplied to three. Viewing it simply, the situation is desperate. But if the White Whale was truly a horde of monsters, is that really something we wouldn't notice?"

"I don't really get what you're trying to say."

"It must be some kind of trick."

Crusch said it bluntly, turning her gallant face toward Subaru. By nature, having that powerful gaze shooting through Subaru made him stand straighter.

"So we've got to…figure out what it is?"

"We shall render aid so as to buy time for your escape. Either way, we cannot hold for long. We must do something—retreat is no longer an option."

So declaring, Crusch changed the orientation of her land dragon and moved away from Subaru.

Making a wide turn, she circled around the White Whale glaring down from above as she showed her face to the scattered units of the expeditionary force, raising her voice.

"Stand! Lift up your heads! Seize your arms! What have you come this far for?!"

"……"

The gazes of the men, seized by misery and despair, rose.

Before them, Crusch grandly drew her treasured sword and raised it to the heavens as she cried.

"Look at that man! He carries no weapon. He is helpless, so weak that the wind alone could carry him away. I have seen this powerless man battered down with my own eyes!"

As Subaru ran, Crusch pointed him out with the treasured sword of her house as she cried louder still.

"He is weaker than any of you!"

Yes. Everything Crusch said was true. Subaru was weak. Weaker than anyone.

He had no power to fight. He had no ability save that of surviving. He had been crushed over and over—a man who had been beaten down and defeated many times.

"Yet, it is the weakest among you who was the quickest to yell it is not over!"

It was the most helpless man there who had grit his teeth and said he could still fight. He held back his tears, coughed out his blood, and in spite of that, stood up to resist for all to see.

"Then why are we hanging our heads low?"

"……"

"Our power is weak. Even all together, I know not if we can reach the demon beast's throat. Even so, if the weakest among us has not surrendered, how can we be allowed to fall to our knees?!"

"Y-yeah…"

The broken men with knees that would not stop shaking looked to one another, encouraging one another to stand once more.

They picked up their fallen weapons and drew close to the land dragons waiting at their riders' sides.

They reached out with their hands, took the reins, and where they had been kneeling now appeared knights astride their land dragons' backs.

The mounts neighed as the knights drew their swords and cleared their throats once more.

A great shout arose—a battle cry to take pride in their own souls, as if to rally their own hearts.

Behind the weakest man on the battlefield, they let out a ferocious roar, driving away the foolishness that lowered their heads.

—People call this emotion shame.

It was the fear of shame that made the knights lift their heads, cut through the various emotions holding them in place, or give in, and gave them the strength to step forward.

"Let's go!! Charge!!"

"Ooooo—!!"

With their once-yielding souls reinspired, the knights resumed their advance.

The force of land dragons kicked up a cloud of dust. Though the expeditionary force now totaled just under fifty souls, they ferociously charged the two White Whales within reach of their swords, with Crusch at the head.

Listening to the upsurge in the expeditionary force's morale, and to the scolding from Crusch that had sparked it, Subaru couldn't keep the corners of his lips from making a strained smile.

"Rub in how much of a weakling and a beaten dog I am, why don't you...?"

The fact that he couldn't bring himself to refute it only proved the severity of his case.

They could call him what they liked, use him as they liked. It was the truth that Subaru was helpless, a loser, broken and flung about, and thus he had arrived at that point.

It was because Subaru understood it that he could bellow then and there: Losing didn't mean it was over, being broken didn't mean you had to submit, being flung about meant there was still time, and being helpless…was not allowed.

"I'm counting on you, Patlash. Go right up close one more time, to the tip of its nose!"

The land dragon leaned down at an angle, clawing the ground and making repeated sharp turns, crying out as it rushed the White Whale.

With the White Whale trying to shake Rem off before their eyes, Crusch and mixed split-off squads went on the attack in support. The knights' swords kicked up sparks as they rent the White Whale's outer hide, and they pulled away so that mounted dragons running parallel could add explosions via magic crystals.

The White Whale let out a cry, slapping the ground all around it. Even that act of writhing in pain was a difficult-to-evade violent force to the human beings around it. One land dragon and mounted knight pair was sent flying by the attack; crushed by a very heavy weight, the sound of bones breaking scattered about.

Blood spurted, and a single human life was snuffed out—Subaru burned the sight into his eyes.

A chill ran up his spine. He could not have saved him in time, but this was the result of Subaru's decision.

It was the result of Subaru choosing to start that battle. He could not look away.

The instant Subaru rejected that fact would be the moment he lost to the emotion of shame.

When he'd lost to his own heart, when he'd faced his most despicable weaknesses, he deeply, gently rejected those weaknesses even so. That was why he could pamper himself no longer.

With a shudder, he tasted the sensation of blood draining away as he cut through the wind, trusting fully in his land dragon.

—The annihilating mist spewed by the countless mouths was right beside them as they grazed past.

If even a single one of his fingers should have touched it, Subaru's existence would be erased and brought to an end.

His entire body would be engulfed in a sense of loss different than death, and he would vanish, ended without even anyone to remember him.

However...

"El Fulla!" "Like we'll let you!!" "Where do you think you're looking?!"

...wind magic swept the mist aside. Blades rising with a bellow, and mauls with a roar, pounded and crushed the mouths spewing mist.

The knights' support slightly thinned the barrage of mist. Even so, the mist's firepower was cause for despair, but Subaru's entire nervous system had grown finely attuned to the aura of impending erasure.

Leaving their course to Patlash, Subaru's flesh took evasive action atop its back. He sprang onto his arms and pushed up. In so doing, Subaru evaded the mist pressing upon him from the rear, but having completely thrown off his balance, he was on his way to a fall when—

"G-guuuuuts!!"

Gripping the reins, he thrust his knees onto the saddle, barely averting the fall. The gripping power he'd honed swinging a wooden sword, something meaningless in his original world, allowed his hands to just barely hold on rather than slip from the shaking and vibrations.

Subaru hung on to Patlash, clawing along the ground, as they broke past the barrage.

Their vision cleared, and when the considerate land dragon slackened the pace, Subaru reseated himself, ending what must have looked like the most disgraceful sight ever. His endurance, never great to begin with, had fallen, and at that rate, next time would be one-sided—but Crusch and the others advanced on the White Whale, launching their attack.

"Gotta rack my brain... Haaa, shit, don't just put your life on the line—think, damn it!"

Even as he breathed raggedly, putting his life on the line to earnestly act as a decoy once more, Subaru's thoughts wandered to the trick Crusch had brought up during their prior conversation.

Where the White Whale's "ecology" was concerned, Subaru was the least informed person there. He had no way of appreciating the damage the being had wrought beyond the extent of the words *Great Expedition*.

There had to be something Subaru could notice, something that only he could notice, that others could not.

Wilhelm had been chasing the White Whale for fourteen years to avenge his wife. The notion that the Sword Devil, having nursed that grudge to arrive at that field of battle, could overlook such critical information as "There are multiple White Whales" was simply unthinkable. Naturally, that meant the phenomenon was unknown.

Then *why* hadn't anyone been told? —No, why had it escaped their knowledge?

"Why did more come out all of a sudden? …The premise that there were three to start with is just weird."

He felt like he was about to catch on. But before he could, Patlash's earnest sprint had brought them within smelling range of the White Whale.

Crusch was chasing the White Whale, adding slashes from her treasured sword to it, but its gaze was shifting heavily toward Subaru. Simultaneously, it opened its mouth, releasing a roar that seemed to shatter the air along with the dense, vastly destructive mist that had filled its oral cavity.

Patlash stomped down, sharply changing directions. That got them out of the oncoming tyrannical mist's immediate reach but was half a step short in getting them out of its effective range—yet…

"We'll handle this!" "We won't let ya!!"

…Hetaro and Mimi intervened, buying them the time to take that last half step.

The twin cat people opened their mouths, unleashing overlapping roars of "Wa!" and "Ha!" The sound waves intermingled to combine into one, entwining as they transformed into destructive power. Then, the vast oscillation wave rippled across the plain, striking the onrushing mist head-on and blowing it apart.

"Whoaa!! That's awesome!!"

"Oh yeah, oh yeah, oh yeah! Praise me more! Woo-hoo!"

"There you go again, Big Sis…"

Subaru's honest praise made Mimi puff her chest out, her cheeks loosening in satisfaction. Running alongside her, Hetaro exhaled, the two sandwiching Subaru as they darted close to him.

"We will support you. Without you, Mr. Natsuki, I do not see any way of winning this battle," Hetaro said.

"So can we go bam, boom, badaboom, and stuff?" Mimi asked.

"Big Sis, we've been going bam, boom, badaboom, but we still need Mr. Natsuki's help."

"Heh!"

The low-stress conversation continued with Subaru stuck in the middle.

Leaving aside Mimi acting like she didn't grasp the situation in the slightest, Subaru turned his head toward the receptive-looking Hetaro and said, "That team-up attack, that's the one you smacked the White Whale with midway, huh. Can you do it again?"

"Mana is tight, so one more and I will be at my limit—Big Sis and I will defend you until the captain finishes healing up."

"That Ricardo guy, he's alive?!"

When Subaru raised his voice at the unexpected good news, Hetaro said yes as he nodded.

That gesture spread the relief in Subaru's heart. When the liger Ricardo had ridden was cruelly slain, he'd seen the large amount of blood and feared Ricardo might have been blown away without even a trace.

"Our gravely wounded captain had a message for you, Mr. Natsuki."

"A message... It's not something like, 'You owe me big'?"

"I believe he will say this to you later from his own mouth, but... it goes as follows. Ahem. 'Wha—? It got lighter. Fact I ain't dead is proof o' that.' End of message."

Hetaro conveyed the message, mimicking Ricardo down to his Kararagi dialect. Subaru made no comment on the quality of the portrayal as he mulled over the meaning of the words spoken to him.

It was a message Ricardo had literally put his life on the line to get to him. If he could only wrap his mind around the meaning within, and the real message behind it—

"You don't sound anything like him."

"Yeah, not one bit! You have no talent for this, not at all!"

"Is this the time to say something like that?!"

Mimi innocently concurred with Subaru's insensitive remark. Hetaro refuted their thoughts with a voice on the verge of tears, but Subaru let that slide off him and looked up at the sky.

Two of the White Whales were still tangling with the expeditionary force, engaged in fierce combat. On the other hand, the White Whale floating in the sky, with a commanding view of the battle, was calmly watching from up high.

Subaru felt that its behavior was somehow…unnatural.

The expeditionary force had lost its main fighting strength, and the diminished squads were split apart, fighting on two fronts. Even with Subaru fulfilling his role as a distraction, if the White Whale floating in the sky were to join either front, it would be enough to decisively shift the course of the battle. If either force was gobbled up, they were finished.

And yet, that White Whale did nothing. Why…?

"Ricardo's message…"

Lighter, Ricardo had said.

He was conveying the reason he hadn't died after putting his life on the line.

So what did that mean? Lighter, but what was lighter? His life? Certainly life was lighter on the field of battle, but he didn't think that's how it was meant. Lighter, lighter meant…

"This is a heavy, hard situation. What the hell can be lighter…?!"

He put all his weight on Patlash and charged toward the tip of the nearest White Whale once more.

With Crusch and the others all over it, the White Whale's oral cavity aimed their way, but an invisible slash from Crusch at the magic crystals lobbed into it inflicted explosive damage.

A cry went up among the knights. Even as their numbers diminished, one here, one there, they were currently maintaining the battlefront on inexhaustible morale alone.

Was this how strong human beings became when they resolved to defy death before their eyes?

After all, the expeditionary force had challenged the White Whale with its full roster. Having lost their main fighting force and even much of their numbers, the fact that they were still resisting by force of arms could only be said to be the power of will—

"You can't expect even the power of will to explain all this, though."

Having thought that far, Subaru gasped, lifting his face.

He looked back at the White Whale left in the lurch behind him, glaring at the demon beast's distant visage.

Then, he realized what felt so off.

"If that's the case…!"

Subaru gritted his teeth, a chill running through his entire body when the possibility rose and coursed through him.

Transmitting his intent through the reins, Patlash made a sharp turn and ferociously approached the other White Whale.

Rem, fighting furiously with her full Oni power unleashed, rode a liger as she smashed hole after hole in the White Whale's torso. Even with her apron dress sullied by demon beast blood spatter, she smiled firmly when she sensed Subaru's approach.

Seeing that happy expression while she was daubed in whale blood was disconcerting, but imprudent as it was, Subaru watched Rem with fascination. Even with the situation at such a disadvantage, Rem trusted in Subaru's reckless resolve.

Her faith, her love, could not go unanswered.

"……"

Without any exchange of words, Subaru's land dragon crossed Rem's liger, with Subaru going toward the tip of the White Whale's nose, and Rem turning her mount toward its tail.

There was no need to stop and discuss it. Both knew that Subaru had his own role to play, and Rem had hers.

When Subaru circled to the front of the White Whale, the demon beast, sensing his approach, shifted his head in his direction. Above its gigantic eye, multiple mist-spewing mouths appeared, drooling as they emitted white mist.

"Ta-daa! Ba-baam! Whoosh, scatter, scatter!"

The liger Mimi rode jumped to the left of Patlash, to the right, above, and all around. As Mimi made decisive poses and voiced sound effects atop the big dog's back, the staff in her hand glowed, blocking the mist with a magic wall, buying Subaru and Patlash enough time to evade before the barrage reached them.

"This is gonna cost you big, mister!"

"I'm grateful enough; when this is over I'll thank you a hundred times over!"

"Okay, then!"

At Mimi's laconic reply, he turned his back and ran parallel in pursuit of the White Whale. Then he overtook it, and got out in front.

Subaru turned, and he and the White Whale glared at each other. The demon beast, its one eye dyed crimson, let out a high-pitched cry at the defiance of the boy, as annoying and small as a pest. But the beast's appearance lent conviction to Subaru's own thoughts.

Neither that White Whale, nor the one facing Crusch and the others, had a left eye.

"Just like I thought! There ain't three of ya, damn it—you split apart!"

The one floating in the sky was surely wounded in the same places as the first, including the loss of its left eye.

—The missing left eye was the battle wound Wilhelm had inflicted on the White Whale in the early fighting.

It was crystal clear there could be only one reason the same wounds were on not a single beast but the two others as well: The one in the sky had split itself, bringing the other two into being.

"The hits are lighter because the offshoots only have a third of the fighting power! That trick explains why we can fight them even with way fewer people!"

It explained why Ricardo, struck in the surprise attack, was not killed in the process. So, too, did it explain why the expeditionary force, diminished in numbers, was able to keep fighting against multiple White Whales.

Subaru had abandoned the convenient thinking that would peg it on the miraculous power of will. And it was precisely because Subaru was such a contrarian that he had arrived at the offbeat answer.

The power of the annihilating mist was absolute. Accordingly, the White Whale had increased its manpower at the cost of its own endurance. If the tyranny of numbers broke the spirit of the expeditionary force, the battle would surely end there.

Subaru had a hard time believing that the White Whale understood the weaknesses of the human heart and had resorted to the tactic with that knowledge. But the White Whale having the power to split itself was an incontrovertible fact.

What would have happened if Subaru hadn't rebelled against surrender when he did?

Subaru could not grasp what would have happened had he not howled. The current Subaru would not allow himself to perceive a future where he hadn't.

He never wanted to stare at the White Whales' ugly mugs so long ever aga—

"—What the...?!"

Before Subaru, forming that conclusion, the movements of the White Whale pursuing him changed. Where it had once floated in the sky, it now rubbed against the ground, as if some foreign object inside its body was causing it agony.

"Big Sis, now!"

"Mimi understands! It's hard when you have an itch you can't scratch, huh!"

Hetaro, sensing a favorable opportunity, leaped forward, and Mimi, misunderstanding the White Whale's movements, followed suit. The twins matched their movements in a pincer attack on the White Whale from right and left, opening their mouths at the same time when—

"Wa—!" "Ha—!"

The howling waves from left and right greatly warped the White Whale's torso, and the shock wave punched through the outer hide to the innards. They bounced off the hardened hide, cracks ran across it, blood flowed out, and the next moment—

"—Zuaaaaaa!!"

The part of the belly that rubbed against the ground's surface swelled from the inside, only for flesh and blood to break part. Reddish-black fluid flowed out like a muddy stream and spewed out; riding that stream was...

"Wilhelm?!"

The Sword Devil, his survival uncertain after being engulfed by the White Whale, had returned.

Subaru rushed over to Wilhelm while the expeditionary force restrained the thrashing White Whale. Wilhelm, his entire body smeared with blood, fell to one knee, holding half his body up with a sword.

"I was...rash...and...careless...!" he groaned.

"You don't need to talk! Aw, crap, I don't know what to do here, but at least you're alive. Let's get back to Ferris first thing!"

When Subaru reached out with his hand, he drew in his breath; the state of Wilhelm's wounds was far beyond his expectations. He still had the willpower to grip a sword, but he was knocking on death's door, his mangled left arm included.

The torch of his life threatened to burn out at any moment if Subaru didn't find a healer, pronto. And yet, when Subaru rushed over, Wilhelm politely refused his hand. Planting his weight on the sword he leaned upon, he clenched his teeth, trying to stand on his own power.

"Not...yet. I can still...fight..."

"This ain't the time! You'll die in front of the whale! So none of this 'it's not enough to kill me,' or 'I'm sleepy' crap! When it comes to life-and-death, I know more than you do!"

"What...are...you saying...?"

Scolding the mangled Wilhelm, Subaru grabbed his body and dragged him up. During the time the two bickered, the cat-people siblings linked back up with them.

"The old man came out!"

"Mr. Wilhelm, are you all right?!"

When the twins came rushing and saw Wilhelm's grave injuries, both instantly went into action. Mimi applied simplified healing magic to the aged swordsman's wounds, and during that time,

Hetaro looked up at Subaru and said, "Even Big Sis's healing magic cannot do much to heal these wounds. Mr. Natsuki, can you get Mr. Wilhelm as far as Mr. Felix?"

"Yeah, I can see for myself Wilhelm's in bad shape! If he isn't treated, it'll be too late! I really wanna bring him myself, but…"

Subaru glared at the White Whale as it began to rouse itself once more.

The belly wound ran deep, and the bleeding from the opening hadn't ceased, but the demon beast continued to spew mist from the mouths all over its body, showing no more sign of giving up the fight than Wilhelm had.

There was no mistake: At present, Subaru's distraction was no small part of their fighting strength against it. If Subaru carried Wilhelm off, the fighting would only take a turn for the worse.

"Even besides that, I might end up leading the White Whale straight to the wounded. Can I leave Wilhelm to the two of you?"

"We can do that with our ligers…but do you have something in mind?"

Hetaro accepted Wilhelm from Subaru, groaning a bit at the disparity in body weight as he put the man onto his liger. After that, he looked up at Subaru, taking the hand of his blissfully laughing sister as he said, "If there is a chance to win, I will listen. If not, I must take my sister by the hand and flee."

"Ehh, why?! We haven't beaten them yet!"

"Big Sis, be quiet."

Her little brother's statement made Mimi pout her lips in visible dismay.

Watching the exchange between the twins, Subaru said, "I suppose so," and accepted with a nod.

"You're mercs. You're just working for money, not like me, Crusch, and the knights with a grudge against the whale… No obligation to risk your lives."

"Do not misunderstand. We are not obligated to *throw away* our lives."

His face and demeanor were meek, but Hetaro gave Subaru his opinion with fortitude. Gazing down at the little beast people, not even reaching his own hips, Subaru exhaled deeply.

"Sorry, but there's no time," he said. "I think there's a chance to win. For now, just get Wilhelm to the rear... I've gotta...talk to Rem and Crusch."

With Patlash beside him, Subaru practically jumped onto its back, straddling it as he ran his gaze overhead.

He looked up at the sky above, glaring at the abominable, fish-shaped figure leisurely swimming therein—

4

"The White Whale split itself, then?"

"Yeah, I don't think there's any doubt. The locations of the wounds and the combat strength bear that out. Put bluntly, you and the other people fighting it directly must've felt it, right?"

"For my part, I was in a daze, but...you may well be correct."

Subaru had regrouped with Rem and Crusch, and both made accepting faces and nodded as Subaru explained.

Having entrusted Wilhelm's retreat to Hetaro's liger, he'd joined the twins, now riding on the same liger, and had just finished explaining the "trick" to the battlefield's main fighting force.

With the main force out of action, the cavalry unit and the Iron Fangs were keeping two of the White Whales busy. Their high morale and excellent teamwork oddly glossed it over, but there were mere minutes of time available for a strategy meeting—

They had to come up with a plan to defeat the White Whale during that time.

"—I accept your hypothesis that they are weaker than the original, single one. But what does comprehending this avail? Even if they are wounded and weakened, the menace to us is greater than before. Even with Ferris's healing, we cannot hope for those who have withdrawn to return to the battle lines."

"It hurts not to have Wilhelm and Ricardo, but I'm not asking the impossible. We've gotta win this without them."

"So we must kill three White Whales. It is easy to say but a high wall."

"We don't need to kill three—killing one should be enough."

With a twitch, Crusch raised an eyebrow at Subaru's words.

Subaru returned her look of deep interest with a nod and pointed at the demon beast in the sky above.

"Whaddaya think that bastard's doing, making its two offshoots fight every which way while it watches from high up there?"

"Perhaps it is refraining while it heals its wounds...?"

Subaru shook his head at Rem's unconfident reply.

From what Subaru could see, demon beasts were not so different from other creatures. At the very least, the White Whale didn't seem to possess any kind of off-the-charts self-regeneration ability.

If that was so, the role of the White Whale high in the sky was—

"That is the main body, then?"

"That's how I'm seein' it."

Subaru nodded, concurring with Crusch, arriving at the same conclusion as he.

Put plainly, it was all no more than a guess. But it was pretty certain that the White Whale high in the sky was the original out of the three. And when considering how to defeat the additional White Whales, the fact that it was playing a waiting game was beyond all dispute.

"I think the fact that it doesn't come down and help either of its buddies can only mean one thing—that it can't let itself get taken down."

"The reasoning matches up. However, put differently..."

"It might mean that killing the bottom two might not even hurt the main body."

Even if they defeated one at great pains, there was no guarantee the corpse would not simply be replaced by a new version. If that was so, the battle would plunge into an infinite loop with no end in sight. As a result, in contrast to the White Whale, playing with infinite continuations, he could see them crying uncle soon enough.

Hetaro, quietly observing, posed a very realistic question.

"So the reason it does not descend is linked to how to defeat it. But what should we do, then? We don't have any way to fly that high and attack it."

The little cat's question made Crusch shift her sharp, amber gaze to the White Whale overhead as she said, "Even using my blessing, my blade cannot attack at that range with appreciable force. I might be able to strike it, but the White Whale shall not fall from that."

The White Whale had fled to the upper sky, reaching an altitude roughly equal to the clouds. It was as if the White Whale was displaying its nastiness by occupying a position higher than when it had first appeared.

At that range, even the accuracy of magic crystal cannons would surely take a heavy hit.

"Rem, could you, say, float a mountain of ice right up close to the bastard...?"

"I am sorry. Mana is more difficult to control the farther away it is. I think it would be possible for Master Roswaal, but my skill is..."

Rem appeared chagrined, feeling the limits of her own power with a plan to break the deadlock before their eyes.

Subaru gave her reply a wave of the hand to say, *It can't be helped,* and looked up to the sky.

—He'd thought up a plan.

Given Crusch's reply, Hetaro and Mimi's reply, and Rem's reply, the best plan was out, leaving the next best, one he hadn't wanted to use.

"I have a plan, but it depends a lot on rolling the dice... Wanna give it a shot?"

Closing one eye, Subaru checked how far the girls were willing to go before revealing that next-best plan. But one might even call it a rude thing to ask.

The very fact that they stood in that place meant they would not shirk from any gamble...

...for they were a pack of great fools—a fact of which Subaru was well aware.

5

—From far in the sky above, the White Whale quietly watched the conflict below.

The battlefield was neatly divided into two halves, right and left, by the tree at the center that seemed to pierce the sky.

On both sides, little humans were clinging to the demon beasts' enormous frames, stabbing with the steel they gripped in their hands, brandishing stones that created light, defying the beasts in a superficial manner.

As flames rose up and the demon beasts' anguished cries reached it from below, the White Whale swam through the sky, spewing mist.

The mist it poured onto the plains was the ally of the offshoots beneath its gaze, steadily but surely whittling down the diminutive foe.

The figures scurried around, but as time passed, their numbers dwindled; one here, one there, swallowed by the mist, their existence erased from that world.

Everything would be swallowed up, and the end of that fruitless battle would not be long in coming. It was only a matter of time before the opposing fighting force began to develop fatal cracks and collapse.

If the White Whale possessed human intellect, it would surely have thought this, certain of its own victory. But in fact, the White Whale possessed no such thing.

The White Whale was simply following instinct, acting to destroy the opponent so as to preserve itself. There was no use asking a beast's instincts why it delivered such a judgment.

In accordance with its instincts, the White Whale calmly, purposefully set about toying with and killing its prey.

"—!!"

It spewed mist, progressively dyeing the surface white.

Though pests had interrupted it, the White Whale's mission was to cover the world in mist. This, too, was the command of its instinct, and doing so was the purpose of the White Whale's existence.

Thus, the White Whale's mind pulled away from the spectacle

below when suddenly, its enormous eye shifted about, its mind reorienting toward the earth once more.

Having detected mana gathering with enormous force, it looked at the flow with its naked eye.

"*Al Hyuma.*"

A blue-haired girl was standing in the center of the vast vortex of mana.

Over time, the mana swirled around her legs, building up as the girl gave it direction, gently constructing a very long lance of ice with a sharp tip protruding from it.

The vile frozen weapon was in the thirty-foot range, and its sharp spear tip was aimed at the center of the White Whale.

Even from a distance, its might appeared menacing, but the White Whale noticing it before she fired it was fatal.

"—Please!"

The girl shouted a prayer as the icy spear launched from the ground toward the sky.

Of course, its target was dead center in the torso of the swimming White Whale. The icy bloodlust accelerated rapidly with force sufficient to break through the sky—but the time it took to achieve that acceleration, and being seen at the moment of its launch, meant the plan had failed, its objective unfulfilled.

The White Whale waved its tail, swimming through the sky by slicing the wind. That alone threw off the icy spear's aim. The pathetic spear of ice sailed wide of the mark, passing by the White Whale's flank on its way to the distant sky—

"......?"

The instant the icy spear passed by, the very gentle sound of something shattering reached the White Whale's hearing. Taking into account the vast disparity in mass between the two, that was little short of a miracle.

That devil-wrought heavenly miracle told the White Whale that it was the sound of an irreparable mistake.

"—Heya. I've gotta say, it feels real icky seein' you up close like this."

An exceedingly light sensation mounted the White Whale's nose.

At the same time it realized that a being had landed atop its brow, the icy spear, supposedly flying past, vanished without a trace, and the White Whale caught a scent of the wave of scattering mana.

—And next, he discovered the source of the unbearably foul odor was right on top of it.

"You're coming with me. Gotta warn you, I'm a man considered too annoying to ignore."

A wicked smile came over the source of the foul odor as the White Whale listened to his words.

6

To summarize Subaru's wild scheme, he'd ride an ice spear from Rem's magic up into the sky, whereupon he would break a mana repulsion crystal to get off it—and climb aboard the White Whale.

Of course, Rem fiercely objected, but he got his way with repeated cries of "I trust you, Rem!" wearing Crusch and the others down by insisting it was not reckless, procuring a mana repulsion crystal from them in the process.

They'd anticipated that the White Whale would evade obvious great magic, and it was therein that Subaru laid his trap. To the contrary, had the White Whale not evaded, it was possible the icy spear, with Subaru clinging to the end, might have hit squarely and smashed to pieces. In one sense, it was the greatest danger to befall his life in that battle.

"But if I'm gonna say that, I'm in a pretty big pickle now—this is really scary!"

Desperately clinging to the tip of the White Whale's nose, Subaru got a good feel of its rough hide and body hair on his palms while his face grimaced from the wind in the upper sky and the raw scent of the mighty creature.

The clinging Subaru—in other words, the concentrated scent of the Witch—brought an about-face in the state of the White Whale. From its posture of solemn observation, the demon beast had clearly fallen into an agitated state, with mist, drool, and loud laughter flowing out of the entirety of its mouth, giving the rude Subaru a hearty welcome.

"—Okie."

Accepting the White Whale's unhappy greeting, Subaru took a deep breath and calmed his heart.

Of course, Subaru did not have any special attack with which to send the White Whale crashing to earth. He wasn't naive enough to think that a bit of enlightenment and resolve were enough to bring that about, and even if he smacked it with Shamak at great cost to his body, he'd probably slip like a brain-dead idiot, falling to his death—so that was out.

So Subaru was clinging to the White Whale for one thing.

"Well, let's give this a try—hardened resolve an' all."

Before the White Whale shifted to action, Subaru let go and slid down the body's stony hide—entering a free-fall course. He hadn't slipped like a brain-dead idiot, but he'd begun falling to the ground nonetheless.

The White Whale shifted its head toward the sight of Subaru committing a spectacular act of suicide, making a slight movement of its body to pursue, but then, it stopped, as if something had made it hesitate.

If it just watched Subaru go, its advantage from air supremacy would remain unshaken. The White Whale instinctively understood this, halting, as if it was resisting the lure of the scent.

I see, stubborn instincts. Well, that's inconvenient.

Accordingly, he played his trump card.

"At this height, there's no worry about anyone else hearing. Listen up! Big freebie here. Thanks to you, Rem died and I went through huge trauma, you bastard!!"

The instant he said it, Subaru's flesh, buffeted by the gale, was disconnected from the world. All the senses of his body grew distant, and his mind, ruled to that point by the feeling that his internal organs were floating upward, lost track of reality. He was invited to a place where the notion of time did not exist.

The next moment—

*   *   *

"I love you."

He felt like someone had whispered in his ear.

An instant later—ferocious pain shot through Subaru's entire body, as if a thunderbolt were turning him to ash.

From a place he could not see, the hands had invaded from the back side to grab his heart, wringing it roughly, but with care, as if checking to make sure it was still there.

He truly felt the organ that governed his life being treated roughly, the foreign sensation of having someone else freely manipulate such a vital part.

At the end of the world, not even allowed to let out a scream, the sounds of the wind and his own scream told him that…

"I'm…baaaack!!"

"_____!!"

Before Subaru's eyes, the White Whale's huge mouth was open as it ferociously plunged after him.

His confession of the taboo had increased the scent of the Witch, and the increased hatred had overridden the demon beast's instincts.

It let out a roar, its eye losing all sanity, seemingly forgetting about the conflict below as the White Whale came rushing, seeking to erase Subaru's existence alone.

Shrouded by a whirlwind, the White Whale rapidly closed the distance between them, making Subaru afraid. In that situation, unable to do anything but free fall, Subaru had no way to evade the charge. At that rate, before ever reaching the ground, the White Whale would catch him, and he'd hurdle toward BAD END 11: "Whale Food."

At that rate, anyway.

"—Rem!!"

"Yes, Subaru!"

Subaru's shouting voice seemed to die on the wind, but she replied loud and clear.

Simultaneously, with the White Whale focused exclusively on Subaru, a flying spear of ice flew in right from the side and collided—intruding upon its open mouth, breaking a number of its yellow teeth, and dulling its movements.

Seizing the opportunity, Rem, on Patlash's back, wrapped her morning star around Subaru's free-falling body.

The chain wrapped around his hips, forcibly twisting him off his crash course and sending his innards to one side. *"Gwah!"* was the cry Subaru raised as he remembered tasting the same impact once before.

It was the second time Rem had saved his falling body in that fashion. The first time was when Subaru's feet had slipped from the dragon carriage on their way to the royal capital.

"I guess you can get used to anything..."

After all, this time he had managed to avoid fainting.

Manipulated by the chain, Subaru's body fell somewhat roughly onto Patlash's back. With Rem spreading her arms wide to receive him, Subaru ended up flying into her bosom.

With a soft impact, Subaru's head was buried in a warm sensation as he exhaled.

"I'm saved!"

"You are getting a treat."

"What are you saying?!"

Subaru's cheeks reddened, and he hurriedly lifted his face from the embrace of Rem's breasts.

Right beside them, the face of the White Whale moved past—

"—!!"

The White Whale had crashed into the ground headfirst, its momentum undiminished. With a great roar, the surface of the ground exploded in a cloud of dirt, the force making the earth shudder.

As they became enveloped in a gust like a blast of wind, Subaru directed Patlash to sprint full force—and behind them, the White Whale was taking flight, bursting out of the dirt cloud.

The incredible force had messed up its head, and on top of that, the White Whale forgot itself, raising a scream as it bore down on Subaru.

In its tremendous excitement, he saw not even the slightest trace of when it leisurely swam in the sky. Its swimming had grown choppy, and its speed, outstripping the wind, was a good match for Patlash.

But in raw vigor, it was overwhelming.

The earth split, and as its tail slapped the earth, the White Whale ferociously chased them from behind.

Subaru put all his weight forward, entrusting his life to Patlash's reserves of strength. This was the land dragon that had earnestly and desperately exhausted all efforts for Subaru so far. Though it had been a short time, Subaru held enough faith to put his life on its shoulders.

"I'm counting on you, Patlash! You're a dragon, right?! Show me how cool you are!"

"—!"

Patlash neighed, and it felt like the speed went up a notch.

The roar of the White Whale resounded, and from the violent shaking of his eardrums and the world going blurry, he knew.

Straight ahead. Straight ahead. We just need to run and go right past it.

The White Whale swam, ferociously chasing down Subaru to devour him whole.

And then—

"Take this, damn it—!!"

"_____!!"

A second roar reverberated, and right after, there was a series of sounds like something was being ripped apart.

The intervals between the flagrant sounds narrowed, drew closer, and finally, a mighty shadow was born, making a very heavy sound as it—the Great Flugel Tree—fell straight toward the White Whale.

"_____!!_____!"

Magic crystal cannons, invisible blades, roaring attacks—destructive forces piled one on top of another had gouged out the roots of the Great

Tree, which had grown over the course of four centuries and had been planted by a sage. As it came down, it crushed the enormous body of the demon beast flat.

The great weight of the tree jutting to the heavens crashed straight into the White Whale, pressing into it from above. Against an attack that was in a different dimension compared to everything that came before it, even the defense from White Whale's tough outer hide was rendered meaningless.

A scream and an incredible shock wave ran across the Liphas plains, with the blast blowing the mist away.

Crushed under the Great Tree, the immobilized White Whale shrieked in anguish, curling its tail. And yet, its vital energy was such that its body had sustained a blow so great, but its life had not been extinguished.

The White Whale writhed, trying to escape from the super-heavy mass, when at the tip of its nose—

"—I dedicate this to my wife, Theresia van Astrea."

Raising above his head the treasured sword he had borrowed from his master, a lone Sword Devil swooped down—to lower the curtain on that ferocious battle upon which hung life or death, vindictiveness spanning fourteen years, and a history of conflict between man and the White Whale spanning four hundred.

CHAPTER 5
WILHELM VAN ASTREA

1

—Let us speak of the man named Wilhelm Trias.

Wilhelm was born the third son of the Trias family, a family of local nobles in the Kingdom of Lugunica.

The Trias family was an old, storied family granted land along the kingdom's northernmost border with the Holy Kingdom of Gusteko. This said, its fame as a family of warriors was a thing of the past; by the time of Wilhelm's birth, it had become a small, weak baronial family, with only a meager fief and a tiny populace to its name.

In real terms, it was no more than an example of nobility fallen from grace.

Wilhelm's brothers were well removed from him in age, and his upbringing had no connection to inheritance of family leadership. Furthermore, he, lacking the aptitude for civil government of his brothers, encountered wielding the sword as his one path leading to a future.

The sword decorating the great hall of their mansion had once been used by a string of men in the Trias family to gain fame as warriors for the kingdom, but to the present Trias family, it was simply a treasured sword to be admired on a wall.

Even Wilhelm did not remember what triggered it.

But when he drew the treasured sword, which he had never before even set hands upon, out of its scabbard, the way he was instantly captivated by the beauty of the steel—that, he remembered distinctly.

Before he knew it, he'd been taking the family sword on his own to the mountains out back, swinging it from morning till night.

The first time he touched the sword, he was eight; he became accustomed to the length and weight of the blade, and when his limbs grew so that they were no longer mismatched, Wilhelm was fourteen, and the finest sword wielder of the domain.

"I'll go to the capital and enter the royal army. Then I'll become a knight."

And it was at fourteen years old that Wilhelm spoke those words and ran off from home, carrying the brainless dream any boy had thought of at least once.

The trigger was on the night of a storm when he had an argument with his oldest brother. His brother had begun a "What will you do for your future?" lecture to Wilhelm, immersed in only the sword and minded to associate with brats and scoundrels in the territory.

Through swinging a sword, he'd felt himself growing stronger and stronger, and that by itself had made him happy. And so, the older brother's words toward his younger, lacking any ambition for the future, were very strict. He had piled sound argument upon sound argument, and Wilhelm, deficient in words, spoke those words as the prelude to his flying out the door.

He followed them with his trademark phrase, "You can't understand how I feel!" and left, and in truth, the result was that Wilhelm left his family with nothing but a sword and a small amount of money.

It was an unplanned departure, but Wilhelm was able to safely reach the royal capital.

Wilhelm, triumphant as he arrived, made his way to the Royal Palace with all haste, and records note that he entered the royal army as a common soldier.

If it were the current era, a stray ruffian arriving in an attempt to pass through the castle gate under such circumstances would have been rightfully and properly turned away. However, at that time, there was a civil war with an alliance of demi-human tribes centered upon the eastern lands of the kingdom—the Demi-human War had long continued, and the urgency was so great that no number of volunteers seemed enough.

It was then that a boy appeared, selling himself as having fair skill in the sword. He was welcomed with both hands, and Wilhelm entered the royal army without the slightest hindrance.

Thus, unconnected to setbacks or travails, Wilhelm stepped onto the field of his first battle.

There, for the first time, the boy came to know the wall called reality. His skill with the blade, unmatched on his home soil, served nothing against veterans of the field of battle, and he was confronted by his own recklessness and conceit.

Such was the hardship of youth, the baptism of one's first battle.

—Yes. By rights, it should have been like that for anyone.

But in truth, without ever having faced live combat, Wilhelm's skill with the sword easily surpassed fifteen normal youths put together.

"What? They really weren't as tough as I thought."

In his first battle, the boy soldier had built a mountain of demi-human corpses, and from atop that mound, he thrust his sword into his attackers.

No one could behold him and not feel afraid of the bloodstained future that awaited him.

Wilhelm's abnormal strength in the sword was multiplied over the days he swung a sword in his homeland. From morning to evening, until his energy gave out, Wilhelm had lived by continuing to swing the sword—every day, from age eight to fourteen, six years without pause.

Even once he had entered the royal army, his lifestyle of devoting every free moment to the sword did not change.

Within the same unit, there were perhaps one or two people who reached out to Wilhelm, but he rebuffed their overtures, immersing himself only in the sword for days and months until the boy became a man.

Unbroken by reality, yet unsatisfied with himself, Wilhelm continued to swing a sword on the field of battle, unable to quench the feeling of gloom within him.

With his blade, by rending the flesh of others, bathing in their blood, and taking the lives of his opponents, he proved that he was stronger—and he knew that only in those moments did a dark joy sprout within him.

As knowledge of his skill with the sword spread, the name of the rural-born swordsman who refused all promotion, to knight or anything else, became known in both the royal army and the Demi-human Alliance by the alternative name of Sword Devil—a devil of the sword, rushing across the battlefield, and smiling only when cutting a person down.

It was a name that became synonymous with fright and hatred, and both friend and foe steered wide of him.

His exploits were beyond counting, and yet, there was no question of promoting Wilhelm to knight.

He did not associate with others, stoically devoting himself to the sword, rampaging on the battlefield without regard for his allies, leaping into the enemy formation, dancing as he made flowers of blood bloom.

Such a man could not be worthy of a flowery title such as "knight."

In a kingdom with a long tradition of chivalry, Wilhelm's existence was loathed as an interloper regardless of his many services to the nation.

And Wilhelm himself never once thought of changing that circumstance.

He did not think like a knight, with their high pride, regard for the lives of others, and their tendency to polish the nobility of their own souls. When he fought, he killed people; he made their blood flow and smashed their lives to pieces. He, who took more joy in that than anything, was not suited for knighthood, and if it stopped him from being able to enjoy that, he wanted nothing to do with being a knight.

His longing for battle was warped, but over a great deal of time, the heart of the young man named Wilhelm rotted.

And it was when he was eighteen—when he had been in the royal army for three years, and when none in the army knew not the name "Sword Devil"—that a gap in that heart was born.

2

She had beautiful, long red hair, and from the side, her face was so pretty it made him shiver.

With the enlargement of the battle lines, Wilhelm was temporarily sent back to the royal capital from the front lines, forced to take leave that he suggested was unnecessary.

Separated from the battlefield, and the rampant smell of blood, gunpowder, and death, Wilhelm, with too much time on his hands, slipped out of the castle gates with his beloved sword in hand, heading for the lower parts of the capital.

Since running out on his own family, the treasured sword he had taken with him in lieu of a parting gift of coin had become greatly worn, but over the course of ten years, he was used to that beloved blade like none other. It was not that he could not use other swords, but when he was bent on taking the lives of others, that sword was indeed best.

Walking all alone, Wilhelm headed down a street in the lower quarter with no sign of life. His destination was the very edge of the royal capital, a run-down district that had been abandoned midway through its construction.

The capital went from the Nobles' District through Market Street, continuing through the Commons, and the abandoned district had apparently been conceived a ways back, but construction had been aborted quite some time prior with no sign of resuming anytime soon. The word was it would likely stay that way until the civil war was resolved.

"......"

In the morning, the unfinished district had no signs of human life, and if any did exist, it would be scum gathering there for no good purpose. They were cowards that would scatter like baby spiders if a little antagonism hit them.

Of late, not even those outlaws had come close to the Sword Devil, wholly devoted to the blade, unafraid and unawares when he entered the unfinished district on his days off.

"Just as well, I suppose."

The reason Wilhelm swung his sword in the lower city rather than at the parade grounds of the Royal Palace was so that his ears would be undisturbed by annoying voices, immersing himself.into a silent world where he was alone.

Wilhelm no longer sought to measure his skill by crossing swords with others.

He turned toward the swordsman he imagined in the back of his mind, counterattacking his unleashed steel. The training he had continued since his youth always had Wilhelm crossing swords with the person he considered his greatest foe.

"Aren't you a bad looker?"

His eyes oozed with bloodlust; his lips were contorted in madness.

The empty-eyed swordsman with whom he crossed swords every day was his reflection in the mirror.

—To Wilhelm, his greatest enemy was always himself.

This was not in a philosophical sense but rather, a realistic view of his might.

On the battlefield, he confronted his opponents—in other words, he took their lives. Having survived the battlefield, on the edge of life-and-death, there had been none on the field of battle to date that was mightier than he.

Then what worthy rival was there to cross swords with than he, a man he could not kill no matter how hard he tried?

Therefore, during his leave, he went to a place devoid of others to immerse in a sword dance against himself.

For it was only there, in a sword drama none should ever yearn for in reality, that he truly felt what it meant to be alive—

"Ah, I'm quite sorry."

That day, the sight of a beautiful girl was the foreign element wedging itself into the Sword Devil's world.

To swing his sword and meet himself in deadly combat—Wilhelm, on his way to the unfinished district with that aim, stopped when he noticed a different guest ahead of him.

Normally, the heart of the unfinished district Wilhelm used was a completely empty space. The footing was comparatively level, and the breadth made it an ideal place for him—and yet, a foreign element rested in Wilhelm's place of relaxation, tilting its head slightly toward him.

"To think someone would come to a place like this, and so early in the morning—"

"_____"

The girl addressed Wilhelm with a little smile.

But Wilhelm responded to the greeting with a simple slap of his antagonistic aura to drive her away.

He felt as if he was shooing away an annoying insect. An amateur amid such antagonism would beat a hasty retreat; even a man of skill would likely perceive Wilhelm's level of skill and do likewise.

But the girl did nothing of the sort.

"...What is the matter? Such a scary face."

She parried Wilhelm's antagonism, continuing her words as if it were nothing.

Wilhelm felt annoyed, clicking his tongue.

This was an opponent upon whom such hostility was ineffective— in other words, someone completely unrelated to the martial arts. At the very least, someone upon whom violence was effective would have shown some reaction to Wilhelm's antagonism.

But to someone unconnected to such things, it was simple coercion.

Depending on the opponent, someone might even receive it with a simple narrowing of the eyes.

In the case of the individual before him, she was a shining example of the latter.

"Woman, what are you doing here on a morning like this?"

He hurled abuse at her, but she had yet to release Wilhelm from her gaze.

The girl made a little "hmm..." at Wilhelm's words, then said, "I would like to ask you the very same thing, but that would be a bit too mean, yes? Your face says you have no sense of humor."

"There are many dangerous men in this area. I cannot approve of a woman for walking around it alone."

"Ah, are you worried about me?"

"It is possible that I am one of those dangerous men..."

Wilhelm replied sarcastically to the girl's lighthearted comment, making a sound with the hilt of his sword to announce the presence of his weapon. But the girl did not turn an eye to Wilhelm's action, pointing behind her as she said, "Over *here*."

The girl, sitting on a stairway, shifted her finger to a building opposite that against which she leaned. As it was a place Wilhelm could not see from his position, his brows furled at being invited to come closer.

"It is not that I do not wish to see, but..."

"Never mind that, come on, come on."

Wilhelm's cheek twitched at the tone, like that used when coddling a child, but he calmed himself and went over to her. He walked alongside the woman higher up on the stairway, leaning forward to peer at what lay on the other side.

"......"

On the other side, the hot rays of the morning sun were shining on a broad, yellow flower garden.

With Wilhelm at a loss for words, the girl lowered her voice and confessed her secret to him in a whisper.

"They stopped maintaining this district quite some time ago, yes? I thought no one would come, so I planted some flowers. I came over to see the results for myself."

Wilhelm had walked that way many times, but not once had he noticed the presence of the flower garden, even though all it would have taken to see them was for him to stretch his back a little higher and broaden his vision.

With Wilhelm's mouth remaining closed, the girl looked at the side of his face and asked, "Do you like flowers?"

He turned to her, seeing the small, gentle smile her face made as he stared.

"No, I hate them," he replied in a low voice, curling his lips.

3

From then on, Wilhelm and the girl continued to encounter each other from time to time.

On his days off, Wilhelm would walk to the unfinished district in the morning, only to find her having arrived ahead of him, bathed in a quiet wind as she gazed at the flowers.

Then, when she noticed that Wilhelm had arrived, she would ask him, "Do you like flowers now?"

He would deny it with a shake of his head, immersing himself in swinging the sword, acting like he had forgotten her very existence.

When his sweat flowed and he raised his head, finishing his deadly struggle with himself, he would see the girl still there.

"You really have a lot of time on your hands," he'd always say in a sarcastic voice.

He thought that, bit by bit, the amount of time they spent speaking gradually increased.

They always spoke after he'd swung his sword, but he began to exchange a few words before swinging his sword as well, and the conversations after he swung his sword also became a little longer.

Gradually, he went to that place at an even earlier hour, sometimes arriving to the flower garden before the girl. "Ah, you are so early today," the girl would say, a regretful smile coming over her.

—It must have been three months since meeting her like that before they'd exchanged names.

The girl called herself Theresia, adding, "For now," sticking out her tongue a little.

When Wilhelm replied with his introduction, she pouted when he said, "I've been calling you Flower Girl until now."

He thought that exchanging names meant intruding onto each other's circumstances to some small degree. To date, their exchanges had been harmless and inoffensive, but their quality steadily began to change.

One day, Theresia asked him, "Why do you swing the sword?"

Without a moment's concern, Wilhelm replied, "Because it is all I have."

As was typical, Wilhelm's return to military duty was greeted with days filled with the scent of fresh blood.

In due course, the civil war with the demi-humans had intensified; over and over, he casually carried out his missions, slipping past an enemy's magic into his flank, slicing him from toe to chin.

He rushed overland, broke through the wind, flew into the enemy camp, and sent the general's head flying. He returned to his own camp with the head impaled on the tip of his sword, and bathed in gazes of acclamation and fright, he exhaled.

Suddenly, he realized that on the battlefield below his feet, even as blood flowed, there were flowers blooming, swaying in the wind.

And now, without being conscious of it, he took care not to tread upon them.

"Do you like flowers now?"
"No, I hate them."
"Why do you swing the sword?"
"Because that is all I have."

It was his ritualistic exchange with Theresia—when they spoke about flowers, Wilhelm was able to reply with a small smile. But when they spoke of the sword, somehow, it felt painful to give his stock reply.

Why did he swing a sword?

I have nothing else, he thought day after day, and there, his thought process had ended.

When he seriously pondered the question in search of an answer, Wilhelm turned back all the way to the day he had first held a sword in his hand.

At the time, Wilhelm was yet to know that the sword in his hand would be bathed in blood.

When Wilhelm saw himself reflected in the light gleaming off the pristine steel blade, what had he thought?

One day, still in a vortex of thought, unable to come up with an answer, his feet took him to the usual place.

His steps grew heavy, for he was filled with gloom at how he would face the girl waiting for him.

Perhaps it was the first time in his life that he had worried his head about such a thing.

Had he not continued swinging a sword without needing to think?

Just when he had resolved to give such a nasty reply...

"—Wilhelm."

...the girl, there in place ahead of him, looked back with a small smile as she called his name.

—Suddenly, his soul shuddered.

His feet halted, and he could not help feeling nauseous.

Suddenly, Wilhelm was assailed by a realization that seemed to crush his body.

When he sought to cast everything aside with such a conclusion, that he had swung the sword without a thought, a variety of things he'd stopped thinking about and set aside suddenly spewed forth.

He didn't understand the reason. The trigger wasn't set in stone. That moment, the bulwark he had raised so long ago had abruptly reached its limit.

Why did he swing the sword?

Why had he started to swing the sword?

He yearned for the glimmer of the sword, the strength, the purity of living by the blade.

There was that, too. There was that also, but surely, it had begun somewhere else.

"I have to do what my older brothers can't."

It was because swinging a sword was a field largely neglected by his older brothers.

Yet even so, it was because his brothers sought to protect their family in their own way that he, so useless to them, sought his own, different way to defend them.

Was that not why he was captivated by the strength and glimmer of a blade?

"Do you like flowers now?"

"...I do not hate them."

"Why do you swing the sword?"

"It is all I... I could think of no other way to protect others."

Ever since, the previous ritualistic exchange of words ceased to be.

In place, he thought that their topics shifted around quite a bit. Before he realized it, he was heading there not with the aim of swinging a sword, but to meet Theresia.

In a place where he should have been swinging his sword without a thought, his head somehow came to find that insufficient, and topics shifted to places away from the sword.

Until then, his fighting style had been to charge single-handedly into the enemy formation and take as many heads as he could, but somewhere along the line, that changed to him running around with a focus on diminishing harm to his allies any way he could.

The sight of him prioritizing his companions' safety over slaying the enemy naturally resulted in a change in how others saw him.

Old war comrades that had stuck with Wilhelm since his bad-behavior days were both delighted at the change in him and conflicted by it...

...for the number of people who spoke to him and that he spoke to both increased.

Previously unheard-of calls for his promotion to knight arose, and he spent only a small amount of time weighing the matter before accepting.

Deep down, he, too, found having such prestige better than not.

"There were calls for my promotion, so I became a knight."

"I see. Congratulations. That makes you one step closer to your dream, doesn't it?"

"Dream?"

"You took up the sword to protect people, didn't you? And a knight is someone who protects others."

He felt that, among the things he wanted to protect, her smiling face stood out.

4

More time passed.

Having become a knight, and coming into contact with more people within the army, the information reaching his ears naturally increased.

The deeply bogged-down civil war continued, with an advance on one front matched by retreat from the next. Wilhelm, too, experienced not only victorious battles but defeats as well.

Along the way, he spent his days continuing to struggle to protect those within reach of his sword, while bitterly regretting those things that were beyond his reach.

It was by happenstance he heard that the fires of war had shifted to the land of the House of Trias.

That fact casually reached Wilhelm's ears from a newfound companion inside the army. Namely, that the civil war that had begun in the kingdom's east had broadened, reaching all the way to the Trias domain in the north.

There was no order given.

So long as a knight did not forget the position allotted to him, it was impermissible for him to act on his own. But to Wilhelm, embracing once more his feelings from the time he first grasped a sword, such things meant nothing.

By the time he rushed to his beloved homeland, the advancing enemy army had already turned it into a sea of flame.

When the scenery that he had abandoned over five years before faded before the reality of more familiar sights, Wilhelm drew his blade, raised his voice, and dashed into the bloody mists.

He cut down his foes, trod over their corpses, and shouted until his throat grew parched as he bathed in blood spatter.

The enemy's numbers were overwhelming. There were no reinforcements, and it was a land weak in fighting strength to begin with.

Until that point, he had meant to fight in battle on his strength alone, but he learned the price, taking one wound and then another—becoming unable to move.

Collapsing atop a pile of corpses, crushed before the numbers of the enemy force that still showed no signs of running dry, Wilhelm understood that death was coming before his eyes.

The beloved sword that had long been with him fell by the wayside, for his fingertips were too numb and lifeless to hold it aloft.

With his eyes closed, he looked back at half his life, during which he had done nothing but swing a sword.

It was a lonely life—a life with nothing.

Along with that conclusion came a momentary sight—and along the way, one face after another flashed before him. He remembered them one by one: his parents, his two older brothers, the bad friends he had hung out with in the domain, his comrades and superiors from the royal army—and finally, that of Theresia, with flowers behind her.

"I don't want to die..."

It should have been his true hope to live by the sword and die by the sword. But faced with the actual result of his way of life, devoting everything to steel, Wilhelm, with the end he should have desired before his eyes, was stricken with an unbearable feeling of loneliness.

The enemy soldier that had cut down so many of his comrades

would not honor the final words he had let slip. Inhumanly large in body, they mercilessly swung their great sword down at Wilhelm—

"_____"

—He would eternally remember the beauty of the slash that lashed out.

A storm of swords blew, and in course, the demi-human's limbs, head, and torso were cleanly severed.

A great uproar spread among the enemy force, but the racing silver flash was faster, easily inflicting death in large quantities.

Splattered blood rose up, the death cries did not cease, and the demi-humans' lives were shaved away.

The all-too-vivid slashes did not register even with those struck by them, managing no expression as their lives were snuffed out.

Whether such acts were cruelty or mercy, no one knew.

As to what was known, there was but a single thing—

—Surely he could not reach that realm of the blade in a lifetime, or even eternity.

He had lived by swinging a blade, devoting the majority of his not-overly-long life to that purpose. And because of that, it was Wilhelm who could keenly comprehend the heights of the swordsmanship repeated over and over before his very eyes.

So, too, the fact that it was a realm he, a man of no talent, could never reach.

If Wilhelm had created a valley of bloody mist in his homeland, it was truly a sea of blood that spread before his eyes. The literal mountain of corpses piled atop one another had no comparison.

The silver flash did not cease its dance until every demi-human invading the Trias lands had ceased breathing.

Having witnessed the overwhelming slaughter to the end, he was carried out by late-arriving comrades from the royal army. They shouted various things and tended to his wounds, but Wilhelm never took his eyes off the sight.

Finally, the slender long sword wavered, and the sword fighter finally walked off.

Wilhelm shuddered when he realized that the sword fighter had not been bathed in a single drop of spattered blood.

He reached out with his hand but could not reach the back moving away.

Most likely, the distance between them was not a physical one alone.

It was when he returned to the royal capital that he heard the true name of the one bearing the alias of Sword Saint.

It was around the same time that the name of the Sword Saint began to reverberate in every land in the stead of Wilhelm the Sword Devil.

Sword Saint—once upon a time, that was the legendary being who had cut down the Witch bringing calamity to the world.

To that day, the men beloved by the sword god were of the blood of that single family, and it was through that direct bloodline that one generation's superman was born after another.

The name of the Sword Saint of that generation had never been public even once—so, too, until that time.

5

It was several days later that his battle wounds had healed and he made his way to the usual place.

Gripping the hilt of his beloved sword, Wilhelm quietly trod the soil as he headed for the flower garden.

He was certain she would be there.

And in accordance with his firm belief, Theresia was sitting in that place, no different from before.

"......"

Before she could look back, Wilhelm drew his sword and leaped at her.

Just before the semicircular cut would have split the girl's head—she caught the tip of his sword with two fingertips, bringing it to a halt.

A sound of wonder caught in Wilhelm's throat as a malevolent smile came over his lips. "Humiliating."

"...Is that so?"

"Were you laughing at me?"

"......"

"Go ahead and laugh, Theresia...no, Sword Saint—Theresia van Astrea!!"

With all his might, he raised his sword high and sliced at her again, but she evaded by a single hair in an undisturbed motion.

A moment after the dance of her red hair stole his eyes, his feet were swept from under him, unable to break the fall as he was cruelly sent crashing down.

Even without a sword in her hand, the Sword Devil's blade could not reach the Sword Saint.

An impregnable wall, a preposterous difference was now evident between them.

"I will not be coming here anymore."

Several times more, Wilhelm went slicing after her, and each time, he was struck by a counterattack and beaten to the ground.

At some point, his beloved blade was snatched from him, and as it rested in her hand, he was beaten by the hilt until he was unable to move.

So far. So very weak. He could not reach. It was not enough.

"Don't hold a sword with...that face..."

"I do, for I am the Sword Saint. I did not understand the reason why I was, but I understand now."

"Reason, you say...!"

"You swing the sword to protect others. I think I can do that, too."

It was Wilhelm who had given Theresia, the girl who loved flowers, who could find no meaning in gripping a sword, that reason—all the more because she was stronger than anyone, the furthest beyond the reach of anyone's sword.

"W-wait, Theresia..."

"......"

"I'll take your sword from you. As if I care about your blessing or your role. Don't underestimate swinging the sword…or the beauty of the blade, Sword Saint…!"

The woman did not stop. Her back grew distant.

All that was left behind was a lone, foolish devil, speaking of the sword to her, who was loved by the sword.

Afterward, the two would never meet there again.

6

The Sword Devil vanished from the royal army; in his place, the name of the Sword Saint spread within it.

A knight worth a thousand men—with hard fighting by Theresia, the embodiment of those words, the civil war tilted in their favor. Though a single person, her martial feats were beyond the realm of any individual, and the alias of Sword Saint resounded—even the demi-humans versed in the old legends despaired.

It took two years after the Sword Saint emerged on the battlefield for the civil war to end.

The Demi-human Alliance lost those who carried it upon their shoulders, and when peace talks were carried out somewhere between the current leaders on both sides, it announced that at minimum, the fight between those bearing swords had come to an end.

Blessed by the end of the long-running civil war, the royal capital gently opened up and began to flower.

A ceremony had been planned where a powerful, beautiful Sword Saint would be granted several medals. People throughout the kingdom traveled to the capital to glimpse the sight of Theresia, the red-haired Sword Saint—the hero whose passion had single-handedly brought the long suffering from wild war to an end.

—It was then that the Sword Devil unexpectedly descended, as if to slice that passion asunder.

The soldiers on guard became agitated from the incredible antagonism rising from a man with a naked blade in his hand. But it was none other than the Sword Saint, the flower of the ceremony, who checked them and advanced to the fore.

Each turned their sword toward the other, almost as if walking onto a prearranged stage.

When her long, red hair fluttered in the wind, none failed to hold their breath at the sight of her facing the intruder. It was difficult to find words for an appearance with such refined beauty, yet so at one with the blade.

The malevolent antagonism of the individual facing the Sword Saint was the polar opposite. Both the brown mantle over him and the skin underneath were filthy all over from rainwater and caked mud. Even the sword in his hand was meager compared to the ceremonial holy blade the Sword Saint held in hers. The blade of the well-made sword was crooked, with reddish-brown rust all over it.

Though the king was seated on the same stage they were on, he halted the knights attempting to go to the Sword Saint's aid. When the Sword Saint stepped forward and her swordplay glimmered, all pulled their chins back, and none raised a voice, watching in silence.

At the beginning, no doubt many found the two figures having vanished from their sight.

Blade recoiled from blade again and again; high-pitched sounds shot past the spectators.

There was a chain of glimmers and sounds of steel as the two figures danced upon the stage at a dizzying speed.

Soon, those witnessing the spectacle had lost their voices, their hearts going to and fro, overwhelmed with a vast sense of admiration.

They battled with incredible force, switching where they stood, from the ground to the walls to the very air as the swordplay of the two sword fighters blurred. Some even realized that the sight had brought them to tears.

But as they listened to the orchestra of echoing steel, they instinctively shuddered, intoxicated by the sublime sight.

They thought, is this really a realm that people can reach?

Can the beauty of the sword truly instill such deep feelings in others?

Their swordplay intermingled, with locked swords, flashing tips, and repeated recoils.

And finally...

"_____"

...the discolored blade snapped in half, its tip sent flying, spinning round and round in the air.

Then, the hand in which rested the Sword Saint's ceremonial sword—

"Victory..."

"......"

"Victory...is mine."

The holy sword audibly dropped to the ground, and the broken sword's warped tip came to rest just short of the Sword Saint's throat.

The spectacle made time stop, and all knew.

The Sword Saint had lost.

"You're weaker than me, so you have no reason to wield a sword."

"If not me...then who?"

"I'll carry on your reason for swinging a sword. You just need to become...my reason to swing one."

He lifted up the hood of his outer garment. The sullen face of Wilhelm glared at Theresia from under the dark, filthy cloth.

Theresia shook her head a little at Wilhelm's behavior.

"You are a terrible person. You've made a person's determination, resolve, everything all go to waste."

"I'll carry on everything that's gone to waste. You can forget about gripping a sword and just take it... Yes, that's it. You can raise flowers and live in peace and quiet behind me."

"Protected by your sword?"

"That's right."

"You'll protect me?"

"That's right."

Theresia placed her hand against the flat of the sword thrust toward her, taking a step forward.

The two faced each other, close enough to feel each other's breath.

Tears welled in Theresia's damp eyes, but they only conveyed her little smile as they fell.

"Do you like flowers?"

"I stopped hating them."

"Why do you swing the sword?"

"To protect you."

The distance closed as their faces drew close; finally, it vanished.

When she drew back from the touch of their lips, Theresia's cheeks were red. She gently stared at Wilhelm as she asked, "Do you love me?"

He averted his face and bluntly stated, "—You know I do."

Just then, the people enthralled by the dancing of swords regained their senses, and a great throng of guards pressed close. Wilhelm's shoulders sank when he saw familiar faces among the soldiers rushing over.

Theresia's cheeks puffed up at his dismissive demeanor.

Their smiles were like those they had exchanged during the days they spent gazing at the flowers.

"Sometimes a woman wants to hear the words."

"Er."

Scratching his head with a guilty expression on his face, Wilhelm reluctantly looked back at Theresia, drawing his face close to her ear as he whispered, "Someday, when I feel like it."

And thus, he glossed over the embarrassing words.

7

—He raced like the wind, and the gleaming, treasured sword rent the stone-like hide with ease.

"Oooooooooooo—!!"

The shout the aged swordsman raised seemed to trail behind him. Whale blood spewed from the fresh blade wound, dying the sky scarlet.

He appeared wounded all over his body.

Then as before, blood seemed to be dripping from his left shoulder, but the blood spatter drenching his entire body had mixed with his own blood, turning its color to black.

Over such a brief period of time, no more could be expected from healing magic than stopping the bleeding and restoring a small amount of endurance. He was still in a gravely injured state, told he must have complete rest.

But seeing Wilhelm as he was that moment, none could laugh him off as an old man on death's door.

Seeing the gleam in both his eyes, seeing the strength in his steps as he raced, seeing the vividness of the slashes of the sword he wielded, hearing the earsplitting cry echoing forth, and captivated by the glimmer of his soul, none could laugh off the old man's accumulated life as that of a fool.

His blade ran, a scream rose, and the White Whale's enormous, suffering body was wracked with intense pain.

With the demon beast crushed under the Great Tree, unable to move, the Sword Devil racing along its back did not hesitate to use his blade. The slash begun at the tip of its head ran down its back and reached its tail, and when the Sword Devil stood upon the ground, he turned right around, rending its belly on his way back to the head.

In one swing—sharp, deep, and very, very long—the single flash of silver cut the White Whale in two.

With a leap, the Sword Devil came down onto the tip of the unmoving White Whale's nose once more.

He shook the blood off his drenched sword as he and the White Whale looked each other eye to eye—their two fates merging together.

"...I have no intention of speaking ill to you. There is no use explaining good and evil to a beast. Between you and me, there is only the law of life and death: The weak are cut down by the strong."

"_____"

"Sleep—eternally."

Leaving behind one last little murmur, light faded from the White Whale's eyes.

Its enormous body went limp, and when it collapsed, the earth shuddered; the droplets of its fresh blood formed a muddy river.

No one could put the feeling of blood running underfoot into words.

A silence befell the Liphas Highway. And then—

"It's over, Theresia. It's finally..."

Atop the head of the immobile White Whale, Wilhelm turned his face skyward.

When the treasured sword fell from his hand, he brought that hand up to cover his face, and with a quivering voice, the weaponless Sword Devil said, "Theresia, I..."

The voice was raspy, but there was boundless, undiminished love within it.

"I love you—!!"

They were words of love only Wilhelm knew. Things he had never told her.

They contained feelings accumulated over many years, words he had not spoken even once to the one he loved most, right up to the day he lost her.

Finally, after the passage of decades, Wilhelm had voiced the words with which he should have answered her question so long ago.

Atop the corpse of the White Whale, his sword fallen from his grasp, the Sword Devil cried out his love for his departed wife, and he wept.

8

"—Here, the White Whale has fallen."

Haltingly, the sound of a stirring voice echoed across the silence of the nighttime plain.

At that voice, the men, lost for words, lifted their faces.

Their gazes poured over a young woman calmly advancing to the fore on the back of a white land dragon.

Her long, green hair was frayed, and she was cruelly adorned by wounds suffered at the height of the battle, her face sullied by her own blood, a most sorry state for her to be seen in.

And yet, in their eyes, the girl had never shone brighter.

That was natural for those who judged the worth of others by the glimmer of their souls.

"……"

With the knights gazing upon her, the gallant young woman lifted her face and took a deep breath.

Having lent her treasured sword, Crusch's scabbard was currently empty.

Accordingly, she thrust her fist toward the heavens, as if to show her closed hand to all present as she announced:

"The Demon Beast of Mist that menaced the world across four centuries of life—has been slain by Wilhelm van Astrea!!"

"—Aye!!"

"In this battle, we are victorious—!!"

With their lord loudly proclaiming victory, the surviving knights raised shouts of joy.

With mist clearing over the plains, signs of night returned once more—a proper night, with moonlight illuminating the people on the ground far and wide.

And there, after four hundred years, the Battle of the White Whale came to an end.

CHAPTER 6
THE ROAD TO THE MATHERS DOMAIN

1

An elated clamor spread across the moonlight-filled plains.

The light of the moon reflected off the swords the knights raised high, with the glow of that light making the scene beautiful indeed.

The White Whale's enormous body rested on its side beneath the Great Flugel Tree as a zealous throng rushed to surround it. Everyone exulted in victory, with tears of gratitude flowing that their long-cherished wish had been fulfilled.

As if to pour water over their joy...

"————!!"

...two powerful roars made the air over the Liphas Highway shake, as if to paint over everyone's pleasure.

Separate from the White Whale that had been slain, there were two White Whale offshoots that had lost the main body.

Acknowledging the death of the main body, the offshoots above the ground writhed around, and their vastness and solidity began to diminish.

With their supply of mana from the main body severed, they were increasingly unable to maintain their flesh. They looked pathetic; left to their own devices, they would surely dissipate within minutes.

"Crude."

With that one disparaging word cutting them off, an arm swung, unleashing an invisible blade.

Accompanied by a gale, the slicing wind entered one whale through its head, slicing the agonized White Whale's outer hide in half with ease—and with its giant body neatly divided into left and right, the being literally dissipated.

With a single blow of an expeditionary force magic crystal cannon, the remaining whale broke into the mist from whence it came, its mana blown away, melting into the wind, whereupon its enormous body vanished completely.

That told them, in a true sense, the battle to subjugate the White Whale was at an end.

However—

"We cannot simply exult in this."

Touching a hand to her breast, Crusch was aware of the jubilation inside herself, but she shook her head, refusing to let the deep emotions show on her face.

With everyone's cooperation, they defeated the evil demon beast, and everyone lived happily ever after, the end.

In reality, the tale would not end so neatly.

Such an ending was only permitted in fairy tales. Reality continued after the end of the tale, with a never-ending supply of things that had to be done.

They had to provide relief for the wounded survivors and courteous burials for the dead, leaving no corpses behind.

And when Crusch thought of such follow-up, she realized…

At a place a little removed from the White Whale, a man who had served with distinction was desperately raising his voice.

2

"Rem! Rem, open your eyes…!"

Subaru lifted the girl in his arms, his face pale as he desperately called out to her.

The land dragon came right up to them, nuzzling them with its black nose in an act of concern. But at that moment, Subaru harbored a sense of nervousness so great that he did not respond to even that land dragon's consideration.

—Subaru's plan to make the White Whale chase his scent and crush it under the Great Tree was a splendid success.

Some had raised their voices in objection, reluctant to cut down a historical tree. But the beast-man mercenaries were rationalists with no such compunctions, and when even Crusch deemed it necessary, opinion easily shifted to his favor.

Accordingly, Subaru, drafter of the plan, saw the operation through, shouldering no small risk in the process, resulting in achievement in battle that one might call second to none.

But if this was the price he had to pay, it was the smallest of small comforts.

"This…is no good… Please, Rem…if…you're not here…!"

Before his eyes, Rem calmly rested with her eyes closed, completely unresponsive to Subaru's voice.

There was no sign that conscious will was conveyed to her limp limbs, and the tearful voice calling her name seemed to pass right through her ears, a cry into empty space.

—Under ferocious pursuit by the White Whale, they'd raced as the falling trunk of the Great Tree loomed near.

The heavy weight of the Great Tree struck the demon beast squarely, with a loud crash to earth and a shock wave that flew indiscriminately throughout the area—and amid it was the sight of Subaru and Rem, running right alongside.

They were engulfed by the shock wave, losing track of which way was up, and Subaru recalled that he was protected by a warm sensation during that. The instant he grasped that feeling, there was a roaring sound from an incredible impact as he, and the sensation, were slammed onto the ground.

Slipping through the gaps of Subaru's vague consciousness was the realization that he was lying on the ground. And lifting his head, he realized who had embraced him—and that it was her body that had embraced his to the very end.

"...Suba...ru..."

"Rem—?!"

With a twitch, her eyelids shuddered, and Subaru was reflected in the dim gleam beneath them.

Reflected in her eyes, he looked so very weak, almost as if he was subconsciously recognizing the reality of what was unfolding before his eyes, when he said, "I'm so g... Yeah, it's me. You know, Subaru. Rem, your body..."

"Subaru...I'm so glad...you are safe..."

His throat choked up. For Rem, seeing Subaru unable to even get out the tearful words of concern for her the way he wanted, was smiling at him in visible relief—as if taking no heed of her own injuries, happy so long as Subaru was safe.

"What happened to...the demon beast...?"

"...It went down. We nailed it. It worked out. Everything worked out! I'm...not hurt, either... It's all...thanks to you..."

"Is that...so? Then, Master Roswaal and...Lady Emilia...shall... surely be all right..."

"It'll work out. Leave it to me. So, Rem, you don't have to say anything right now, just rest... No, don't...close your eyes... Aw, crap, what should I do...?"

She didn't need to force herself to speak. But if Rem spoke no words, he couldn't wipe away his own unease. Subaru was nervous, almost as if the relentless coercive power of Fate might yet snatch her life from his hand.

He didn't know what he ought to do. He didn't know what was best to do.

Not knowing what to do, Subaru couldn't help holding her hand and embracing her with his other arm as strongly as he could.

"That…hurts, Subaru…"

"Sorry, my bad. But if I don't do this, you'll go off somewh…"

"I shall not go…anywhere… I shall be at…your side, Subaru…"

Rem gave Subaru a little smile, like that of a mother consoling an unreasonable child in tears, when strength suddenly left her body.

Subaru's throat froze in fear as he felt her body go soft in his arms.

Inside his ears, he heard the sound of blood draining, of anything and everything leaving him behind.

"Rem…? Rem! Please, Rem…open…your eyes…"

"Somehow, I'm very…sleepy… I'm sorry. Let me sleep just a little, and when I wake…soon, for your sake, I shall be…"

"Never mind all that! You don't need to do anything. It's fine if you're just together with me…so please, Rem…!"

Even though she was right within his arms, Subaru wrung out his voice, desperately trying to hold fast to her as she began gradually slipping away. And yet, though Rem was right before his eyes, his voice did not reach.

"May I say something…selfish?"

"…! Say it, say anything! I'll listen to anything, I'll do anything, so…!"

In a broken voice, in a frail tone, Rem looked up at Subaru and made a little murmur.

"I want you to say…that you…love me."

Tears welling up forced Subaru's eyes open as he shook his head side to side. Then, he drew his face close to hers and told her:

"I love you."

"……"

"I really love you. Of course I do… I can't…manage without you."

They were words from his heart of hearts.

Subaru poured all his unembellished true feelings into the words he spoke that instant.

He couldn't have made it that far without her. He couldn't live without her.

"Ah…I'm so happy…"

Receiving Subaru's confession, tears came out through her closed eyes.

Rem's cheeks suddenly reddened as she happily accepted the words tossed toward her. With that, Subaru felt that the last of her strength had truly left her.

"Wait…"

"I love you, Subaru."

"Don't kid around—stay with me! Am I gonna have…nothing but regrets again?!"

He could not bear a future that did not have her in it.

He understood that well before, and now, her existence loomed far, far larger. That was why…

"I don't wanna…laugh and talk about the future without you…!"

"In that future, can I be by your side?"

"…Of course. I won't let you be anywhere else."

Closing his eyes, Subaru wiped away the rising tears before staring straight at Rem.

And then, he stated firmly, "You're mine. I won't…hand you to anyone."

"—I shall take that…as a commitment."

"Huh?"

Abruptly, Subaru let out his voice like an idiot at the highly intellectual reply.

As he did so, Rem slowly opened the eyes she had kept closed all that time, proceeding to sit up inside his arms. Then, with Subaru dumbfounded, unable to grasp the situation, she tilted her head and smiled at him.

"You have promised I shall be at your side, Subaru… You cannot take it back now."

Where had the sight of her dying gone…?

In a teasing, toying way, Rem closed one eye and gently touched Subaru's lips.

Crestfallen, Subaru's strength gave out from his shoulders down as he sank to the ground.

"Why you…you, you…youuuu!"

"Yes, I am Subaru's Rem. In name and fact."

Hearing her trademark reply, now even more brazen, Subaru could not follow up his words.

Even so, even if by rights it was a scene where he ought to be shaking with anger, the fact that the girl before his eyes was safe took precedence, leaving him too happy to do so.

"We've both aired our true feelings, so that's really overkill..."

"Girls are strong when they become honest about love, Subaru."

Subaru was flustered by how Rem no longer had any intention of hiding her love for him. More embarrassed than anything else, Subaru's face reddened as he let out a small breath and confessed, "...If you'd died, I was about to die, too."

"I am a lucky woman that you think so much of me."

"I'm not kidding, either."

Rem replied with a little smile, but Subaru had answered with his true and sincere feelings.

If Subaru had lost Rem, he would have most certainly attempted to do it all over again. Even if the chance to do things over was not granted to him, there was no doubt he'd have tried anyway.

That was how large a place Rem's existence now occupied in Subaru's heart.

"I absolutely must not die, then."

"Darn right. I won't let you die, even if it kills me."

Subaru drew his face to hers, and their foreheads touched as they looked at each other from so very close.

Rem gazed adoringly at Subaru's gesture, and it was hard for Subaru to just stay there with her close enough that their breaths touched. Naturally, his gaze was drawn in by her pink lips, and he felt his heart beat just a little faster—

"—Could you two wrap it up already, *meow*?"

Ferris, looking exasperated from having watched from a distance as the two flirted, butted in to break things up at the most important juncture. Apparently, he'd been watching the whole time.

Subaru was sure he'd done it on purpose.

3

"You're so cute, Subawu, calling out to her so desperately, *meow*...I can't live...without you...!"

"Shut up, you're annoying! You should reflect on your bad taste of staring so much!"

"In the first place, if you thought about it calmly you'd have understood, *meow*. Ferri has to go around treating the wounded immediately, so that meant Rem's injuries weren't life-threatening, *meow*!"

"Like I can think about it calmly! An important girl...who told me she loved me...was hurt and unconscious. Of course I couldn't think straight!"

"Boys are so pure of heart, unable to say certain things except in a few places, *meow*."

As Subaru vented with angry shouts, Ferris smiled flippantly as he turned his palm toward Rem, a blue glow coming over it. Even while the look on Ferris's face struck Subaru with unquenchable annoyance, he couldn't conceal his relief at how Rem's expression gradually grew softer.

There were many things in what Ferris said that he couldn't just come out and agree with, but the part about triage, prioritizing healing the most heavily wounded, was no doubt the honest truth. Giving shabby treatment to Rem, part of another camp's fighting strength, and to Subaru, both key players in bringing down the White Whale, was not something his master would ever permit.

As Subaru's thoughts reached that conclusion, that very same master—Crusch—appeared, calmly stepping over grass.

"You are all right, Subaru Natsuki?"

Even sullied by blood and mud, the sight of Crusch walking straight with her back tall was beautiful.

Naturally, the elegance she had in no way lost wafted around her, and so, too, the vestiges of the battle; the beautiful woman seemed like the living embodiment of the word *Valkyrie*.

"Somehow or other, yeah. Glad you look all right yourself."

"I am. But the expeditionary force is depleted to no small extent. Nor will those slain by the White Whale return."

When Subaru responded, waving up to her, Crusch drew her chin in, shifting her head pensively. Her gaze shifted toward the corpse of the White Whale, still crushed under the Great Tree.

Over there, the survivors of the expeditionary force with comparatively light injuries had gathered together. Apparently, their first order of business was to get the Great Tree off the White Whale.

"What are they doing over there?"

"We must transport the White Whale's corpse. With even the Great Flugel Tree sacrificed for the operation, some sort of evidence is required. It is what comes after the battle that concerns me."

"Transport...that huge corpse?"

Subaru wanted to make sure he hadn't misheard, but Crusch's demeanor was unchanged. Subaru hurriedly returned his gaze to the White Whale, observing the giant body over maybe one hundred and fifty feet in length as he remarked, "Doesn't seem doable, does it?"

"Failure is not an option. The creature was a menace that swam through the skies for four hundred years. At worst, we may have to return with the head alone."

Crusch's words seemed like an exaggeration, but Subaru thought it over and realized her judgment was correct. To begin with, from Crusch's point of view, the subjugation of the White Whale was a success she wanted all to see to advance herself in the royal selection.

Naturally, Crusch was not someone of such low character as to prioritize achievements over all else, which the battle had amply demonstrated. But the achievement was simply that grand.

She was already the most influential of the royal candidates, with high support among the populace, and if this earned her favor with the merchant faction, which had been the final holdout, Crusch's position would be even more rock solid—

"Wait, did I wind up pushing us into a bad spot...?"

The degree of aid he had provided an opponent finally dawned on Subaru. There was no going back, either. He'd done everything so that he could return to Emilia's camp, but he wondered if he'd overdone it even so.

Fearing as much, Subaru held far-too-late regrets.

"Your face has become rather dark—it does not look like the face of the hero who brought down the White Whale."

"I'll get raked over the coals as Emilia-tan's biggest traitor... Er, what...did you say just now?"

"The hero who brought down the White Whale—I do not wish to be so shameless as to claim your exploits as my own house's feats."

Returning her gaze from the corpse of the White Whale, Crusch's expression seemed to impale Subaru like a sword.

Subaru blinked at the sincere glint in her eyes, turning to face her squarely. As he did so, Crusch gently put a hand to her own breast and stated, "I cannot thank you enough for your cooperation. Were it not for you, we would have failed to subjugate the White Whale, and I would have surely fallen halfway along my path."

Speaking those words, she adopted a stance of deep thanks toward Subaru.

"_____"

Subaru unwittingly froze at the heat of the noble Crusch's sincere gesture of thanks. He had no memory of any human being in her kind of position speaking such words to him ever.

"Er, ah...no, cut that out. I...didn't do anything big like that..."

"You discerned the time and place the White Whale would appear; by your efforts, the expeditionary force, insufficient in strength, was bolstered; when the knights' morale was broken, you roused them; you proposed a plan to rescue the hopeless situation at great danger to yourself, and on top of that, you executed it splendidly, guiding us to victory."

When Subaru replied with halting words, Crusch enumerated Subaru's actions during the battle and their results.

Told of his own actions in such an orderly manner, and examining the result, Subaru could only conclude, "Sounds like nothing but the work of a crazy man, if I do say so myself..."

"Perhaps it would not be accurate to compare your actions to that of a ferocious, raging lion. However, there is no mistaking that you were the driving force behind this battle. If others should belittle your actions, I swear upon my honor that I shall correct them."

Crusch extolled Subaru honestly and with a serious look, without any calculation or hesitation. Surely she, the living embodiment of sincerity, truly had not a single smidgeon of falseness in the words of gratitude she had spoken.

Thinking back to the relationship he had with Crusch until the night before their departure, Subaru could only make a strained smile.

"I'm surprised. Seems like your assessment of me has improved quite a bit."

"This is nothing to be modest about. And I am compelled to recognize that my view of you until a short time ago was very mistaken. Properly speaking, a suitable repayment for such achievements would be to welcome you into my own house, but..."

"I'll have to pass on that."

Crusch had narrowed her eyes and, in a low voice, invited Subaru to her own side. But Subaru raised a hand and interrupted her cordial invitation.

"It's not the same thing as loyalty, but my trust's already been put where it ought to be. I genuinely feel like you're a good person, and you'd probably do a great job if you became king, but..."

Crusch would no doubt be a king to nobly lead the people more than any other. Such was the extent of her character, and he knew just a tiny bit about the powerful reason that compelled her to act in such a manner. A proper reason, and the resolve to endure, was probably something she'd inherited, entrusted by another.

This included, everything had served to shape the lone woman known as Crusch Karsten. A small human being like Subaru who'd continued lying to everyone could only look at her dazzling form in admiration and envy.

"—I will make Emilia king."

"_____"

"Not for anyone's sake. It's what *I* want to do."

"...Though I understood as much, to think your reply would be to that extent."

Subaru's reply made Crusch's lips break into a broad grin as she drew her chin back. Then, she uncrossed her arms, hardened her white fingers into a fist, and pointed it toward Subaru.

"Very well. Your exploits shall be repaid in a different form. I swear upon the name of Crusch Karsten that this promise shall be fulfilled."

So solemnly declaring, Crusch opened her hardened fist and looked at her own palm.

From then, the tone of her voice dropped slightly as she said, "Now that I think of it, this is the first time I have felt so good about having an invitation of mine rejected. It is a most refreshing sense of defeat, and I can make no show of being troubled by it."

"...Crusch, I think you're an incredible person. If I were out here on my own, I think it's a sure thing that I'd let that hand prop me up."

If he had nowhere to go back to, with nothing certain in his life, and someone on Crusch's level offered him her hand, he'd likely leap at the chance without hesitation and cling to her, relying on her for everything.

But the current Subaru had someone else whose hand he wanted to reach out and hold, someone with a wavering back he would support with his own palm.

Thus, he could not take her hand, but...

"I'm counting on you for the alliance thing. Even if we've gotta become rivals in the end, we can probably get along nicely till then, so let's do that."

"—Subaru Natsuki, I shall correct one thought of yours."

Subaru's reply made Crusch's smile vanish. She put on a solemn face and pursed her lips.

Surprised at feeling the atmosphere grow tense once more, Subaru's eyes widened as he looked at Crusch. To him, Crusch raised a finger, then pointed it at herself.

"I shall regard you favorably, even when the time comes to determine my mate," she remarked.

"_____"

"Even if the day we must part ways shall inevitably come, I shall never forget my debt of gratitude toward you this day. Furthermore, even should a time of rivalry come, I shall regard you with the greatest favorability and respect."

Crusch lowered her arm with the raised finger downward, firmly declaring it in a crystal-clear tone of voice.

This time, her conduct sent a chill running up Subaru's spine.

It was not a negative feeling. It was simply his feeling overpowered by something so grand.

—This was the woman named Crusch Karsten, Duchess of the House of Karsten.

"This would be a pretty dangerous spot if the number one and number two places in my heart weren't already taken..."

"—Hmph. I am not thinking as far as accompanying you as a woman. Though my heartstrings have been tugged upon in certain places, my heart is set on fulfilling a dream—and so it shall remain, until someday, I achieve the dream he yearned for."

Subaru tried to gloss over his agitation with flippant words, and Crusch smiled thinly as she replied. But the latter half of her words became extremely soft, and those did not reach Subaru's ears.

With a blink, Crusch forgot that sentiment, going, "Now, then," as she continued her words with a sober glance.

"If possible, at this juncture I would like to return to the royal capital with the wounded and the White Whale's corpse. But it seems some mission yet remains for you."

"...Can tell that 'cause of the blessing, huh?"

"The power of the blessing is not necessary. I know that look in a man's eyes."

Crusch closed one eye, peering into Subaru's eyes as she replied thusly. Then, she checked Subaru's appearance from head to toe and said, "Surely you are not without injury. So you have something you must do in spite of that."

"I've gotta do it whether I'm hurt badly or not. In one sense, the whale hunt was so that I could do it. I feel bad saying it like that, though."

"Oh, really, after subjugating the White Whale?"

He said it in a way that surely came off poorly, but Crusch showed no sign of annoyance. She seemed curious about the objective Subaru spoke of so seriously.

"Most interesting—you surely took the alliance with our house in account for that. If so, it is hardly unthinkable for you to request something of us... You require aid?"

"I do. But...to be honest, I didn't think it'd be *this* tough, so..."

Subaru's shoulders sank when he looked over the expeditionary force members wounded far beyond his plans.

With the subjugation of the White Whale finished, it meant returning to the Mathers domain, where Emilia awaited, and confronting the abominable group there. Fighting such a powerful foe required Crusch's power, but—

"With all these people hurt, I won't ask anything reckless of you. Besides, you have to see this with not just your personal feelings but your place as a ruler. Asking you to lend a hand beyond this is just..."

"—Then how about using these old bones until they fail?"

Abruptly, a tall figure walked over with quiet footsteps and interrupted the conversation—Wilhelm, the aged swordsman still appearing as ghastly as before, his entire body bathed in demon beast blood.

The Sword Devil approached, walking with a gait that showed nothing of the wounds to his flesh, and offered the treasured sword in his right hand to Crusch.

"Lady Crusch, I return that which you lent to me. In addition, let me offer my thanks concerning this matter from the bottom of my heart. It is because of your cooperation that my long-cherished wish has been granted, Lady Crusch—thank you very much."

"Your long-cherished wish and my objectives aligned, that is all—you may hold on to that sword for a little while longer. You can serve no role unarmed."

"—As you wish. My thanks."

Crusch responded briefly to Wilhelm's words of thanks and looked at Subaru. Accepting her reply, Wilhelm turned his head back to Subaru as well.

"_____"

Now that they were in close quarters again, the stench of blood wafting around him was incredible, and Subaru felt nervous from that surging, aimless antagonism, which felt like a slender blade poking into his liver.

But the tense atmosphere from before the battle—*that* had been lifted, and it was a fact that Wilhelm seemed like his spirits had been lifted with it.

The aged swordsman looked straight at Subaru and, after that, fell to one knee on the spot. It was a gesture demonstrating the greatest of all respect to another, one he had seen the night before they'd set out.

And then—

"Sir Subaru Natsuki. It is because of *your* cooperation that this subjugation of the White Whale was successful. It is you who has granted meaning to all the long years of my life until this day. I thank you. I thank you—I offer my thanks, with the whole of my being on the line."

"......"

This was Wilhelm, he who had offered half his life to the sword and then spent over a decade of life devoted to vengeance. Subaru, engulfed by the vast passion of the gratitude such a man directed to him, was so afraid of blurting out the wrong thing that he was at a complete loss for words.

It took a while to settle his mind, waiting for the proper words to direct to the old man before him to coalesce—for it would not do to have Wilhelm, a man of such resolve, put on such a shameful display.

"It's your own sword that did it, Wilhelm. You thought about how to fight the White Whale, you studied it, you trained, you didn't give up, you fought it..."

Having tasted setback after setback over and over, he must have been on the verge of giving up his grudge. Subaru didn't think he'd thrown everything away, never once attempted to abandon those deep-rooted convictions.

It was Subaru, who knew more than anyone about the weakness of the heart, about being defeated, about being obstructed by the irrationalities of fate, who could understand the suffering Wilhelm had undergone until his strong feelings went fulfilled.

"You stuck with it until the White Whale went down because you reaaaally loved your wife. If I helped with that even a little bit, I'm glad. I'm not sure this is the best thing to say, but…congratulations. And—well done."

"_____"

Prompted by Subaru's words, Wilhelm lifted his face, his blue eyes opening wide.

Subaru had arbitrarily drawn comparisons between what he felt and what he imagined Wilhelm felt. He didn't think his brief words from just then could convey that, and for Subaru to speak as if he understood probably didn't amuse Wilhelm.

But Subaru couldn't restrain his desire to say it anyway—words to thank Wilhelm for his love for his departed wife still burning fourteen years on, and for his labors, continuing to fight Fate day after day until they led him to victory…

"—I thank you."

Briefly, and with a quavering voice, that was how Wilhelm replied.

After that, he leaned forward slightly, and after a silence of but several seconds, he rose to his feet. Then, he turned his gaze to Crusch, and when she nodded, he said, "I have received Lady Crusch's permission. Sir Subaru, I place this body in your hands. Please use it to the fullest for your objective."

"That's super-helpful, but you're serious?"

When he glanced at Crusch to make sure, she drew her chin in and nodded affirmatively. When he looked Wilhelm over in all seriousness, he felt both the dependability and the fearsomeness of the man, his antagonism undiminished in spite of having one arm wounded.

—To Subaru, Wilhelm's cooperation was a wish come true.

In the current situation, where every bit of fighting strength was desperately yearned for, he wanted the Sword Devil's strength enough that a hand might sprout from his own throat. But even an amateur like him could see that Wilhelm's injuries were grave.

In the face of Subaru's doubts, Crusch shook her head.

"That is not a problem… Ferris!"

"Yes, Lady Crusch!"

When Crusch called sharply, Ferris seemed to instantly glide into view in response.

With a skip in his step, he lined up alongside Crusch, and as the kitty ears on his head made a little flutter, he said, "What is it, Lady Crusch? Ferri's in the middle of going all around and doing a big job, but of course I'll prioritize anything Lady Crusch has to ask before everything else!"

"Hey, don't drop your responsibilities halfway through the sentence!"

Ferris, the butt of Subaru's comment about easily casting aside all sense of duty as a healer, made a sour face. He was still like that when Crusch gazed at the expeditionary force and asked him, "How many of the wounded are in mortal peril?"

"I'm treating gravely wounded people, but I can clearly say the number in peril is zero. Other people's field dressings were excellent, and I'm a capable kitty, so it's okay to praise me, *meow*."

With Ferris flirtingly touching a finger to his cheek, Subaru put a hand to his chest in relief. At the very least, Rem didn't seem to be in any serious danger. The exchange after the battle had been decided had put him at ease, but hearing all over again that she was safe was a relief nonetheless.

In the meantime, Crusch nodded as she stroked Ferris's head. "Understood. So the remaining wounded can be transported. Ferris, you can leave the existing healing as it is, then. Afterward, you will accompany Subaru Natsuki and fulfill the role of his ally."

"—Eh?!"

It was Subaru who raised his voice in surprise at the order Crusch issued.

She was splitting Ferris off and making him accompany Subaru.

That order meant nothing less than prioritizing her ally, Subaru, over her own camp's wounded.

Of course, Ferris would object to Crusch's decision to split him off from the Crusch ca—

"Understood. Ferri will accompany Subawu from here. I'll have to heal Old Man Wil on the road anyway, *meow*."

"Quite the trouble for you."

"Old Man Wil's the one swinging his sword, so that makes it about even, *meow*?"

There was no beating these people.

Ferris accepted the order like it was a matter of course, and Wilhelm betrayed no expression of surprise at the order, either. Subaru couldn't conceal his bewilderment at the interplay between the two servants and their master.

With Subaru in such disarray, Ferris glided his eyes over to him and said, "So that means half of the people left in the expeditionary force look all right...? About twenty people, give or take? They'll be coming to cooperate with you, Subawu. Take good care of us."

"That's putting it pretty lightly! You're okay with this...?"

"Okay with what, *meow*?"

"Whaddaya mean, what...? Lots of things. Can you trust my judgment...?"

As far as he could remember, back in the royal capital, there had been none he'd come into contact with that had acted to gouge more wounds in him than Ferris. No matter how friendly a smile came over his face, no matter how adorable the attitude he dressed it up in, Subaru somehow understood that he harbored a deep disdain for Subaru's weakness.

Subaru naturally thought that he'd feel reluctant to follow such a person, but...

"It's not that I trust you, Subawu. It's that I have faith in Lady Crusch's decision that Subawu is to be trusted. It's not like she's wrong, *meow*?"

"O-oh...thanks."

"—? Did you…say something just now?"

"—Why?!"

"But!"

"But—I do not want this. It hurts. I cannot bear it."

"When you are in distress, Subaru, I want to be the one offering my hand faster than anyone. When you hesitate along your path, I want to be the one pushing on your back. When you challenge something, I want to be at your side, stopping you from shaking. That is—that is all I wish for. So please…"

"You don't need to worry 'bout any of that stuff."

"Eh?"

Naturally, Rem's tearful-sounding voice weaving those lovely words brought a bashful expression to Subaru's face. Supporting her shoulder, he gently stroked her head as he said, "You've been holding my hand nonstop, and you've pushed my back lots of times. When I'm shaking, just thinking of you lets me manage somehow—you've been saving me all this time."

"…Ah…"

"It's all right, Rem. I'll manage somehow, all of it. I'm your hero. I decided this was the first step toward that. So you don't need to worry."

When her quivering eyes looked up at Subaru, her cheeks grew red and hot. With her like that, Subaru turned a smiling face toward her, baring his teeth as he smiled ferociously.

"The whale hunt's done already. Your hero's super-bedeviled, I guess."

"Suba…ru…"

Unable to restrain the emotions welling up inside her, Rem's call of Subaru's name faltered midway. From there, she seemed to anguish, as if restraining her impulses over and over, and after breathing in several times, the tears she could not hold back trickled from the corners of her eyes.

"—Yes. My hero is…the greatest in the whole world."

She cried with a smile on her face.

4

Crusch gathered up the wounded, Rem included, and the head of the White Whale, and departed for the royal capital.

Half of the remaining expeditionary force escorted Crusch and the others, and the other half went with Subaru, heading for the Mathers domain.

Headed by Wilhelm and Ferris, the expeditionary force accompanying Subaru amounted to twenty-four souls. It was somewhat below the numbers Subaru had hoped for, but it was reassuring fighting strength nonetheless.

Besides, it was not just people from the expeditionary force accompanying him but also—

"Captain! Mimi! Mimi worked hard, too! Worked incredibly super-hard!"

Two beast people were riding ligers as they quarreled loudly.

One was Ricardo, recovered after withdrawing from the battle lines after being wounded shielding Subaru. The other was Mimi, who had not lost any of her childish extravagance, even amid a battle with her life on the line.

It was not only the two of them joining the battle but also the ten-odd surviving members of the beast-man mercenary band, the Iron Fangs. Apparently, the other lieutenant, Hetaro, had taken command of the wounded, returning to the capital with Crusch.

"Come to think of it, how'd your little bro get that wiped out when you're that full of energy?"

"Hetaro's a little weakling! Goodness, so pathetic!"

Mimi cackled, laughing loudly as she made sport of her little brother's weakness. But Subaru judged that it was probably just the older sister's stupid amount of endurance.

She was the berserker type who couldn't help laughing in battle—or more precisely, an extremely positive thinker who saw fun in everything. Subaru couldn't help being envious.

"Welp, I didn't do much for the last half of the whale butt kickin', but don't worry. The Lady Anastasia asked nice an' proper. I'll be doin' plenty for the real job comin' up."

"The real job— Wait, you know what I'm trying to do...?" Subaru said.

"Tangle with the Witch Cult, right?"

The words Ricardo quietly spoke made Subaru's throat tighten.

Naturally, when he strongly gripped the reins of Patlash, the land dragon bearing his weight, he heard the pitch-black dragon make a little sound of concern for him.

Seeing the side of Subaru's tense face like that, Ricardo bared his sharp fangs and smiled.

"Go ahead an' look surprised. To merchants, fresh info comes number one, and the miss has us on the payroll for a reason. We don't have these ears for nothin'. They pick up lots of things, not just 'bout you."

"That's right! Mimi's awesome!"

"I wasn't talkin' 'bout you, runt."

Mimi's reaction threw Ricardo's joke off on a tangent, earning a strained smile from him. While standing on the side, Subaru scratched his head, feeling surprised at Anastasia's poor actions.

That said, now that they were sticking together thereafter, sharing info with Ricardo and the other Iron Fangs was inevitable. If possible, he'd love to sit everyone down, expeditionary force included, and properly talk things over. And along with them, the insurance Subaru had arranged before departure, though he didn't know if it would work, or—

"Oh, looks like we can link up."

"Ah?"

Beside Subaru, sunk in thought, Ricardo's eyes faced forward when he suddenly spoke those words. Subaru's gaze quickly followed suit, but he could see nothing through the darkness of the plains at night. Unable to see what Ricardo did, all he could do was tilt his head.

"You don't hafta strain like that; I can tell they're waitin' for us. Relax."

"So says the guy who can tell, sheesh. Showing off and all."

"Hey, if you've got it, flaunt it. —They're a bit far, but comin' from thataway is the other half of our band of mercs."

"Half?"

Subaru knotted his brows at Ricardo's words. The other half of the Iron Fangs ought to have meant the wounded withdrawing to the royal capital, but...

"By half, I mean exactly that. We put only half the members o' the Iron Fangs on bringin' down the White Whale. The other half had the other half to do."

"Doing what?"

"Had to make sure no other humans on the highway got involved in the fight, right? So they were shuttin' off the highway from the other side. They set out durin' last night, so ya never had a chance to meet any of 'em."

Hearing Ricardo's explanation, Subaru accepted it, drawing in his chin.

He wasn't exactly thrilled they hadn't devoted all their forces to subduing the White Whale, but they had lent Ricardo and Mimi, their main combat strength. Considering that the subjugation failing might have meant complete annihilation, Anastasia wasn't wrong to hedge against that risk. He just didn't have to like it.

It was Subaru's envy at work, for he had few cards in his hand and no options save tossing fastballs full force.

"So the ones coming now are the rest of your buddies. Who's leading 'em?"

"Mimi's younger brother TB! He can do combo boomies with Mimi just like Hetaro! Incredible!"

Mimi stuck her chest out as she proudly replied to Subaru's inquiry. Just from hearing her vague, energetic reply, he had some concerns about their remaining comrades.

"Er, but that younger brother was a straight shooter. Does this younger brother take after the sis, the bro, or is it fifty-fifty…?"

"I get why yer worried, but TB's the smartest o' the bunch. He handles our accountin' and negotiations, and he's the lady's right-hand man. He's an expert at handlin' Mimi, so he's a step up over Hetaro there!"

"Don't say that, I'm gonna feel bad for Hetaro…"

The various rankings the older sister and the captain had issued made Hetaro something of a tragic figure.

Either way, setting pity for him aside, Iron Fangs reinforcements was good news. It was surely best to link up with them, then talk to everyone and think about what was to come. A strategy session aimed at the awaiting Witch Cult—Wilhelm and the others from the Crusch camp had likely surmised the circumstances. The problem was how Subaru would explain it.

Just like with the White Whale, he had to explain things without touching upon Return by Death.

"But that's not an easy thing to do…mm?"

As Subaru's brain agonized, he saw a pack of ligers kicking up a dust cloud up ahead. Just as Ricardo had said, this was the other Iron Fangs group linking up with them. However, Subaru felt unease.

"_____"

With a corner of his head giving off an uneasy feeling, Subaru's eyes strained, and then, he discovered the source.

Among the pack of ligers, there was a single figure to the fore with characteristics differing from those around it. As the distance closed, and as those vague contours became better defined, Subaru understood that those characteristics were that of a land dragon.

And mounted atop that blue land dragon was…

"—Why are *you* here?"

"That is quite a thing to say to one's reinforcements. Most typical of you."

Both groups stopped, and Subaru, still on his land dragon, faced the individual.

His pale-violet hair was meticulously combed, his body was clad in the solemn, white armor of a Knight of the Royal Guard, and the corners of his handsome mouth were curled up in a thin smile.

Subaru stared at the elegant figure before him, connected to him by karma—Julius Juukulius.

5

As Patlash furled the folds of its nose, the blue land dragon before it screeched with a sharp glare. Subaru stroked its neck, trying to pacify the comrade that felt the same way he did.

Though they had not yet been together long, the bond between Subaru and Patlash had been strengthened by escaping the edge of death together. Subaru felt like Patlash's thoughts were conveyed straight through the reins.

"This might trouble you at an inopportune moment, but could you stop soliciting my land dragon? Your land dragon seems quite fine as well, but such invitation goes too far."

"Hey, Patlash! Why, you— You're flirting?! I go thinking we feel the same way and you betray me?! Chasing tail before a do-or-die battle?!"

"Hey, bro, that land dragon don't wanna hear that from ya. You were checkin' it out so much before we left and all. Besides, bro... your land dragon's female."

"Wait, you're a lady?!"

Patlash, the center of discussion, looked annoyed at Subaru's surprise over his partner's gender.

Seeing Julius shrug his shoulders at the exchange, his statement just earlier seemed to be an unfunny joke. Subaru was about to yell at him for it, but before he could, Ferris cut in.

"Why, it's quite something to meet you in a place like this, Julius. We were fighting for our lives until just a few hours ago, *meow*."

"I have nothing I can say in my defense. However, I must correct you, Ferris. I am not the individual known as Julius. Let us see... I shall call myself Juli."

When Ferris stared and offered sarcasm, Julius toyed back with a serious face. Everyone was giving him cold looks for his meaningless use of an alias, but he accepted their gazes with a slight, serene smile and said, "If, for argument's sake, an individual of knightly rank were to join a band of hirelings, it could only mean he had fallen to the station of mercenary. Thus, it is untrue that the knight named Julius Juukulius has joined the Iron Fangs, but rather the lone man before you named Juli."

"I see, *meow*. Typical, families with proper chivalry are so much twouble. Ferri's so glad to be from fallen nobility."

"I do not think of being a knight as troublesome at all. I

believe the only problem lies in the willingness to help out a friend—coincidentally, I should also declare that the punishment by house arrest received by Julius Juukulius was last night, so whereupon the day has changed, it has been lifted."

"Puttin' up all those stupid distractions... Is there even a point to an alias, then?"

Listening to the conversation between Ferris and Julius, Subaru clicked his tongue and levied abuse. Averting his gaze with a twist of his lips, it felt like he was pouting, but given that this was actually the case, he could make no excuse for it.

Hearing such abuse from Subaru, Julius abruptly looked his way, advancing his land dragon forward to take a position directly facing Subaru when he remarked, "It is good you are in better spirits than I expected—I wondered about the condition of your body."

"—!"

Julius's statement of concern for his physical condition made something in Subaru's brain audibly snap.

Although Subaru's humiliation was nearly two weeks ago from his perspective, if only a few days from Julius's, the question, which could only come off as some kind of dry sarcasm, was more than enough to make him remember.

As a slap in the face, the statement delivered like nothing else could, and Subaru just barely managed to lock his jeers in his own throat, holding his anger in.

He cleared his throat, took a deep breath, put on a calm face, and gave his short forelocks a little flick.

"Yeah, well, it was just a scratch, right? Like, a little spit and polish and I was all better? Anyway, aren't you a little late to think of yourself as reinforcements? What? Were you busy writing apologies to the higher-ups because you got serious against an amateur?"

Subaru countered with his specialty, fanning the flames, using a guess based on the house arrest punishment he'd previously heard discussed. As he did so, Julius's face grew sterner, ever so slightly daunted.

"I did not wish to speak of that but rather, the valiant wounds sustained from the subjugation of the White Whale...but it is good that those scrapes have healed as well. In the first place, the wounds should not have been as severe as they appeared...though you rolled around in exaggerated pain, specializing in earning sympathy as you are."

"Ha-ha-ha-ha-ha."

"Hu-hu-hu-hu-hu."

As the two exchanged dry laughter between them, the atmosphere began to feel like a powder keg.

When Subaru thought of how those around him were taking this, he saw that Ferris and Ricardo were watching with the look of amused bystanders, while Mimi mingled with the other group in search of her younger brother.

Naturally, the duty of calming things down fell to...

"It is good to warm over old friendships, but perhaps this is not an appropriate time?"

Advancing to the fore, riding a land dragon and making that argument, was an aged swordsman—Wilhelm.

Reproaching the two as they glared at each other, his calm, blue eyes reflected Julius within them as he said, "I cannot thank you enough for coming in aid. Our fighting strength is rather depleted from the battle with the White Whale... As a man coming along for his own self-satisfaction, I was concerned."

"Wilhelm, that's not..."

When Wilhelm lowered the tone of his voice and stated that, Subaru interjected.

To Subaru, subjugating the White Whale was the first must-clear hurdle on his list.

Subaru had intervened firmly out of his own self-interest, so he could not possibly think of Wilhelm as a burden. It pained him that he could not explain everything, but he at least wanted to wipe away that sense of being indebted.

But before Subaru could raise his voice—

"It is a fine face that you have become able to make, Master Wilhelm." In a quiet voice, it was Julius who addressed Wilhelm. Moved by Wilhelm's eyes, which no longer looked haunted, he nodded deeply and said, "It is as if you are a different man from the one I met previously... Surely, this shall also be some small comfort to Reinhard."

"I...suppose it might."

Wilhelm put a hand to his chin and lowered his eyes.

How deep, Subaru wondered, must the conflict within the old man's chest have been to give rise to that momentary hesitation?

The various people around them took their exchange in a variety of ways. Sympathy, relief—knowing the circumstances, many must have had those reactions. Subaru, the only one not to know, was left behind.

"Regarding that, I was unable to face up to it. Even if he did no wrong, even if he meant no harm, I could not forgive him—one day, I shall pay the consequences."

"Even those thoughts alone are surely enough to ease his heart."

Wilhelm held back something bitter in his reply, but Julius took his words well. Then he slowly turned a gentle gaze back toward Subaru, as if all was water under the bridge.

Naturally, Subaru girded himself for a resumption of the earlier war of words, but...

"I must give you my thanks."

"—Ah?"

In front of Subaru, unwittingly raising his voice, Julius lightly hopped off his land dragon onto the ground. Then, he looked up at Subaru, still riding Patlash, and went down on one knee.

"Properly speaking, this subjugation of the White Whale was the longstanding desire of the Knights of the Royal Guard. For bringing a final end to the disaster neglected by every nation for many years, I thank thee."

When he proceeded to display his gratitude with an elegant gesture, Subaru, who had held only enmity toward Julius to date, was unable to muster an immediate reaction.

Meanwhile, beside the perplexed Subaru, Ferris interjected.

"Now, hold on! Don't misunderstand, the subjugation of the

White Whale was led by the Duchess of Karsten—so it's Lady Crusch's achievement, *meow*. And importantly, Old Man Wil's the one who slew it."

"I understand very well that there is no power within him to directly slay the White Whale, having crush—having heard from Julius, who crossed swords with him directly."

Julius showed every sign of sticking to the notion that he was the mercenary Juli to the bitter end.

But having recognized Ferris's statement, he continued his words.

"However, there is no mistaking that his existence was a major impetus for the subjugation of the White Whale. Ferris, is it not right that you, too, acknowledge this?"

"*Meow*!! That's... Well, that may be so, *meow*..."

When that was pointed out to him, Ferris hemmed and hawed as he wilted. Having put those kitty ears in their place, Julius turned his gaze to Subaru once more.

"Thanks to you, people can forget the days they spent in fear of the mist—Lady Anastasia shall surely be overjoyed as well."

"Even though I can accept the first half straight-up, it's a lot harder to accept that second half as is."

"And my friend can...begin to put his regret of many years behind him."

Subaru understood that by "friend," he probably meant a certain red-haired hero, but Subaru didn't know the fine details of what regrets that complete super-human had harbored for many years.

Did someone like him really have a past he needed to regret...?

At any rate, Subaru had no intention of fiddling with how to take all those words. It was right to be happy for Wilhelm having achieved his long-cherished desire, and at the very least, he recognized that his own cooperation had been useful to that end.

But even so, Subaru felt extremely conflicted having Julius praise him so.

"_____"

He put on a strong front, but he couldn't wipe away his weakness, flinching and recoiling from the handsome man.

Even had he overcome his own weakness, all that awaited him was the unsightly image of a rebellious child having a tantrum. Even though he felt genuinely grateful for the reinforcements, the fact that it was Julius was hardening Subaru's heart, enough that deep down, he wanted to give his superior, Anastasia, a piece of his mind.

Taking pains not to let such negative emotions come out onto his face, Subaru exhaled at length.

"So in the end, what are you doing here? What'd you come for?"

"—You really pulled it off, didn't you?"

"Ah?"

Julius did not reply to Subaru's question, but somehow, Julius's murmur sounded like he was deeply moved. When Subaru prompted him, he commented, "Nothing," and shook his head before saying, "I wished to ask if you comprehend that the contract with Lady Anastasia lends the Iron Fangs to Lady Cru— Rather, to you, only during the subjugation of the White Whale?"

"Huh? Was that the deal? But I'm sure the lady said that…"

"Big Sis, please be quiet."

Hearing Julius's declaration, Mimi tried to interject, but a little feline beast man with identical facial features sitting right beside her stopped her from doing so. That was probably the talented younger brother.

Glancing sidelong at the exchange, Subaru grimaced at Julius's words.

"What are you trying to say exactly?"

"It is a simple story. Having succeeded in subjugating the White Whale, we no longer have any reason to cooperate with you. The job is done—yet here you are, trying to take them somewhere this very moment?"

"Ah-ha-ha-ha-ha! Julius, you're so forgetful! The lady said this and that before we left and everything! Mimi's forgotten what it was, though!"

"Be silent."

Though the kitten-sibling interplay tugged at his mind, Subaru finally grasped what Julius was trying to say. In other words, it went like this:

"You want me to choose, here and now, whether to let the Iron Fangs pull out or stay on as reinforcements."

"I am under instructions to sell our services at a high price, you see. Or perhaps our strength is not necessary at this juncture?"

Julius indicated the others watching from behind him, pressing Subaru to decide.

In spite of himself, Subaru could not easily permit his irritation to slip into the decision. It would be simple to give in to anger and chase them off, but that would be a fool's choice, diminishing his fighting strength while the tallest hurdle loomed ahead of him.

That said, readily accepting the "high price" Julius had invoked brought its own problems. It was a bad move in negotiations to make promises you couldn't keep, and moreover, Subaru's decision had numerous lives, and the future of a particular girl, hanging on it.

"......"

With Subaru pushed into silence, Wilhelm and the others beside him watched without saying a word. Even if Subaru had requested support from them at that juncture, it would turn the negotiation into the Iron Fangs entering the employ of the Crusch camp. But that would only serve to create one obligation to satisfy another.

At present, Crusch was lending support to Subaru from a position of equality between them; put bluntly, he didn't want to upset that balance.

"......"

When he looked next at the mercenary band under Ricardo's command, Ricardo was folding his arms, keeping his silence. Beside him, Mimi copied her captain, folding her arms as she twitched her ears.

When he thought back to Ricardo's earlier display of willingness to fight the Witch Cult, it all came together. He was getting in Subaru's good graces in anticipation of this negotiation with Julius.

"That's dirty. You Kararagi folk sure play dirty..."

"That's a harsh thing to say to someone, ya know. By the way, I ain't really into this whole 'takin' advantage of people's weaknesses' thing. I just like money more, so..."

"You're so shallow it's depressing! Not that I was expecting more to begin with!"

Even if he was boss in name only, he still had no intention to seek aid from Ricardo, part of the enemy camp.

At any rate, it was disgustingly obvious that the negotiation left Subaru no option but to say yes. Unlike the Crusch camp, lending him help so they could call it even, Anastasia was creating a one-sided debt. It was a painful decision, but there was no move to make save for grudgingly accepting the situation.

Declining reinforcements would be a far stupider decision.

If only there was some magical means to make the Iron Fangs fight the Witch Cult under the existing contract—

"Magic, magic...? Mist, White Whale...and the contract for the highway..."

Subaru, searching for some kind of convenient means, suddenly lined up side by side what had been mere words in his head. Upon examination, they seemed to be unconnected terms, but that little nudge made his thoughts burn white-hot.

Bit by bit, a vague image began to take form inside Subaru's mind, turning into a coherent answer.

And then—

"...How about this: The subjugation of the White Whale...ain't over yet."

"—That is an...interesting statement."

Julius narrowed his eyes as he replied to Subaru's desperate-sounding words.

Subaru's statement unsettled not only the Iron Fangs behind him but the expeditionary force as well. Among them, Wilhelm's wide-eyed look tugged especially strongly upon Subaru's conscience.

But in a meaning separate from Wilhelm succeeding in his long-cherished aim, it was his idea for addressing a problem that could not be set aside.

"It's possible that the White Whale is a demon beast acting for the Witch Cult. I'm...aware of people in the Witch Cult saying something like that."

—It was the third time around, in other words, the final scene before that world came to an end.

Facing off against Petelgeuse in the forest, he'd lost to the madman's Unseen Hands. After that, Subaru thought Petelgeuse's kicking of Emilia's remains was like he intended to force Subaru to feel powerless.

At the time, as the madman's filthy mouth berated Subaru, he definitely ran his mouth to the effect of...

"—*The highway is sealed by the mist, so there is no one to interfere with my love!*"

How did he know that?

Why did he speak of it like it was his own doing?

And buttressing that was a word spoken afterward by the Beast of the End, freezing the world over with its breath.

"Someone who knew the White Whale called it 'Gluttony.' If I'm not wrong in thinking that means something to the Witch Cult, the cause of the demon beast appearing is where I'm heading."

If Petelgeuse had called the White Whale to the highway, obstructing entry to and exit from the Mathers domain, his objective could have only been to further his own mad ends.

In other words, covering the highway in the White Whale's mist was preparation for the attack on the mansion—and Emilia.

"The Witch Cult's got a chip on its shoulder, so we've gotta knock it off. With this added, that'll be four centuries of failure set straight. When we've done that, then we can say we've finished taking care of the White Whale."

"_____"

Subaru looked Julius's way as he continued with a strong declaration, "The job of the employer is to give orders and dish out rewards. Don't cut out on me midway, merc. Or are you gonna pay compensation for cutting and running?"

The basis of his statement was so thin that, on the inside, even he was amazed. But Subaru was now able to maintain a bold, smiling exterior while saying such a thing.

He'd gathered scattered bits of information from each repetition, piling them together to hazard a guess. He'd had that experience several times before, but this time, the guess was on spectacularly thin ground. After all, the crux of the information was gleaned from things he'd overheard while his mind was clouded.

Even linking them together in some semblance of coherence, he had no idea if it would sway them. If it could not, at least it could be the thread leading to further negotiations—

"Mm, I think I shall grant you a passing grade."

"Huh?"

"You could make it sound a little better for our ears, but in general, your claim passes muster. Nor shall Lady Anastasia lose face."

"W-wait a minute!"

Subaru raised his voice in haste at Julius's know-it-all reply. In response, Julius casually looked at the agitated Subaru.

"What is it? You need not be concerned; the Iron Fangs shall continue their assistance in accordance with the collateral that has already been paid to Lady Anastasia. There is no problem, is there?"

"That easy...? I mean, what's with that know-it-all stuff! Why, you...!"

When Subaru began to voice the words that were to follow, he came to realize a very disagreeable part of himself.

Julius had considered Subaru's circumstances, cooperating by taking Subaru's guess at face value. Subaru just hadn't wanted to notice his benevolence.

Subaru wanted Julius to be a hateful person he could never see eye to eye with.

—He realized the vulgarity of his own feelings in wishing that it were so.

"Well, it ain't like we're doin' this for free. A dumb robber only takes from ya once, but a clever one gets as many chances to take from you as he likes."

"Doesn't change that in the end, you're getting hosed, huh..."

Ricardo wedged himself into the conversation, and fortunately, he was on Subaru's side. In so doing, the easy way became easier, and Subaru hated himself for running from it.

When Subaru's self-hatred mixed with the self-hatred of others, things only got worse and worse. But even Subaru knew that. He'd learned it long before.

"I'm...in the wrong... Crap, sorry. Aw, damn it, that's not even what I wanna say. Even back then, I knew I was..."

Putting a hand to his forehead, Subaru finally voiced the logical answer he'd agonized over. However, even though he understood in his head, it was hard to find the words for it.

This was where he ought to be thanking Julius for bringing reinforcements and committing to the fight. Now that he could look back at it calmly, he could understand just who had been in the wrong, and that the previous antagonism between them was the result of Subaru's quick temper.

Or perhaps even the reason Julius had done what he did at the time was—

"_____"

Julius simply waited, saying nothing to Subaru's difficult words.

He surely understood what Subaru wanted to say. If Subaru couldn't say it, and he wanted to get out in front and voice a reply, surely he could.

But he did not, and Subaru could not help hating him for not doing so. It would have been so much better if he could simply keep hating the man through and through.

"I...was wrong. Sorry. I apolo...gize."

To Subaru, they were abominable memories to think back upon, but he'd have had to face them sooner or later, and that was the place, in front of the man he'd have to settle things with someday.

Julius closed his eyes at Subaru's apology, slowly drawing in his chin.

"Allow me to apologize for my own rudeness. I do not take back everything I said and did in that place, but even so, I take back my belittling of you, from the bottom of my heart."

Those were the words with which Julius answered Subaru's apology.

Sincerity flowed from Julius's words, and Subaru knew that the resentful, hateful feelings inside of him had melted away with exceptional ease.

Understanding this, he dismounted, standing on the same ground as the knight before him, squarely facing him on a level playing field.

He was reflected in the other's yellow eyes, and Subaru's own black eyes reflected in the knight's as Subaru admitted, "I was wrong. But…"

"Mm."

"I really hate you—I think badly of you, and right now I'm thankful you came, but I *really* hate you. I truly, from the bottom of my heart, hate…your…guts!"

The last sentence of his rude declaration was broken up, with shakes of his head to the left and right for extra emphasis. And slammed in the face by all that hostility, Julius looked taken aback.

Then, his expression abruptly collapsed.

"That is well. After all, I am not very minded to become your friend, either."

With that, Julius snobbishly stroked his hair upward and laughed.

6

"Ahh, to be honest, this sort of thing really işn't my cup of tea. It's like, having people watch me with those serious looks is gonna make me blush…"

With the group of fifty sitting in a circle, Subaru stood at the center, embarrassed, as he let those words slip.

The place was the Liphas Highway; the time was before daybreak, and the participants were everyone in the expeditionary force.

The group that had persevered through the battle with the White Whale had been joined by reinforcements, the Iron Fangs under Julius's command, making them a rather large gathering, but the time had arrived when it was necessary to share the objective and information concerning it to all.

For that purpose, Subaru had proposed to sort out all their information in one sitting, but—

"I didn't think I'd be standing in the middle of all these people for it, though..."

Surrounded by veteran soldiers, beginning with the likes of Julius, Ferris, Ricardo, and Wilhelm, Subaru could not help flinching.

In the first place, he'd often anguished over his low interpersonal abilities since back in his old world. He was well aware that he lacked experience in standing before people like that, let alone the character to stand above others.

But even if Subaru was timid from having them look at him with a certain level of trust in their eyes, he didn't mind it at all. It just put him in quite a bind.

"Anyway, let's straighten this out. Ahh, from here on, we're heading to the Mathers domain...or rather, Roswaal Manor. There, the Witch Cult will probably—no—definitely show up."

"The Witch Cult, you say..."

When he invoked the name of the Witch Cult, conflicted emotions came over the expressions of various people. Given conversations to that point, there were surely many among them resigned to where it would lead, but even so, it was a different feeling knowing for sure who you were up against.

Though, Subaru did not know exactly what this world understood of the Witch Cult or how they would act on his information.

"As far as I'm concerned, though, they're the worst of the worst."

Based on everyone's reactions, they all seemed to share that thought.

When Subaru took comfort in that, Julius addressed him casually.

"Subaru. How did you come to realize the White Whale and the Witch Cult are connected?"

Ever since Subaru aired his real feelings about their quarrel, Julius's demeanor had softened considerably. To be frank, that transformation left him conflicted in and of itself, but at the moment, answering the question took precedence.

"Burns me to say it, but I had a run-in with disciples of the Witch Cult. I didn't get out unscathed and I have a pile of bad memories from it...but there was one guy who ran his mouth," Subaru explained.

"I see... It would seem the knights' guess was not in error."

"I suppose not, *meow*. The research Old Man Wil put together seemed to come to the same conclusion."

"Wait, you knew?"

Julius accepted Subaru's words, and Ferris nodded and concurred. Their behavior surprised Subaru, but Wilhelm gently shook his head and said, "It was mere chance that I noticed the connection. I thought it was unnatural how often the distribution of the White Whale's appearances coincided with records of the Witch Cult's activities—it was nothing firm enough to call concrete evidence, but..."

"To Old Man Wil, the White Whale was the main course, and the Witch Cult is like dessert, *meow*. Ferri wasn't sure to believe it or not when hearing about it the first time, either..."

"There has been similar talk among the knights. Though to be precise, they were never considered anything but old wives' tales, tales to amuse one another with."

As Julius shrugged his shoulders, Wilhelm replied, "That is a small wonder," and exhaled.

Listening to their exchange, Subaru roughly scratched at his head and said, "For starters, it's lucky for me that there's a foundation for you to believe what I'm saying. Either way, if we believe what that Witch Cult guy was saying... Er, that might not be very trustworthy, but I think it's almost certain they're connected to the White Whale. The Witch created the White Whale to begin with, right?"

"So it is said. The existence and origins of demon beasts are mysteries to us. Some propagate in the same manner as ordinary living creatures, but some suddenly appear out of nowhere like the White Whale. Though, properly speaking, the only exceptions on par with the White Whale are the Black Serpent and the Great Hare."

"Feels like some words I shouldn't just let go are flying around, but they scare me, so is it okay if I move on?"

Everyone nodded as if to say *no problem*. Seeing this, Subaru cleared his throat and advanced the conversation.

Now that everyone knew that they'd be facing the Witch Cult, there were things that had to be known to all.

"The Witch Cult's target is Emilia. They intend to burn away the mansion, the nearby village, and everyone inside. That's why we have to drive the bastards off somewhere."

"Drive off? Subawu, you're saying a really naive thing, *meow*."

Ferris narrowed his eyes in a flirtatious manner; there was a suggestive inflection to his words as he looked at Subaru. It was a sensual gesture that sent a cold shiver up Subaru's spine. However, it still came from a guy.

"Whaddaya mean, naive?"

"Shouldn't you just cut down every last one of a bunch like that? Given what they've done until now, isn't that the proper and just way to deal with them?"

"_____"

Hearing Ferris unflinchingly propose slaughtering the lot of them, Subaru's mouth opened in surprise.

It was not the extreme statement that surprised him but the statement that he himself was naive. He, who had gone over and over in his head that they ought to die and had to be killed, was surprised at the change in his mind-set that had made him use such soft words.

That was probably because the order of what ultimately mattered most had changed inside of him.

"Right now, to protect the people in the mansion and village, that's fine. Whether it's driving out the Witch Cult, blowing them away, crushing them, beating them to death, twisting their heads off, turning them into mincemeat, roasting 'em, pounding 'em to little bits…"

"I…understand. I see that you're very angry toward them, so…!"

"—Er! Darn it. No, you're wrong. I didn't go picking a fight out of anger and hatred. And it's unjust to say I got close to Emilia-tan just on account of that!"

"No one said anything like that, *meow*!"

Subaru's anger was gradually rekindled as he spoke, with Julius and Ferris ending up calming him down. However, he also gathered that it was unnecessary to smooth such things over. During the previous go-around, people had tended to distrust Subaru, but apparently, this time people didn't feel even a hint of suspicion about him. *That's wrong somehow*, thought Subaru, wrapping his head around it, but…

"After bringing down the White Whale at so much risk to yourself, no one's saying anything unjust like that, *meow*? Subawu, you're surprisingly untrusting of people."

"I'm not being untrusting…"

In fact, he'd experienced Ferris and Crusch doubting him in just those words. But he hadn't just frivolously smiled and acted to hide his misgivings from them. Perhaps that transformation, too, reflected a change in Subaru's way of thinking and acting.

"In any event, surely there is no room to doubt that the Witch Cult is on the move. Given their faith and their past activities, it was anticipated given the fact that Lady Emilia has publicly declared herself a royal selection candidate."

Separate from Subaru's internal thoughts, everyone seemed to be concurring with Julius. Their knowing reaction made Subaru finally voice a question he'd neglected to ask at previous opportunities.

"I've wanted to ask this for a while. How did you go from Emilia's name going public to accepting that the Witch Cult is on the move? It's a bit weird to me how everyone just accepted that so easily… I thought the Witch Cult was pretty much a mystery to everyone?"

"You're saying that considering *you* know which way the Witch Cult is moving?"

Subaru had expected to be laughed at for his ignorance, so he paid no mind.

"Well, there's no time, so let's get on with it. So how'd you get there?"

"Ain't it weird for the one not knowin' to put it like that…? …Well, ya know to the Witch Cult that the Witch of Jealousy, Satella, is more important to them than life itself. Y'know that, right?" Ricardo said.

"More or less. To be honest, I've only touched on that. I read it in a picture book, that's about it."

"Well of course, it ain't like there's anyone left who's actually seen her. I've only heard of 'er, too. Well, if y'know that the Witch Cult disciples worship Satella, it's all good. So ya knew that Satella witch is a half-elf, right?"

"That, too, kinda."

That information hadn't been written in the picture book, but he'd heard it when Beatrice had explained the Witch of Jealousy to him. Besides that, even in the royal capital, the issue of Emilia's appearance compared to that of the Witch of Jealousy had come up time and again.

Each time, Subaru had indignantly insisted that it was no reason to put her down, but...

"Emilia's outside appearance is a dead ringer for the Witch, right? So back to the Witch Cult... It's simple to them—a half-elf is in the way, y'see."

"What?"

Subaru, beside himself, unwittingly let his voice jump out of his throat. But from the reactions of those around him, no one else thought anything special of Ricardo's attitude. In other words, it seemed to be a shared opinion.

"Why's that? By any normal thinking...not that I'm sure these guys think normally... But normally, why would you persecute someone who's a half-elf, the same as your dear, precious Witch...?"

"It's 'cause they worship her and think there ain't nothin' better than her, that they can't allow someone else that's the same kind. That she's kind of the same but not the same—an imposter."

The voice was exceedingly cold, infused with bloodlust down to its frigid core.

Subaru blinked hard and instantly looked toward the individual who had let that voice loose. As he did so, that individual turned to Subaru as well, and the two ended up staring eye to eye.

Subaru flinched from that gaze, as if it could see everything inside of him, when the individual said, "Well that's the guess Ferri just wanted to try and see, *meow*."

The expression easily crumbled as he stuck his tongue out, acting like the atmosphere just then had never existed.

Subaru couldn't form the words to follow up on that virtual about-face in his demeanor, but with him so rocked back, Ferris put on an innocent look and leaned forward as he said, "In the first place, the Witch Cult guys being weird in the head isn't a recent thing, so is it a big deal, *meow*? With the Cult after Lady Emilia, the real problem is who's leading them."

"An Archbishop of the Seven Deadly Sins, I reckon."

"—?! Wait, you know that name...?"

When Ferris changed the subject, Ricardo concurred, and Subaru bit on the term that came out.

Archbishop of the Seven Deadly Sins—that was the position Petelgeuse had claimed to have, though he had also babbled about being charged with Sloth on top of that...

"The Archbishops of the Seven Deadly Sins of the Witch Cult, are they pretty famous?"

"Well, at least enough people figure they exist. Plus, way back before the Witch of Jealousy went on her big rampage, the titles belonged to witches besides Satella."

"Pride. Wrath. Sloth. Greed. Gluttony. Lust. Six witches bore the names of those deadly sins, it would seem. Either way, it is said that once Satella claimed the mantle of Jealousy, she swallowed all of them."

In other words, "Witch" meant Satella, the Witch of Jealousy, and other witches of the deadly sins no longer existed within that world.

"But—and I do not know if this is the proper wording—I have heard that those in the Witch Cult acting as leaders have taken the names of those deadly sins in place of the lost witches. Satella is the symbol of Jealousy, which is what they worship. In other words, besides that, there are six—six Archbishops of Sin."

"Six..."

Listening to Julius's explanation, Subaru's breath caught at how little was known of the Cult they were facing.

Since Petelgeuse had claimed to be Sloth, he'd expected that there were others charged with different deadly sins. To Subaru, they were wonderful, familiar words straight out of rich middle school subculture. That said, what stopped the term from making his heart flutter was that his first-hand impression of sloth was just too awful.

—Were there really five more people like that?

"But we brought down the White Whale that was supposedly Gluttony, so the other Archbishops of the Seven Deadly Sins should show their faces in the Mathers land where we're headed. It's our chance to take 'em all out in one shot."

"Whoa, so stwong~! But Ferri agrees with the view that this is a chance to squish those Witch Cult weirdos. They've really underestimated Lugunica, huh?"

"As with the White Whale, they have inflicted damage the world over. The knights have also long suffered at their hands. Many other knights are surely as grateful as I for this opportunity."

Ferris and Julius concurred with Subaru's view, and Ricardo made a belligerent smile as well. Wilhelm responded with merely a solemn nod.

That being the case, what Subaru needed to do was make good use of his future information to draft a plan using the fighting strength currently on hand—though really, the plan itself was exceedingly simple, for all the necessary pieces were already on the board.

"Worst case, I'd have to pull this plan off with half the people we have now, but with Julius and them linking up, no more worries about being short on people. I think we can do this."

"I would like to correct you about one thing. My name is Juli. Certainly, I am on close terms with the eldest son of the Juukulius family, but I would prefer you pay that heed."

"In a nonpublic setting, that's just in the way, you know! It's holding back the conversation!"

"The key to not slipping up at a critical juncture is to pay heed even during normal times."

"If you wanna warn people about normal, don't come dressed as a Knight of the Royal Guard! You're out of character!"

After yelling at Julius for his thin commitment to the ruse, Subaru breathed raggedly while looking at everyone's faces. Then, he cleared his throat.

"All right, let's start this—Witch Cult Hunting Made Simple, so that even a monkey can do it."

With a twist of his mouth and a villainous laugh, Subaru laid out his plan.

The moonlight waned, and one could begin to see daybreak over the Liphas plains.

It was a quiet beginning to the morning of the last day of that loop.

AFTERWORD

Hey, everyone! Hi, Tappei Nagatsuki here, the Mouse-Colored Cat to some.

Thank you very much for sticking with *Re:ZERO -Starting Life in Another World-* for one more volume! With the tale now reaching its seventh volume, the books are really starting to pile up. I hope that, just like my characters in the story, I have grown as an author day after day. That sounds less like growth than getting older, though…

Now then, this time I have an unusually big announcement, and thanks to give.

I believe many of you are already aware of this, but this work, *Re:ZERO -Starting Life in Another World-*, has been slated for an anime release on television!

This, too, is thanks to all your support. Really, really, thank you very much!

I've already written this in afterwords several times, but this story began as a web novel via a website known as Let's Become Novelists!

It was over three years ago that I began my submissions, read by numerous readers, but it feels like it was only yesterday when someone approached me about putting the series into print. In reality, it was more like two years and a month ago, but really, since then, I've reached the point of being so busy day after day that it makes my eyes spin.

I am exceedingly grateful for being blessed enough to reach seven regular volumes and two side-story compilations. Along the way, the possibility of adapting it into an anime came up, and now that I can report that to everyone, my happiness and my gratitude know no bounds.

Truly, thank you very much.

Mind you, turning it into an anime wasn't the end goal—the work still has a long way to go.

With the work half-finished, it's still midway through the stories of the characters and through my growth as an author, so I can't stop now. As before, I'll be striving at full throttle, and I will be very pleased if all of you who have read this far continue running along with me.

Thanks to the anime release, even more people will know about the work, making me want to keep up the good work writing interesting stories, so best regards going forward!

Now then, all that fervor won't fill out this space, so here come the other thank-yous.

First, Mr. I the editor. Without your cooperation, Mr. I, *Re:ZERO* would never have begun to go into print, let alone reach where it is today. Truly, thank you for giving me the gift that is *Re:ZERO*.

Otsuka-sensei the illustrator. Otsuka-sensei, it is because you give these characters the greatest shape and color that their charm may shine. Thank you very much for yet another incredibly impactful cover illustration! I can't help being glad that the characters you have drawn will soon go into motion!

Kusano-sensei the designer, you have been exceedingly helpful. Thank you not only for the cover and logo but for many other places related to *Re:ZERO*'s publication! For future help as well, many, many thanks!

And thanks to Daichi Matsuse-sensei and Makoto Fugetsu-sensei for drawing the world of *Re:ZERO*, sometimes adorably, sometimes painfully. I've had so many people say the manga hooked them into the work; I can't lift my head before the two of you! Thank you so much!

Besides that, to everyone at the MF Bunko J editorial department, sales managers, copy editors, bookstore salespeople, you have truly been a great help. Thank you very much.

And finally, my greatest thanks to all you readers always reading my books and sending such warm support that gives me strength as an author. Please accept my best regards going forward.

Now then, let's meet again next volume!

August 2015
Tappei Nagatsuki
(Still worked up a month after
the anime announcement)

PUBLIC EXHIBIT: MONSTER (?) DESIGNS!!

Illustrations and text by
Shinichiro Otsuka

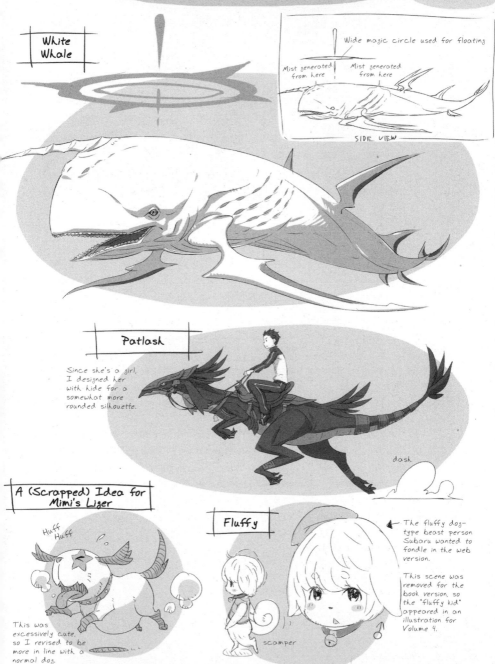

White Whale

Wide magic circle used for floating

Mist generated from here   Mist generated from here

SIDE VIEW

Patlash

Since she's a girl, I designed her with hide for a somewhat more rounded silhouette.

dash

A (Scrapped) Idea for Mimi's Liger

Huff Huff

This was excessively cute, so I revised to be more in line with a normal dog.

Fluffy

The fluffy dog-type beast person Subaru wanted to fondle in the web version.

This scene was removed for the book version, so the "fluffy kid" appeared in an illustration for Volume 4.

scamper

Subaru

"I know you've been the central character for most of the volume, but you doing the next volume preview with me must be fresh stress, huh, Wilhelm?"

"You need not be so modest. Unlike you, Sir Subaru, I am completely unversed in this. I intend to follow your directives in all matters, so please do not hesitate to call upon me."

"Whoaaa, now I feel even more gracious! Okay, let's get into the announcements, then! This is a big one, really big, wow! *Re:ZERO* is getting a TV anime release!! You're sure you want Wilhelm and I being the ones to announce this?!"

"It is the result of so many drawn in, following your footsteps in admiration, Sir Subaru. It is almost enough to make even my chest grow hot…"

"Those footsteps had a lot of pretty embarrassing parts, too, you know…!"

"What, everyone has embarrassing moments in their youth. While I am glad for the anime being decided, there are also comics going on sale, it would seem?"

Wilhelm

"Ah, yes, there are. The second volume of the hugely popular Mansion arc, serialized in *Monthly Big Gangan*, is going on sale in December! And the first volume of the third arc, serialized in *Monthly Comic Alive*, is also going on sale in December! Wilhelm, you'll be appearing in this!"

"I see, so they are going on sale in December simultaneously. It would seem best to buy them both at the same... mm? Sir Subaru, what is...?"

"It's just like you said, Wilhelm, everyone has embarrassing moments in their youth."

"Mm, certainly, I did say as much..."

"So the setting is fourteen years before the main story—! *The Ballad of the Sword Devil*, a side story set during the huge civil war in the kingdom, known as the Demi-human War, is set to go on sale, also in December!"

"So a side-story novel and one volume from the second and third arcs. I was inexperienced and a sorry sight in my youth, but do pick them up if you have some interest in them."

"Oh yeah! Hey, it turned out pretty good in the end! When push comes to shove, we're a good team!"